THE DARK YOUNG MAN

A Novel in Four Parts by
Jacob Dinezon

Translated from the Yiddish by
Tina Lunson

Adapted and Edited by
Scott Hilton Davis

Published by
Jewish Storyteller Press
2019

Translated from the Yiddish Novel
Ha-ne'ehavim veha-ne'imim,
oder, Der shvartser yungermantshik
By Yankev Dinezon (Dineson)
"Akhiseyfer" Publishing, Warsaw
Copyright 1928 by S. Sreberk, New York, USA
(Original Vilna publication date 1877)

Adapted and abridged.

Fire photograph © iStock.com/Pleasureofart

Published by
Jewish Storyteller Press
Raleigh, North Carolina, U.S.A.
www.jewishstorytellerpress.com
books@jewishstorytellerpress.com

Find out more about Jacob Dinezon at
www.jacobdinezon.com

ISBN 978-0-9798156-5-2

Library of Congress Control No. 2018936950

Praise for Jacob Dinezon's *The Dark Young Man*

Then

"Never has such a righteous hatred flamed over all that's bad and evil as over the Dark Young Man, who, with his intrigues, annihilated a family of blameless souls." —I. L. Peretz, Yiddish author (trans. Jane Peppler)

"There was hardly a Jewish home where all the members of the family —old and young, male and female—had not read the novel and not shed hot tears of sympathy for the sufferings of the unfortunate Yosef, Rukhame, and Roza."
—Nachman Mayzel, Yiddish literary historian (trans. Tina Lunson)

Now

"Tina Lunson's excellent English translation (the first ever) vividly captures mid-nineteenth century Jewish life in Eastern Europe, revealing not only its particular culture but also its parallels to today's Jewish experience."
—Philip K. Jason, *Jewish Book Council*

"Dinezon's writing is poignant and haunting; his characters are bright, intense, and unforgettable. . . . Jacob Dinezon is truly a giant in Yiddish literature."　　　—Charles S. Weinblatt, *New York Journal of Books*

"Virtuous heroes and heroines, a delicious villain, and a web of melo-dramatic intrigue in a Jewish novel that remains historically important today."　　　—Ellyn Bache, author of *The Art of Saying Goodbye*

"Jacob Dinezon's *The Dark Young Man* propels the reader back into the intriguing world of a 19th-century Jewish community in Eastern Europe, including a tragic love story, a thoroughly evil villain, and well-drawn supporting characters."
—Deborah Kalb, author of *Haunting Legacy* and book blogger

"Dinezon is a natural storyteller, maintaining humor and suspense through-out the book. His diverse cast of characters . . . jump off the page with a vibrant humanity."　　　—Deborah Miller, blogger at *Books and Blintzes*

THE DARK YOUNG MAN

In honor of Jacob Dinezon's one hundredth *yortsayt,*
the one hundredth anniversary of his death.

TABLE OF CONTENTS

PREFACE

No one was prepared for the success of Jacob Dinezon's first novel, *Ha-ne'ehavim veha-ne'imim, oder, Der shvartser yungermantshik* (*The Beloved and Pleasing, or, The Dark Young Man*), when it first appeared in 1877. Published by the Widow Romm and Brothers of Vilna, the initial printing of ten thousand books sold out quickly, and Dinezon himself had difficulty obtaining a copy. Soon, the novel was in almost every Jewish household, and over time sold more than two hundred thousand copies.[1] Even by today's standards, this would be considered an achievement. But what makes Dinezon's success so surprising is that the novel was written in Yiddish and, therefore, limited to Jewish readers.

Dinezon's *The Dark Young Man* was the first Yiddish novel to present, in a realistic and compelling fashion, the story of several bright and intelligent young people who were beginning to embrace the modern ideas of the *Haskalah,* the Jewish Enlightenment. Dinezon, a follower of the Enlightenment himself, wrote the book while living with a wealthy family who employed him as a tutor and later as a bookkeeper and manager of the family business. As he witnessed firsthand the conflicts that were facing young people as modern ideas challenged their parents' established traditions, Dinezon began writing about what he saw and heard.

Previous Enlightenment authors wrote satires that chastised their Jewish readers for their backward and intransigent ways—especially those living in the small *shtetl* towns of Eastern Europe. Dinezon, on the other hand, turned his attention to the young urban Jews like himself who lived in major cities like Mohilev (then in the Russian Empire), and Saint Petersburg and were trying to break out of the old ghetto-minded traditions of exclusion and conformity that still influenced their parents. He held up a mirror that reflected the plight of Jews drawn to the Enlightenment, and the obstacles, both physical and spiritual, that stood in their way. His main character, Yosef, clearly reflects his own idealism and internal struggle as the poor insulated Talmud scholar chooses to enter the world of business and finance while still trying to hold onto his Jewish identity.

Another conflict Dinezon observed was the growing friction within families that adhered to the traditional practice of arranged marriages. Dinezon poses the question: Should parents rely on the age-old system of matchmakers and marriage brokers, or permit their children to fall in love and choose their own partners? Although he clearly opposes arranged marriages, Dinezon describes the conflict from the point of view of both parents and children. In so doing, he shows us why change was so difficult to achieve.

But for Dinezon's readers, the novel was more than just an Enlightenment manifesto. It was also a complex, emotional, heartrending romance. Right from the start, the title portends the outcome. The first part is in Hebrew: *Ha-ne'ehavim ve-ha-ne'imim* (*The Beloved and Pleasing*), which comes from II Samuel 1:23 as David laments the death in battle of King Saul and his son, Jonathan. The two, says the verse, were so beloved and pleasing in life, they would not be separated by death.

The second half of the title is in Yiddish: *oder, Der shvartser yungermantshik* (*or, The Dark Young Man*). In Yiddish, *shvartser* is black or dark. *Yunger* is young. But *mantshik* is more complicated. It is not exactly "man." The word can mean "vigorous lad," "a newlywed bridegroom," or something much more sinister: a rascal, troublemaker, or evildoer. For Dinezon's readers, there was no question that Yosef's antagonist, the villainous Meyshe Shneyur, was an example of the last definition, and his name became a common term used to label similarly deceitful types in the Jewish community.

For Dinezon, the popularity of his first novel proved to be a blessing and a curse. He had consciously decided to write *The Dark Young Man* in Yiddish, the common language of the home, street, and marketplace. Followers of the Enlightenment preferred to use the sacred and scholarly language of Hebrew to spread their ideas, and they disparaged Yiddish as "the jargon." But Dinezon had his reasons, as he explained years later to the literary historian, Shmuel Niger: "Little by little I came to the conviction that nothing could be more natural than to write in Yiddish for the Jewish reader. And Yiddish began to satisfy both my artistic feelings and my Jewish conscience, which had been tormented realizing I had been writing in the holy language for only a small circle of friends to whom I really had nothing to say. While the thousands and tens of thousands of brothers and sisters to whom my writings might have been useful and to whom my tales might have brought pleasure, could not hear my words or stories, because I wrote in a language which only scholars and the Enlightened understood."[2]

Although *The Dark Young Man* was enthusiastically received by the Jewish readers Dinezon hoped to reach, he was not prepared for the stone-cold silence from those in the Enlightenment community whom he had so wanted to impress. The one prominent editor of a Hebrew journal who did comment, criticized Dinezon for writing in "a corrupt language."[3]

To further complicate the matter, Dinezon was deeply embarrassed by the sudden appearance of imitative works by authors trying to capitalize on his success. "I felt guilty for the whole flood of vapid and dismal novels drowning the Jewish reader," Dinezon wrote to Niger. "I couldn't stop writing, but it didn't cost me effort or mental strain not to publish the finished works."[4]

For the next thirteen years, Dinezon refrained from publishing another novel, although he contributed articles, essays, and translations to Jewish periodicals and remained closely connected to the Yiddish literary world. He befriended and mentored many of the most important Jewish writers of his day, including Sholem Aleichem and Isaac Leib Peretz. When Peretz was disbarred from practicing law by the Russian authorities, Dinezon printed, at his own expense, a small book containing three of Peretz's Yiddish stories. The two men became inseparable friends, and as the years passed, they collaborated on several literary, cultural, and philanthropic projects. Dinezon admits that it was Peretz's strong encouragement that finally convinced him to begin publishing his novels again.[5]

Although none of his later works achieved the success of *The Dark Young Man,* several attained popular acclaim, including *Hershele, Yosele, Tsvey mames* (*Two Mothers*), *Falik in zayn hoyz* (*Falik in His House*), and *Der krizis* (*The Crisis*). During his final years, following the outbreak of the First World War, Dinezon turned his attention to social welfare and philanthropic causes, caring for orphaned children displaced by the fighting between Germany and Russia and promoting secular Jewish education.

When he died in August 1919, tens of thousands of Jews lined the streets of Warsaw to pay their respects to the author who many now consider "The Father of the Jewish Realistic Romance."[6]

A Word About This Adaptation

How does one make a Yiddish novel published in 1877 pleasing to readers of English nearly one hundred and fifty years later? Even with a translation that is faithful to the original of that period, it is often impossible to keep sentences and dialogue from coming across as awkward and difficult to read. For this reason, I have approached Tina Lunson's translation in much the same way a screenwriter adapts a novel, trying to remain faithful to the tone and substance of Dinezon's original and Lunson's translation while attempting to produce a book that will appeal to twenty-first century readers. At all times, I have endeavored to let Jacob Dinezon's spirit shine through.

Scott Hilton Davis
Raleigh, North Carolina
January 2019

Notes

[1] "Jacob Dinezon's Letter" with commentary by Shmuel Niger, in *Di Tsukunft* (*The Future*), trans. Jane Peppler (New York, 1929), pp. 620-626.

[2] Ibid.

[3] "Jacob Dinezon," by Sh. L. Tsitron, in *Dray literarishe doyres: zikhroynes vegn Yidishe shriftshteler* (*Three Literary Generations: Memories of Yiddish Authors*), trans. Archie Barkan, ed. Robin Evans (Varshe: Farlag Sh. Shreberk, 1920).

[4] "Jacob Dinezon's Letter" with commentary by Shmuel Niger, pp. 620-626.

[5] Ibid.

[6] *The Sentinel, A Weekly Newspaper Devoted to Jewish Interests* (Chicago, Ill., September 12, 1919), No. 11, p 8.

Dead flies turn the perfumer's ointment putrid.
—Ecclesiastes 10:1

Present in the city was a poor wise man
who might have saved it.
—Ecclesiastes 9:15

PART ONE

ONE

MIDNIGHT IN THE STUDY HOUSE

The hour is late, and all is quiet and dark in the streets. Shops are closed and lamps extinguished, except here and there, where a sliver of light slips through a crack in a shutter or escapes from a small attic window as someone for whom the day is too short struggles to earn a bit of bread, or sits beside a sick patient who hopes to see another sunrise.

Watchmen on the streets go around bundled up in layers of shawls, old cloaks, or tattered military greatcoats that have already served their time. Occasionally, they shout out their arrival or tap out their familiar knocks, especially when they think one of their employers—who pays them a meager thirty-three or thirty-five groschen a month—is still awake.

Yet, an hour or two later, instead of the tromp, tromp, tromp of footsteps, the only sound one hears comes from the watchmen's deep and delicious sleep. There, in the dead of night, the poor and unfortunate sleep very sweetly as they lie on a stoop in the snow with their heads propped against a door. Perhaps even more soundly than the rich who sleep with their feather pillows and down quilts.

In truth, it is no wonder the watchmen sleep, so long as we do not think they are shirking their duties. A man is not an angel. If he does not eat, he is hungry; if he labors the whole day, he must sleep at night. And if his hard luck does not permit him to sleep like a human being in a bed under a roof, he does not cease being a human being and must fall asleep on a stoop in the glistening frost.

Oh, people! Why do you want someone else to be an angel when you cannot be one yourself? Tell me, how can you expect this watchman, this weary, toil-worn person who drove a cart all day, or carried sacks of flour on his shoulders, or dug the earth, sawed lumber, swept the streets, or cleaned yards, to walk around all night without closing his eyes as he guards your shop and precious possessions? And for what? For, I beg your pardon, the lowly pittance you pay him? Perhaps, if that unfortunate watchman could feed his wife and children with ten times, or even fifty times, the thirty groschen you pay him each month, he could then, with such enormous largesse, sleep during the day and stay awake all night doing his job.

People, we are such terrible egoists. We want others to sacrifice their lives for us. We want them to toil without rest for our thirty groschen! If we ask the rich to take any pains, it costs us dearly. To a rich man, each tick of his gold watch is worth a whole ruble! But the poor man has no watch. His minutes, hours, days, are like tiny pieces of lead or tin that get tossed into the rubbish or sold as scrap to the highest bidder. The poor man lives a hard, leaden life as he grinds his way to the scrap heap.

But lead and tin are useful materials in this world. We make tools from them to dig the gold, silver, and diamonds that decorate our homes, offices, and bodies.

Poor people are also useful. We employ them cheaply so we may live as princes and capitalists. They contribute to our happiness with their sweat and toil, but when they stand in our doorways seeking a bit of recognition, we shout, "Get out!"

The poor are also useful because they work, make their contributions to the world, and find happiness in their own conscience. Those who do not work, the idlers and the ones who squander money, remain debtors in the world. They benefit from the labor of others and do not fulfill God's purpose that each person should answer to his own conscience, which sooner or later will ask: "How have you spent your life? What use have you brought to others for the use that they have brought to you?"

On that cold and quiet night as the watchmen slept, there sat in a study house in the suburb of the great, old-fashioned Jewish city of Mohilev, a fresh new "idler," or as they are often called in such places, "yeshiva boy," "poor boy," "synagogue studier," and other endearing names that denote the impracticality of their lives. The study house clock, which was always a half-hour slow or fast, had already struck twelve, and the whole place was quiet except for the snoring of the sons of the rich who, thinking they would adopt the scholarly mode of studying all night, lay with their fur coats rolled up under their heads near the Wise Man from Lizshanke.

Incomprehensible words burbled up from the sleepers. The *shammes,* the caretaker of the study house, a Jew from Kurenos with long sidelocks, was asleep on the *bimah.* Near him lay his son, perhaps three years old, who the *shammes* routinely brought to spend the night so his young mind could be imbued with Torah, or with the politics discussed by the followers of the Wise Man of Lizshanke. From time to time, the child gave out a little cry like a bird in the forest dreaming in his nest.

The idler was toiling over a complicated passage in a holy text. He sat wracking his brain, but something was not right, and he could not grasp the meaning. He sat as always, studying with diligence, digging and searching, not noticing how time hurried by. Suddenly he jumped up. Hot wax had fallen on his hand from the candle that had just sputtered out. He looked for the candle stub he had hidden away, but could not find it. He stood and went to the clock to see how late it was, then looked around for a place to sleep. All the places were taken, and he stood for a moment not knowing what to do.

I don't even have a place to lay my head, he told himself. I never imagined such a thing. Not long ago, I was a rich man's son. I, too, came to study all night, but I never took the place of a poor boy who lived in the study house. Now here I am, a poor boy myself. Back then, when times were good, and my mother happily waited for me to come home from *cheder,* could she have ever imagined someone saying, "Your dear child, your coddled little Yosefke, has been tossed out into the wild world where he has exhausted himself."

He knew his mother would wash him in her tears if she saw how he lived and spent his time and health. For what? he wondered. Who can explain this even to me? Mama, how could what you and Father so desired for me as an infant lead to such a place as this in spite of all my sweat and toil? No, I am not a child anymore and can suffer with sealed lips. I will gladly sit and study Talmud as you always wanted for me if only I knew for certain this would make you happy. Because I love you, dear parents, more than life itself.

Unfortunately, I also know that a child, a boy who is a treasure, who knows a thousand pages of Talmud by heart and leads the afternoon service, must still struggle to make a life for himself. Although he may be a great joy and pleasure to his parents, how does he exchange a few pages of Talmud for a loaf of bread, a pair of shoes, a dress for a wife, or clothes for a child when the cash value of his learning has fallen? I know, dear parents, this is a great misfortune for you, a bitter grievance to see what the years of work have brought to your son. I don't blame you. Your eyes have always been bound by trust in God's goodness, and you do not see how times have changed. But I have new books in Yiddish and other languages, and my eyes are half-opened. The blindfold of trust has been torn off, and I cannot play blindfolded anymore!

The idler went over to the cantor's stand and picked up a flickering *yortsayt* candle, then opened a little chest and took out a small book in Russian which he began to read. Akh, he thought, what if a synagogue official caught me reading a Russian book— and by the light of a *yortsayt* candle no less! Fortunately, everyone is asleep, and if the dead man knows I'm using his candle while it burns in his memory, I suppose he also knows the kind of book it is. Perhaps he would even thank me for reading Rabinovich's *Shtrafnoi* by the flame of his candle, instead of lighting my pipe with it the way the good and pious Chassidim do!

He asked himself, Why do people call these books "devil books" or "Berliner books"? Why do Jews call everything "heretical" that is not Talmud or written by some rabbi-genius? Why condemn these books without even knowing what's in them? These books talk about our troubles and offer consolation to Jews who sometimes need to shed tears over the useless suffering of our brethren. Or do they disdain these books because they benefit all Jews, rather than just those who devote themselves to the study of holy texts?

This dilemma confounds me. Just when I think I understand the principles of our faith, I must figure out why it is forbidden to be an educated person who does not go blindly through the world.

I thank you, Rabinovich, for being a holy writer! Every tear that you have called forth from my eyes is like a balm to me, and I understand from you that I must do all I can to help my people.

As the idler pondered this thought, a little song came to his mind and he began to sing softly, "I am a Jew, a son of my people. I want to help with everything I own, with all my flesh and blood. But I am so small, dear God, please give me strength!"

As he finished the song, a boy of about seventeen came over and whispered, "Yosef, I heard you singing in my sleep. You were standing at the cantor's desk praying, and everyone was weeping at your song. Then I awoke and saw you sitting here singing and weeping alone. Yosef, what's the matter?"

"Shimen," answered Yosef, "things are not so bad for me. But you should know that we don't always cry about our own troubles. Sometimes we shed tears when we hear about the suffering of others. Here, let me read something to you."

Yosef read Shimen a passage from Rabinovich's book. When he saw tears in Shimen's eyes, he stopped. "That's enough for now," Yosef said. "I wanted to see if it was only me who wept over a story in a book, or if others would be moved to tears as well."

Shimen looked at Yosef in bewilderment. He began to speak, then hesitated as though afraid. Finally, he said, "Yosef, I want to ask you something, but please don't be offended. I and everyone else here wonder how you came to be in such a situation? How did you come to be a yeshiva boy living in a study house and eating at other people's tables? Yosef, I mean you no offense."

"Shimen, what do you see in me that is different from the boy from Minsk or Horodne or any of the other yeshiva boys?"

"They say one recognizes a person by his clothes," Shimen said, "but I recognize you by your delicate appearance and the way you speak. I don't know why I feel such a strong attachment to you, but

I've felt this way from the very first day we met. Yosef, you must become my brother. Promise me."

"If you are worthy," answered Yosef.

"How can I be worthy?"

"By being diligent in your studies. You must put aside your laziness, leave behind your childish ways, and become a *mentsh*, a real person, a grown-up!"

"So am I not a *mentsh* already?"

"You are a *mentsh*, dear Shimen, no one can deny that, but the word *mentsh* has a broader meaning, and I myself am far from it. One must work hard to be worthy of the name."

"Yosef, it would be enough for me to be like you. Will you be my teacher? Will you tell me your story? I want to know how you got here. You're not a boy from a poor family, I could swear it."

"My history is a long one, Shimen. It's three o'clock and I need to sleep."

"Go lie down on my coat," Shimen said. "I don't want to sleep anymore."

Yosef stretched out on Shimen's fur coat and Shimen sat down beside him on the floor. Quietly, Yosef began to relate his story. "You're right, Shimen, my parents were rich, but not for very long. How they became paupers is a complicated story. We don't have time for it now, but someday I'll tell you everything.

"What I can tell you is that I began to notice my father was worried. He didn't have the money to pay my teacher, and that was hard for me. I began to look for a way to take some of the burden off his weary shoulders. But what could I do? I didn't want to cause him any new problems, and I wasn't wise enough to know what was best for me. All I knew was that my father wanted me to study Talmud. So I thought, does it really matter where? That's the reason I left home: to find another place to study.

"By the time I arrived here, my money had run out, and I was forced to stop traveling. So I decided to stay. But I still don't know whether to thank God for falling into this place or to curse my situation. I can't make peace with charity meals and eating days. I can't get used to this life in the study house or living with so many yeshiva boys. If only I could find a student to tutor who would provide me with room and board and maybe a little pocket money. At least that would give me another year to take the first steps towards my goal."

"I have just the student for you," Shimen said. "My mother has wanted me to ask you for a long time, but my brother-in-law has been opposed to it. Now, he won't interfere!"

They heard the study house clock strike four, and Shimen said, "Go to sleep now. We'll talk more when you wake up."

Yosef slept for over an hour before people began arriving for morning prayers. They climbed over him to find a spot where they could read Psalms, a bit of rabbinic lore, or study a passage from the commentators—whatever struck their fancy. More than once, Yosef felt wet boots near his barely covered body as he struggled to wake up.

"Get up!" yelled a thin young man who looked like a greyhound with wet sidelocks. "Get up, I say! What have things come to? Once we used to study the whole night. Now the idlers sleep here like princes. What do they lack? They have plenty to eat and drink, nothing to worry about, and they hardly study at all. I swear I wouldn't mind being an idler myself!"

Yosef managed to get himself up, and Shimen came over to invite him out for a glass of tea. But Yosef declined. "Listen, Yosef," Shimen said, "my mother already knows who you are. The women in the study house tell each other everything. Last *Shabbes,* one of our neighbors told us that she'd gone to the rabbi to ask a question and that he had called upon you to make the decision. They consider you a blessing, and my mother says it's a *mitzvah* to make a sacrifice for—"

Yosef raised his hand to cut him off. "Thank you for the news, Shimen, but I ask you not to tell me any more. More importantly, it's not proper to sing someone's praises in their presence. When a small pebble falls into a still pond, it stirs up desire. Desire causes the pond to lose its equilibrium. This is also true for the human heart which is not so deep and doesn't go back to stillness as quickly as a pond. Shimen, you must always remember: do not listen to what other people say about you. And do not say anything about others!"

"Yosef," said Shimen, "I have read in books that people can be drawn to each other like magnets. If this is true, then you are my magnet. Somehow, I have become attached to you. I don't know what to call it, but I know there is an attraction."

How often do we find a magnetic quality in a person of strong character who pulls us towards them without any apparent reason for our attraction? This is one of the secrets in the control of one's conduct because without such people there would be no geniuses in the world, and people would remain at the same level they have created for themselves.

As the Chassidim began to pray, the broad melody of their praise-songs filled the study house. Many danced around snapping their fingers to show their devotion.

Clearly, this behavior upset Yosef who stood in his place and prayed. Shimen also wanted to pray without moving and shaking, but he often sang out words that came mostly from habit and not from his heart. Yosef asked Shimen to explain the singsong repetitions in his praying, and thus began the process of correcting what Shimen had learned from his previous teachers and friends.

When the service was over, two young men sat studying at a table. One was Shimen's brother-in-law. Those who knew him well doubted he was thinking about the words in the Talmud. His thoughts were more likely on the matzo ball soup he would be eating for lunch, or how he meant to take advantage of his father-in-law by setting up permanent residence in his home.

Two

THE LETTER

We see our Yosef a few weeks later, again sitting up late at night. This time he is immersed in reading all four sides of a hand-written letter to his mother. As soon as he finishes, he starts reading it again from the beginning:

Dear and beloved Mother!

I know that it has been wrong of me not to write to you until now, but I did not want to ask you for anything. I hope you do not have bad thoughts of me for being so silent. You know how you love me, and your Yosef loves you no less. I knew you were already suffering from worry, and I did not want to grieve you any further. So I took it upon myself to wait out the bad times until I could offer you some good news. Now, at last, dear Mother, I can report something good to you. See how God does not abandon us and how His loving-kindness is everywhere?

I was very lonely here in this city. I had no place to live except the study house. I could not get used to the hard benches, the bitter cold, or the name "idler." I have no regret about the entire business, but I confess that I wanted to come home. I knew you would have taken me in as a guest, but your heart would have wept when you looked at me sitting around without a purpose. The thought plagued me, but at last, to my good fortune, God has sent me a brother. In truth, he is better than a brother, for he has taken me into his home, and here I have found a new family and a new mother.

Dear Mother, you must not see this as a sin—honoring another woman with your holy name. For every person there is only one true "Mother," and you are that mother to me because I am your flesh and blood, and because of your goodness. But what if I told you that God has sent a stranger who has been as kind and loving to me as you are?

This stranger keeps her eye on me day and night. I am ashamed to relate all that she does for me. She does not hesitate to come in the night and cover me with a blanket. If my socks are wet or torn, I find them clean and whole the next morning. She comes in the middle of the night to check on me and fluff up my pillow. I have felt how she lifts up my head with her warm, motherly hands, and felt her comforting lips as they touched my forehead. I have heard her say, "How could a mother let such a child out of her sight? You don't have a mother here, so I will act in her place. Bless me, Master of the Universe, with such a child!"

I heard and felt all this in silence. A terrible sigh tore through my heart. She, too, as if in echo, sighed quietly as she tiptoed away. I was so moved, I could not go back to sleep. Thousands of thoughts were awakened in me. My whole childhood played out before my eyes: how you used to tell me little stories and ask about my secrets, and how I never withheld anything from you. I never lied, and never needed to, because you never punished me for breaking something or making mistakes. You just told me that when you were a child, you were punished for such things, and then showed me how to improve.

You always told me everything that was in your heart. I remember how I tried to free you from all your concerns, and how I tried with all my childish strength not to do anything that would displease you. You were always a wise mother who trained her only son with kindness and love.

Above all else, Mother, I saw your tears at my leaving home—a memory I will never forget. And after all you have done for me, how have I thanked you? I cannot find a shred of evidence that I have done anything in my whole life to repay you for all the goodness you have done for me. The only way I could express my gratitude was with the name "Mother," which you always treasured. Now, I am sharing that name with a stranger because I have no other means to repay her kindness.

Do not begrudge her, dear Mother, and do not begrudge me, and I will find comfort in knowing that I can repay her in this way. I want to be a good and worthy son to her. She wants my love for you to remain as strong as it ever was, but I must love this second mother without limits, too.

I am writing now from her home where I have become a member of the household. I am teaching her son, the one who brought me here. His name is Shimen, and he is an innocent young man, happy as a child.

He has two unmarried sisters. One is seventeen or eighteen years old. Her name is Roza, and her name suits her well. She blossoms like a lovely rose in a glorious garden, or like a clever daughter of good and intelligent parents.

She keeps mostly to herself, avoids unnecessary conversation, and is known as a good person. Most of all, I like that she does not consider herself above the poor or less educated, as others in her position often do. They say she was once quite merry. Now she seems pensive and quiet. We have not had any long conversations, just my explaining a word or two in a book, or the simple exchanges people have who live together in the same house.

The younger sister is Rukhame, a playful name a houseguest once gave her. Since then her original name has been forgotten, although people remember she was named after a grandmother. She is clever, pretty, has blue eyes, blonde hair, and is happy and gay. As a light drives away darkness, her lovely presence drives away cares and sadness. Laughing and singing is heard whenever she appears. I cannot express what a sweet person she is. She is like a younger sister to me and calls me "my Yosefke." I am teaching her to read and write, and she has a good head on her shoulders, although like many good heads she is not always so diligent in her studies.

I have not said anything about my salary. I have room and board, several new friends, and I lack for nothing. I mostly study. I confess I am teaching a lot of Russian and German, although I have to be careful that my second mother, a pious woman, is not troubled by this. And it is worth my effort to protect her from trouble.

I have written Father a long letter about Torah topics. I hope he has made peace with me by now and will write back. I do not deserve his silence. I am an honest child and have admitted that studying Talmud is not my only desire.

Someone else might have denied it and made up false answers. This I cannot do.

Be well, dear Mother. Say hello to everyone.

Your Yosef who loves you as he loves his own life.

When Yosef finished reading the letter, his heart was full. Yet something troubled him. Is it an error, he asked himself, to write to Mother about Roza? What will she think? Oh, God, why do I keep worrying about such things? She knows I can't keep anything from her. Why shouldn't I describe the company I keep? Besides, Roza is worth having in mind because of her good character, and I shouldn't be ashamed of thinking about her. I know myself; what do I have to be ashamed of?

Yosef folded the letter, put out the lamp, and went to sleep.

"Sleep well," we say to him, "as long as you can fool yourself and your thoughts!"

THREE

THE DARK YOUNG MAN

"Unhappiness follows in the steps of happiness," say the poets, and the experienced person knows "no good comes without bad." In our story we see both sayings demonstrated at once. Good fortune had just begun to shine on Yosef like a glowing red dawn, yet barely had the sun risen upon his clear horizon than a cold wind began to blow, and heavy black clouds gathered to darken the sky.

Yes, "unhappiness follows in the steps of happiness." Fortunately, the happy one does not see it coming. For if we saw in our joy the sadness that lies ahead, how could we ever be happy?

If our Yosef had opened his eyes and seen what was taking place, what was being woven for him in the next room, then instead of thanking God each morning for putting him into such a friendly family, he would have wept and begged God to get him out while there was still time. Unaware of what awaited him, Yosef praised His precious Name. We must not be cruel and look away too soon. Let us leave him feeling happy for as long as possible.

When Yosef first met Shimen's brother-in-law, he found him rather intimidating, but the two adopted a more friendly attitude once they were living in the same household. In their conversations, the brother-in-law often deferred to Yosef's knowledge of history—especially Jewish history—which he did not possess. Yosef also wrote poetry and knew about science and nature, things of which the brother-in-law was mostly ignorant. He quickly saw that learning from Yosef would help him become a more accomplished person—the person he bragged he already was.

The brother-in-law frequently invited Yosef into his study and talked with him through the evening. Yet he always referred to him as "poor boy" or "idler." "Idler," he would call out, "excuse me!"

When Yosef finally asked why he kept referring to him in this way, the brother-in-law replied, "I certainly don't mean any offense by it."

"Tell me, dear friend," Yosef said, trying to remain calm. "What is your definition of the word 'idler'? It's as if you want to shame me in some way. Is it a dishonor for someone to go off to study Talmud? Yes, a shabby yeshiva boy may be a disgrace, but a yeshiva student who studies hard and strives to be a scholar has nothing to be ashamed of, even if he doesn't have the money to afford an apartment and must rely on help from the study house.

"Tell me, what should a poor child do if his parents want him to become a Talmud scholar? Should he disrespect his parents? If it were up to me and I was a parent living in a poor situation, I'd prefer to apprentice my child to a craftsman. So what? Not everyone has the same sense. Should I bury my parents alive so I can do what I want? As God is my witness, I could never do that!

"On the other hand, they say if you're going to be a soldier, you'd better get used to the smell of gunpowder. I suppose, since I've agreed to be a yeshiva student, I better get used to the name 'idler.' So call me what you will, it doesn't matter. Look for the person inside the person; not what's in his name."

"So you say," replied the brother-in-law, intent on hurting Yosef for no particular reason. "But ask yourself this: What are today's young women looking for? 'No way an idler,' they say. 'Anyone but an idler!' It's even a stretch for a shoemaker's daughter to take an idler. A schoolteacher might take an idler for his twenty-five-year-old spinster, knowing full well the son-in-law will end up a pauper just like him. Where are you going to find someone who's looking for the 'person inside the person'? Try it—let's say you decide to get married. Who will you talk with about a match? A butcher, a tailor, a schoolteacher? And let's say the match works out and you get a dowry of a hundred rubles. How far do you think that will take you?"

"First of all, dear friend, you ought to know that I'm only seventeen and far from considering marriage. And second, I'm not an idler. In fact, I earn my living from your father-in-law as a teacher in this house. Does staying at the study house for a while make me a worthless person? I'm not ashamed of being a yeshiva student. Why should I care if you call me an idler in front of a hundred people?"

"Maybe not in front of a hundred people," said the brother-in-law, "but what about in front of one girl?"

Although Yosef did not comprehend his remark, he understood it contained poison. Knowing that Roza had likely heard her brother-in-law's views also pained him. He, too, disapproved of idlers, but he also spent time in the study house with them. He knew their situations and how difficult it was for many to better themselves. He felt sorry for them and was indignant when he heard people insulting them.

Jews, thought Yosef, don't you realize that idlers, vagabonds, and beggars are our jewels? Once we were famous for taking care of our own; now we despise them. Whom shall we blame if not ourselves? Who makes the wound yet seeks no remedy to heal it?

Later that evening, Yosef wrote these words in his diary. Nightly, he recorded all the thoughts that came to him during the day, everything that made an impression on him. This is how he came to realize that Shimen's brother-in-law was beginning to persecute him. Yosef wondered, Why is he doing this? Why is he so suspicious? What has offended him? What is he afraid of?

The Dark One, as we shall call him, was named Meyshe Shneyur —always with two names. His countenance, dark as a Moor, made an impression on people when they first met him. This impression was so strong, they immediately forgot his two names, and referred to him instead as "the Dark One" or "the Dark Young Man," as we shall call him, too.

People said he had a good head on his shoulders, and his father-in-law took him for an innocent lad. He had been newly outfitted from head to toe and arrived with letters of recommendation which a teacher had written for him. His bride, Roza's older sister, Leyke, was an old-fashioned girl of quiet demeanor who was afraid to express her inner feelings and let herself be sold into marriage. Yet, we must not weigh her heart, for she has discovered his true nature, and carries her wounds alone.

Since that fateful day when the wedding took place three years ago, the Dark One has moved into the house, and, like a fox, learned how to please his in-laws. His father-in-law, Fridman, was already an elderly Jew. Running his business had become too much for him, and he quickly taught his new son-in-law how to keep the books. One can imagine the difficulties the father-in-law encountered with his new business associate, but, thank God, the Fridman household has prospered.

The Dark One, however, was never satisfied with all that was being done for him. He complained about his wages and how hard he toiled for his father-in-law's family. In his heart, they all became his enemies, and he resented paying their expenses as if the money was coming out of his own pocket. He wanted Fridman to have no more children or sons-in-law so he could become the sole inheritor.

How can I get rid of this family? he grumbled to himself every time he recorded an expense for a new dress, pair of shoes, or tuition payment. You would shudder if we described the dark thoughts that occupied his mind almost every night as he sought a plan to get everything into his own hands. So instead of describing them here for the good reader, we will encounter them only in his dealings with Yosef.

The Dark One's cunning eye noticed everything that went on in the house. He saw how well his mother-in-law treated Yosef, how visitors admired him, and how well he pleased everyone in the family. Yosef's constant thoughtfulness, friendliness, and fine, noble appearance greatly irritated the Dark Young Man.

His eye also noticed changes in Roza. She would slip away when guests began praising Yosef. A certain shyness appeared whenever Yosef asked her to accompany him on a walk. And she was growing more distant from the Dark One himself. As he observed these and other details, he could easily predict what would happen if this new arrival became a permanent member of the family. Yosef was like a bone stuck in his throat, and he began to make plans to get rid of him so he could take over the family business once and for all.

"What will I do if that idler becomes my brother-in-law?" Meyshe Shneyur asked his wife. "What if Roza falls in love and wants to marry him? Your mother already likes him better than me. No! I must make my case before that terrible moment ever comes. I would sooner see him break his neck than let him take away my position in the family."

"But why would you begrudge Roza such a fine husband?" Leyke asked. "Isn't she worthy? Isn't he worthy of her? He is so much better and finer than all the other marriage proposals. I'll tell you the truth, Husband, and I've told Mother as well, I like him. Roza is my sister. Why should I have some ignorant boor for a brother-in-law when I can have a fine human being, which Yosef certainly is before God and before people!"

"He's only a coarse idler!" answered the Dark One in anger. "Do you hear what I'm saying? Would you be doing so well if you had married Gavriel? At one time, everyone made a big fuss about Gavriel, but once I came into the house everyone forgot all about him!"

"But does everyone have your nature?" asked Leyke. "Do you think Yosef will do to you what you did to Gavriel? If you would stop picking on him, maybe he could become your friend. Why does it bother you so much if someone else is happy? Thank God that Father can afford the kind of man that Roza deserves. Why would you ever want her to marry some scoundrel?"

"Fool!" shouted the Dark One, and his crooked nose flared in anger. "You have no sense. Stop offering your opinions!"

But the Dark One's wife did not remain silent. "You simply have no right to get mixed up in these arrangements. Who knows, maybe he's her *basherter,* her predestined one."

"Predestined one?" repeated the Dark One in a rage. "I'll tell you what he's predestined for! I'll make splinters out of that cursed idler. Then I'll throw him out on his ear!"

The Dark One stood and began pacing the room. Leyke prepared the table and set out the meal. Like a glutton, the Dark One threw himself at the food and ate with his nose in the plate as Leyke sat to feed her infant son. "Why don't you slow down and eat like a normal person?" she asked.

"I eat how I eat!" growled the Dark One.

Seeing there was no use in arguing, Leyke stood and pulled the suckling child from her breast. She laid him in his cradle and softly whispered, "Oh, child, if you're going to grow up to be like your father, you should've died in my belly. Before another wife has to cope with all that I've suffered from him, I'd rather bury you as an infant!"

One can feel a mother's breaking heart when she gives her sleeping child such a blessing over his cradle. We know and feel her wound but must remain silent.

FOUR

GOLDE

Matchmakers began pouring into Fridman's house from every side—insensitive people trading in the happiness of innocent and unsuspecting children the way men once traded in slaves by dragging them to the marketplace bound in iron shackles where buyers tried them out by whipping them like horses. Instead of doing business in the marketplace, these matchmakers bring their buyers to the homes of brides and grooms. Their slogan: a bride is like a hand towel; there are a thousand grooms for every bride and a thousand brides for every groom.

Potential brides and grooms are obligated to dress up in their finest clothes and display their hearts and souls to every prospect who is brought to examine them. Who in the world has made so many Jews unhappy as that deceiver, that slave trader, known in our language as "the matchmaker"? For a ruble, they take an interest in two innocent children who have never seen or heard of each other, and by so doing, poison their young lives and make them miserable to their dying day.

In these times when the slave trader is almost unheard of anymore in Europe, and when we are horrified to hear how they conducted their business in Africa, we seem not to notice that family slave traders are still at work in our Jewish communities. The only difference is that the others captured their victims outside their homes and put them in chains before selling them in the marketplace. Our vile slave traders capture and sell them in their own homes! Their hands and feet are bound in chains, yet somehow the couple is convinced their shackles are golden rings, until later when they realize they have been enslaved. And no one seems to care that these two blossoming children have been sold to the highest bidder and are doomed forever.

These were the unscrupulous people flooding into Fridman's house. The matchmakers usually came as partners, one for the groom's side and one for the bride's, and they frequently brought along the potential in-laws. When Roza saw them, she trembled, especially when the two main matchmakers in Mohilev came to call. One was a cantor, a crude man with a big nose named Shleyme. The other was called Meyshe the Madman. Whenever Roza saw them coming, she ran into her room like a frightened child. Her heart told her these men were no good, and she feared what Yosef would think if he found out matches were being discussed for her. Although she would do anything for her parents, she would refuse to dress up for prospective in-laws if she thought Yosef was around.

"Dear Mama," Roza begged Golde one afternoon as tears began to flow from her eyes. "Don't make me do this today. It's so hard for me. I'm afraid. I'm sick; I'm sick inside, Mama. God knows what's wrong with me. Please, not today. Tomorrow I'll do whatever you want!"

"Why are you crying, my darling?" her mother asked. "Everything is all right. I will tell the in-laws you've been invited out today."

"Thank you, Mama. I just want to be free. Please don't sell me."

Before Golde could reply, they heard footsteps on the other side of the door. Is anything more sensitive to hearing and feeling than the heart of someone in love? Roza sensed Yosef was near and wanted to hide her teary eyes. She cried out, "It's him!" and tried to run, but Yosef entered the room with Shimen and Rukhame. Roza's words tore at Yosef's heart.

"Excuse me, Yosef, I was crying," Roza said. "I took a taste of horseradish, and it got in my eyes. What a silly thing to do. Check the horseradish and make yourself cry!"

"They say that after a good cry, the eyes are clearer and you can see better," replied Yosef with a smile. "Your heart is lighter, and you feel better. Isn't that true, Rukhame? You always agree with me."

"True as the day," Rukhame said cheerfully. "Roza, we're all going out for a walk. I'm going, Yosef—my Yosefke—is going, and Shimen is going, too. Why don't you come along with us!"

Roza looked into her sister's bright blue eyes and marveled at how freely she spoke her words, "My Yosefke." Why am I not permitted to say such words? Roza asked herself. How much sweeter and more loving they would sound coming from my lips. If only God would grant me permission.

"Wait a minute!" Roza said as she hurried away. "I have to wash these tears from my eyes. I won't be long."

"Come here, Yosef, I want to tell you something," Rukhame said quietly as she took him by the arm and pulled him aside. "I think Roza was really crying. I think the horseradish was just an excuse. And I think I know what's bothering her. If you tell me your story, I'll tell you about Roza, and then you'll have to admit I understand a thing or two."

"I'll tell you my story," Yosef replied, "but I don't want to hear about Roza. Haven't I told you it's not good to have an open mouth? It's a drawback to know too much, and it's even worse not keeping it to yourself."

"Dear Yosef," said Rukhame, "I promise I'm not going to tell anyone else. But I can't hide anything from you. You're like a big brother to me."

"All right, Rukhame," Yosef replied, "from this day forward we will be like brother and sister. But listen, dear sister, you'll have to respect your older brother!"

"My older brother, Yosefke!" Rukhame exclaimed as she ran to hug and kiss Shimen.

"She kissed me," Shimen said to Yosef, "but I know she meant it for you! Isn't that right, Rukhame?"

"May you be so healthy!" Rukhame replied without taking her eyes off Yosef.

"May I be so healthy," laughed Shimen. "And you too, Yosef!"

"And me too," added Rukhame quietly.

"You see, little sister, how it's not good to have an uncontrolled tongue?" asked Yosef. "God just paid you for it!"

"If only I can live my whole life with no worse punishment," Rukhame replied with a playful smile. "Do you think that I'm embarrassed by it? I would have told you myself soon enough."

Roza came into the room dressed in her street clothes. Her curls were tied back, and she carried a parasol in her hand. The simple dress on her slim young body, her open-hearted countenance, and her lovely eyes under half-lowered lids, pulled Yosef towards her like a magnet.

Seeing her loveliness made Yosef feel like electricity was passing through his body. Yet he did not suffer. Oh, God, he told himself, I must keep my wits and not lose myself in these sensations. I must be cautious and treat her like a devoted brother treats a beloved sister. Then I will be a *mentsh,* a faithful *mentsh.* Even if it's painful, I must tear out these feelings before they get out of hand.

"You seem deep in thought, Yosef," said Roza.

"Sometimes it's not so easy to give an accounting of one's thinking," replied Yosef.

Rukhame hurried over and said, "Roza, you're such a dear sister. First you're crying, and now you're smiling. Would you call that a capricious nature, Yosef?"

"Shall we go?" asked Yosef without answering Rukhame.

"Yes, let's go," said Shimen.

"March!" commanded Rukhame, and they all headed out the door.

As Golde watched from the window, she said a blessing for her happy children as they walked down the street. She saw Shimen and Rukhame strolling in front, and Yosef and Roza following behind. What a lovely couple they make, Golde admitted to herself. Bless me, God, with a son-in-law like Yosef. He's such a diamond! And why not a match with him? Why look elsewhere when God has sent him from heaven right into our home? What does it matter that I don't know his parents, or that Roza would be a wife without a mother-in-law in town? Does it really matter? Is my Leyke so happy with her mother-in-law—a woman she can never please? A mother-in-law who only wants to meddle, give an opinion, and be a dictator!

No one can tell me that Yosef was born from a stone. He has parents, and he often speaks of his devoted mother. So what if she's far away? A mother's heart is always with her child. May my children and grandchildren conduct themselves with such a good name as he does!

Of course, we all want to be part of a good family with a noble descent. But today a person can buy their aristocracy with money. With a thousand rubles, anyone can become an aristocrat! The so-called pedigree from the grave is a lot of trouble, and who needs it when I could be blessed with such an intelligent and faithful child as Yosef for a son-in-law?

Golde sat for a long time looking after her beloved children, watching as they happily walked together in the summer sunshine. Memories of her days as a young girl began to enter her thoughts. How she never went walking with a boy and was even embarrassed to look into a boy's eyes. How she always fought with her brothers and sisters and was always at war with her parents. How she was engaged to be married without her consent, and how in her heart she wanted to see the groom, or at least talk with him before the wedding. How she quietly wept when she learned that her intended bridegroom was a coarse young man, and how she trembled at the idea of speaking out against her parents who only wanted him because he came from a good family with money. How lonely and unhappy she was about him until God stepped in and rescued her by causing a devastating fire that impoverished her family. The wedding was quickly called off when her parents could no longer pay the dowry requested by the pedigreed in-laws.

She remembered with shame the feelings she had for one of her uncle's sons, Leybl, a boy she had been raised with, and how her heart pounded so sweetly whenever she was with him. Oh, how she wished to throw herself into his arms and weep and kiss him! A shudder ran through Golde's body as she recalled the day she attended her dear Leybl's wedding and how she danced with the bride who had stolen him from her until she fainted and was carried away from the celebration. Everyone worried she was losing her senses, and she had to keep everything hidden in her pure, innocent heart. Only by crying alone in her bed for several months was she able to heal from the wounds she had suffered that day. Only God in His seventh heaven knew her grief and how it still remained hidden in her heart to this day.

We were so foolish back then, Golde sighed to herself. What did we know about life? How quickly we went back to playing our little games and singing our little childhood songs. And if there was a marriage in a year, you just did it, because you shook like a leaf before your parents who were always angry with you about something. Why should I deprive my children of a few carefree moments? Let them be their own chaperones. And what if they're not completely honest? Why look for trouble from such pure, innocent, and dear children? Why make their lives a prison? Besides, when do we as women get to live? Once we're married, we're constantly bound up with pregnancy and nursing, or with little ones pulling at our aprons. Enjoy yourselves, dear children, and your mother will rejoice with you. Young people are smarter today. It is a better world. You can be good, smart, honest, and pious as well.

As Golde watched through the window, her children turned a corner and disappeared from view. She stood up with an easy heart and felt as if a new feeling for life had come upon her.

And truly, can there be a greater happiness for a mother than the pleasure of being satisfied with her children? Children who are handsome and good before God and man, and for whom she hopes for an even greater happiness.

Golde was not the only one watching her children walking together on the street. Others looked on from other windows.

Although these good children had never offended anyone or done anything wrong, they were not without enemies. Yet how could they have enemies without ever harming anyone?

Their enemies are all those enviers in the world who hate others for being happy, as if another person's happiness is somehow offensive to them. All those people without God in their hearts who release an angry word at someone who is happy, and then sit in wait until their happiness is destroyed.

FIVE

THE GOD-FEARING WOMEN

Why did the women of the city who saw the happy children walking along together begrudge them their happiness? What business was it of theirs, even if what they said was true that it was not proper for a young woman to be out strolling with a young man on the street? How did it harm them? Did they not realize they were committing a far greater sin by gossiping about these innocent children?

Indeed, they knew their sin, but told themselves, according to the piety of the Jewish multitude, "I may, but you must not." With their corrupt hearts and limited senses, they could not judge themselves. Have pity on them; they must find fault so as not to be envious.

"What do you say about that?" asked Dvorah Basye the tavern keeper who was known as a God-fearing woman with a mean tongue. "What do you make of that little group?" she asked Sterne Gute, the city's busybody, who acted like God's attorney.

"A spectacle, as I'm a Jewish daughter!" replied Sterne Gute, one of those wicked creatures who knew how to ingratiate herself first, then bite to the bone. "How can a person forget who she is? How long was Golde's husband a pauper? How often did she come to borrow something for *Shabbes?* Now look at her children parading down the street! Is that any way for Jewish children to behave?"

"Tell me," said Dvorah Basye, "how does a decent mother let her girls go walking with a grown man? Especially some kind of German in a short coat dragged here by the demons!"

"Do you think anything good will come of this?" asked Sterne Gute. "Just look at Shimen. While he studied with my husband, he was like silk. But now? Where is his shame? How could they take such a young pup for a teacher while tossing aside a scholar like my husband, Reuven Horishker? How many Jews of his stature can you find in a city like this? Why should my pious husband, may he enjoy long life, give up one of his best students to such a hooligan?"

"If your husband would cut off his sidelocks, put on a fancy coat, and be willing to play with the ladies like that little German at Golde's, he would have bread, too," answered Dvorah Basye.

"Better they be done away with before disturbing one hair of my Reuven's sidelocks! It doesn't bother me that my husband is not so pretty. Torah makes wise, Torah makes beautiful, and Torah is always the best merchandise. I remember when I got engaged, people said to me, 'Sterne Gute, you're taking a dark horse for a groom.' But I said, 'Carob is dark, too, and it's sugar-sweet!' My husband is like carob! But would these girls today have the brains to see it? May God let us attend their funerals! *Oy*, look at me. I've been talking to you for two hours and completely forgot that I was on my way to the pharmacy."

"Is someone sick?" asked Dvorah Basye.

"Sick is what my enemies should be! Those who slander me should be sick and diseased. Dvorah Basye, don't you know I help everyone? In truth, who else could Sore the widow ask to get her prescription if not for me? It's not a big sacrifice, and occasionally I add a little contribution of my own to help pay for her medicine. Still, I'm a little short right now, and only the demons know how much it will cost."

Dvorah Basye rummaged through her pockets and found a groschen which she handed to Sterne Gute. "*Nu,* what do you hear about my Feygele?"

"Don't be offended," said Sterne Gute. "I won't hold anything back from you."

"Why should I be offended?" asked the tavern keeper. "Does anyone look at a donation so long as the intention is clear?"

"All right then, I'll tell you what people are saying. Some say your Feygele doesn't want to get married. Others say the reason she doesn't want to get married is because there's something wrong with her mouth. But I've been in your house plenty of times, and never noticed anything out of the ordinary. May my enemies' lives be as twisted as a bagel if her mouth isn't as straight as a violin string," insisted Sterne Gute. "But tell me the truth, Dvorah Basye, do you think it's such a good idea to be chasing after that young man going around in a short coat? You may think he's a good catch, but I know finer and better children. Not only that, I hear people talking about him. But whatever people say, as it says in the Torah, 'It's Messiah's time.'"

"I think that's in the prayer book," said Dvorah Basye, trying to show off her education.

"Yes, in the prayer book, too," the busybody quickly agreed, "where we ask the Master of the Universe that our young men and women will not have to learn for themselves like our elders and parents did. But I still have to say that it all depends on the mothers, and my child would not be alive today if he acted like your potential groom. Mind you, we live next door, and I've seen with my own eyes how he polishes his boots on *Shabbes*. But I won't say anything damaging. That's the greatest sin, to tell gossip. So I will not, God forbid, say anything bad about him. But I don't have to tell you what a quiet boy my Yisrolik is. If he sees a girl, he runs the other way. He studies so well, and I assure you, he knows nothing about fancy shirts and modern coats. He only knows about the study house and how to open a Talmud. What else do you need? Surely, your daughter would be a happy bride if God sent Yisrolik to be her husband. Even my husband Reuven says, 'No one in Mohilev knows what a pearl is growing here.' So do you think that even if Golde gave me a million rubles that I would give my son to that brazen girl who goes walking with that hooligan? I swear they walk hand in hand together. Haven't you seen how they fondle each other?" asked Sterne Gute, trying to convince the tavern keeper to admit to something she never saw.

"I've never seen fondling, exactly," replied Dvorah Basye. "But what's wrong with her head to be out on the street in broad daylight holding hands? Soon they'll be sneaking out of town to do who knows what, God forbid."

"Why doesn't the Messiah come now?" asked Sterne Gute. "What evil edicts await us, may God save and guard us. Just yesterday, Yuda Yenta's week-old baby died. How is this poor child guilty because Golde has taken a German into her house who has bewitched her children? I mean, why should an innocent child have to leave this bright world because of such heretics? Dear Father, may all misfortunes fall upon them and not touch one hair on the rest of us!"

A powerful clap of thunder almost stopped the hearts of these quiet, God-fearing women. Sterne Gute, whose throat was already dry from her long tirade, coughed into her hand, then washed her hands, and recited a blessing for thunder. "God, may your first thunder reach the heretics who stole the livelihood from my husband. I must be going, Dvorah Basye, I'm afraid the rain will catch me before I get to the pharmacy. Will you be in the study house in the morning to hear the new rabbi? I have something else to tell you. Good day!"

"A good year! Go in good health," replied Dvorah Basye. But as soon as Sterne Gute was gone, the tavern keeper grumbled, What a character! What an insolent mouth she has, may she go dumb for saying my Feygele has a crooked mouth. Does she think I don't know what she's trying to do? And all those hints about her Yisrolik's virtues. Does she think I will grab him up as a treasure for my Feygele? Never!

While Sterne Gute was detaining her mother, Feygele was standing at the window watching Golde's happy children pass by. Tears welled in her eyes as she asked herself, Why is the whole world alive? Why is everyone living except for me? Some go out walking, he with her, and her with someone else. They know they are alive in the world. Me, I have no day or night. I go around in my greasy dress without a moment's rest and not a soul to talk to. All day long, I listen to Pintelman's drunken singing, Lielik's loud shouting, some groggy young man's rude talk, and curses from my mother. I'd be better off living in an empty forest! How have I sinned by letting out that walking with a boy is not a crime and that Yosef who lives at Golde's house is good enough to be my husband? Do I deserve slaps and curses and eating my heart out so that I might, God forbid, do who knows what? Roza and Rukhame were born with silver spoons in their mouths. Their parents let them dress like *Shabbes* in the middle of the week. And me, even on *Shabbes* and the holidays, I must sit and guard the Gentile who takes over for mother out of fear he will steal from the cash box.

May God grant me as many healthy, happy years as all the glasses of whiskey my mother sells. For her, it's not a sin. And if she needs to fry fish on *Shabbes,* does she get upset? Doesn't she take them out of the pan herself? Yet she thinks going for a stroll or speaking a few words to a boy is such a terrible sin. To me, it seems a lot worse to be taking the paltry earnings from some discharged soldier's pocket. *Vey iz mir,* that's the thieving way she's collecting a dowry for me!

No, Mama dear, I have no one to learn from. What can I do while you're holding the whip and driving my life wherever you desire? But not for long. Today I'm going into the city to have a dress made and to buy a pair of gloves and a parasol so I can be a human being like other human beings. Even if you're making wedding plans for me with that old busybody's son, he's not getting me so fast. He's going to have to wait awhile! There'll be a lot of water under the bridge before I take such a boor for a bridegroom. The lout couldn't even recite a blessing when they called him up at the Passover *minyan.* But Yosef, how skillfully he read the afternoon service. Just listening to him was such a joy. Roza was so proud, and Rukhame—what a clever girl she is—never took her eyes off me during the entire service as if to say, "Look, your intended bridegroom can't even say a blessing, and our Yosef reads the whole service so beautifully."

How happy I was during Passover that I could tear myself away from the tavern and go hear Yosef's talk. He always talks about so many wide-ranging things, and he's such a pleasure to listen to. But my mother had to turn around and start a whole resentment with Golde's household. For what reason? Why must I be angry with them when I don't even know what they've done? No, I have to write them a note and tell them I'm not responsible for the dispute my mother started. I must let them know that my mother and I are of two different natures. But how will I write it? How will I begin? I'm sure there will be more errors in my letter than words, but no matter, they won't laugh. They're not the kind of people who make fun of others. But if Yosef sees that I can't do any better, maybe he'll think I'm just the kitchen maid. What a hopeless life I have. Look what a mother can do to a child! But to you, Roza, I will pour out my heart, and tell you about all the wounds I carry from my own mother who bore me and suckled me and raised me to be a servant.

Feygele's thoughts began to make her feel ill. The first rumble of thunder startled her, and she hurried back down to the kitchen before her mother noticed she was gone.

Sterne Gute, her head covered with her apron, ran as quickly as she could to avoid the rain. By the time she reached Golde's house, she was exhausted. Taking the apron off her head, she went up to Golde's door and shouted at the top of her lungs: "Good morning, Golde! What do you say to this downpour just as a person is running to buy medicine for a sick friend who lies dying in her bed? But how can I run through a downpour like this? *Oy*, it's raining buckets, and there's thunder and lightening, too. One's heart could stop from fright. Holy Father, send it to the open fields or empty forest!" shouted Sterne Gute as another clap of thunder made the windows rattle.

Golde, who was sitting with her grandson Leybke, ran to open the door for Sterne Gute. When she saw the pouring rain, she cried out, "My children! God only knows where they are. Master of the Universe, perform your loving kindness and protect my children from harmful events, bad people, angry dogs, storm winds, and rain!"

"Don't worry, Golde," said Sterne Gute trying to comfort her. "I just passed your children a little while ago. I hardly recognized your Roza and Rukhame. They glow like stars in the heavens. They are gems, so handsome and good. Is there another in the land as picture-perfect as your Roza? Such a dear child, may no evil eye befall her.

"It's not my business to ask, Golde, but what do you want in a son-in-law? You know that your father's mother-in-law's father-in-law's brother was related to my great-grandfather's father-in-law. Once you figure it out, we are actually pretty close relatives, although I can't say whether it's first or second cousins. My Yisrolik could figure out all these relationships in the blink of an eye. As I've told you before, he's a genius among the greatest minds. My Reuven can ask him a difficult question, and he can answer without even thinking about it. But what was I going to tell you? Can you believe it, as we get older the mind seems to evaporate.

"Oh, yes, I remember now. My Reuven says he's heard you've been negotiating for Shleyme's son, the doctor. Shleyme is an honest Jew all right, although after all is said and done, no one gets off easy. As the Talmud says, even the best doctor will end up in hell.

"I was just over there today. I had to call the doctor to come see Sore the widow. She's sick in bed, may a Jewish home never know of it. This is the third week that I've been trying to take care of her, collecting a few groschen here and there, bringing her a little chicken broth, and running to the pharmacy in the thunder and rain. How, I ask you, does a proprietress like Dvorah Basye the tavern keeper, who is loaded with money, take out a bent two-groschen piece and make a big deal out of it? Even if I asked her for a donation for one of her own kin, someone who is lying on their sick-bed with their soul wavering between life and death, she'd still come up with the smallest coin possible. What do you think? If Avrom the butcher came to her for a donation, would she shame him with the same kind of stingy contribution she gives to me, Reuven Horishker's wife?

"Golde, you don't come from ignorant people. Tell me, do you see in today's generation any people like my husband, or like his father-in-law, may he enjoy himself in Paradise. See, I'm not telling a lie."

Sterne Gute called to Golde's grandson, "Leybke, come here so I can pull your little ear. We're talking about someone who is dead." Then the busybody turned back to Golde. "But between you and me, I've learned how Dvorah Basye got to where she is today: she's been dealing with robbers who bring her their stolen goods. That's your leader of the women in the study house! You can tell the truth about anyone except your own father, and I'm telling you that when she gave me her gift, she told me that she hoped your Shimen would become her Feygele's bridegroom! I won't deny that my Reuven said that if you would send Shimen back to him, he would let another student go, one who is not so talented, because he sees that your young man has a good head on his shoulders. And it wouldn't hurt him to be studying with my Yisrolik. It doesn't matter that they aren't evenly matched. Shimen could still get a clearer understanding of the Talmud by learning beside Yisrolik.

"Tell me, Golde, don't you worry about such a pure heart studying with someone in a German coat? And what about your other children? What will people say? Don't you think people will gossip about his going out strolling with your Roza? Like your neighbor, Dvorah Basye, people don't seem to have enough to do. Just today, she said that if he were her child, she would break his legs. I, on the other hand, know very well that your children are trustworthy; but still, one needs to be careful before people as well as God. Even Shleyme's son, the doctor, may not be the best match for your Roza. He may be very kind, but I would be careful about giving my child to him. A doctor, no matter who he is, has learned to be a doctor in the outside world. He may be more successful, but isn't it better to have a son-in-law who sits and studies Talmud? In any case, God has helped you, and you don't lack the few hundred rubles to get the finest bridegroom. And why not? Your Roza is worth it!"

No longer able to listen to Sterne Gute's ramblings, Golde ran to the door to look for her beloved children. "Protect them, dear God in Your holy heaven," she prayed. "Do not remove your grace from my pure, precious children."

Meanwhile, Sterne Gute sat down beside little Leybke and asked him, "Does your mother like your father?"

"Yes," the child answered.

"Does your father like Roza?"

"Yes," Leybke nodded.

"Does Roza kiss Yosef?"

"Yes," the child replied, licking sour cream off his bagel.

The busybody's despicable questions, which the ignorant little child continued to answer with his unconscious "Yes," gave Sterne Gute enough gossip to talk about for weeks. We will not weary you, sympathetic reader, with more of her tedious ramblings. Let us just say she came away with a fist-full of money that each member of the household gave her for the poor, long-suffering widow.

We beg the indulgence of those dear readers whose patience has been tried with these long rantings that are really no more than a busybody's chatter. Sterne Gute is not a main character in the novel, and Dvorah Basye plays only a small role. But we cannot leave them out because they buzz around our dear heroes, too, and must be addressed in our writing. Unfortunately, there are Sterne Gutes and Dvorah Basyes everywhere, even in positions of power. Perhaps they will be recognized and exposed one day. Perhaps.

But back to our story!

Six

YOSEF AND MEYSHE SHNEYUR

Although Yosef tried to drive from his mind all the bitter thoughts that Meyshe Shneyur provoked in him, he was still disturbed by them. One name, in particular, especially bothered him. In the beginning, as an insult, Meyshe Shneyur called him "idler." Now, he called him "Yosefke" or "my little Yosefke," and in the seemingly affectionate term, Yosef perceived even more poison.

Would I not be better off returning to the peace and indifference of being a yeshiva student? Yosef asked himself. But, in truth, what peace did I have? Didn't I suffer from conflicting thoughts about having my young life consumed by the study of Talmud? Didn't I struggle to find a way out without disappointing my parents who wanted me to become a rabbi? Questions plagued me day and night, and I wept over each one: Why don't others understand what is good, just, and pious the way I do? Why, even with my understanding, did I refrain from doing what was right? And why did I fool myself and others by going along on their dark, slippery road even though I knew it was too narrow and crooked for me?

Dear God, I feel like a man bound in shackles by those who want to tell the folk how to live their lives. But how do I break these chains and accept Your gifts of happiness? How do I remain strong under the yoke that lies over all humanity? The wound I carry is depleting my energy. I don't sleep at night, my thoughts are jumbled, and I can't wake myself during the day. My mind is filled with only one thought: Roza! But no! I must forget her. I must be honest with myself and face my current situation. Where are my books? I must study. I still have time to heal myself.

In the days that followed, Yosef became a different person. He studied harder and with more diligence. He only saw the family for meals, or occasionally in Fridman's garden, which was large and filled with tall, thick-branched trees. Sometimes he lectured there so his separation from the family would not seem so conspicuous as in the house, but these gatherings were cold and infrequent. Whether anyone noticed or not, the change in Yosef served as a kind of cure for him.

Meyshe Shneyur was one person who did notice. He understood Yosef's nature and saw the change in him. As Yosef's separation from the family grew, Meyshe Shneyur began treating him with more kindness.

One day, while studying in his room, Yosef was startled to find a note in his Talmud:

> You do not know that walls have ears, and heaven and earth have eyes. You think that no one knows, but all is known. I write in the name of my father-in-law who wants to drive you out in shame, but the One God knows my loyalty to you, and I will not allow this to happen. My advice, Yosef, is to remember this information but act as if you do not know it. Protect yourself. No one should notice a change in you, and you can gradually remove yourself from the household.

A person like you could easily have a position in the city, so why remain in a house where you are unappreciated until they ask you to leave? They are of the old world and have certain feelings about character and insults. I do not need to write you again. You are lost, Yosef. God is witness to my loyalty.

If you like, you can come to me this evening. I will explain everything to you.

Meyshe Shneyur

Yosef was furious. He thought he would faint on the spot. He sat for a long time with his head in his hands not knowing what to do. He wanted to gather his few possessions and leave, but the image of the resulting scandal flashed through his mind. God, where could I show my face? he asked himself. How could I besmirch the name of that innocent angel, the purest and most lovely? Is she guilty for my inability to keep my mask in place? How could I betray these good people? What if that faithful woman who has been as good and devoted to me as my own mother thinks that I have insulted her and repaid her kindness with shame and dishonesty?

Just as Yosef finished these troubling thoughts, Golde arrived with a glass of hot tea as she always did at the end of the evening. Sensing his anxious mood, she said, "Yosef, the Talmud will not run away. Drink your tea before it gets cold." Then she quietly left the room.

Yosef's heart melted. She's always been so good to me, he thought. How could I be so ungrateful to her? God, please let this dear woman know my truth.

As Yosef sat in the darkness tangled in his thoughts, he did not notice Roza enter the room. She stood by the door and regarded him with a happy look. "Yosef," Roza said gently, "you're so deep in thought. Don't worry, your ship is not sinking!"

"Roza! Excuse me, I didn't see you there."

"Excuse me, Yosef," Roza replied shyly. "I didn't mean to interrupt you. I just wondered what you were thinking. I must learn not to be so curious or try to guess your thoughts."

"Roza," said Yosef, "I have something to tell you."

"Oh, Yosef, not right now. I've been invited to a wedding, and there's a carriage waiting for me at the door. I've come to deliver a letter I've been asked to hand to you personally. Don't take it the wrong way, Yosef. Good night!"

She gave Yosef the envelope and hurried from the room. Yosef walked to the window and watched as Roza got into the carriage and drove off with her mother.

Divine angel, he thought, how can I be ungrateful to you? How can I run away from such a luminous child? Where will I go? Where will your glow not reach me? Where will your sweet smile and pleasant voice not follow me? Oh, Roza, you are in my heart, and I will run away like a shot deer with the arrow still in me!

Lighting a lamp, Yosef looked at the letter Roza had brought him. Although addressed to him, it had not come through the mail. He opened the envelope and began to read:

Dear Friend Yosef!

If you, as an intelligent man, were in my position and could feel what is in my heart as I write this, you would understand that one may not always follow one's will, and not everything that works well for a short time can last forever.

Believe me, I have the greatest confidence in you, and I tell you openly that you fill the largest part of my heart. Most of my thoughts are about you, and if it were in my hands and my power, I would not need advice in making a decision. Yosef, I also have a heart and feelings and know love.

I am, however, under the will of my parents, who have clearer eyes to discern my future life, and I must and will obey them! You are trusted for your honesty. You have not lost my parents' trust, and my friendship to you remains as strong as ever.

What I want—and what is very hard for me to ask of you—is this: if you find another position somewhere or another calling that draws you, I beg of you, please leave and spare us both from pain and trouble. Protect our names from evil talk.

Yosef, you are young and talented. Run off now and become an adult. One can master oneself if one wants to, and I, a sensible girl, show you this example.

Be happy and healthy, Yosef. I ask you not to withdraw your friendship from me. And whatever you decide, may it be calm and not careless. Let it not bring about any gossip. Please protect my name.

Roza

Oh, Yosef sighed, what kind of day is this? The clouds have burst and let out their whole deluge on me as if to do away with me once and for all. Perhaps Roza is not so clever after all. Why did she have to write such a convoluted story? Why did she tell me of her love and then withdraw it? Who asked her to reveal herself to me at this time? Excuse her, dear God, for this foolishness, and for hurting me for no reason. At least now I understand the situation and her words, "I must learn not to be so curious or try to guess your thoughts." That's why she hurried away. The coldness of her letter makes me shudder. She wants my heart to break gradually. She wants me to suffer before I free myself. No, I won't do it! I must get out of here quickly.

With his cheeks flaming and his eyes full of tears, Yosef hurried to see Meyshe Shneyur. Roza's sister, Leyke, invited him in with friendship and love. "Oh, Yosef, we haven't had the honor of seeing you for such a long time. I'm so pleased I decided not to go to the wedding with the others. For some reason, my heart told me to expect an important guest. My heart tells me you're a good friend, Yosef, even if my husband doesn't know your real value."

"I thank you a thousand times, Leyke," said Yosef. "A heart can often tell things in advance. If you feel that I am your friend, then be assured I feel the same way towards you. Your husband is a friend, too, although I don't always understand how to take his friendship."

"Yosef, are you ill?" asked Leyke. "Your voice is shaking, and you talk as though you're in pain."

"Yes, I've been sick, but I'm beginning to feel better now."

Meyshe Shneyur opened the door to the dining room where he was eating a large meal. He brought a chair to the table and invited Yosef in. "Sit down, Yosef," he said. "I'm glad to see you. You haven't come to see us for a long time. You used to sit with me here day and night."

"So it was, dear friend," answered Yosef. "In good times we forget old friends, and in bad times we remember them. Thank God I've run back to my old friend before it's too late."

"Thank you, Yosef, for considering me a friend. But tell me the truth, do you really consider me a friend, or are you just being polite?"

Before Yosef could answer, Meyshe Shneyur called out in the voice of a master speaking to his servant: "Leyke, go out for a while. Yosef and I have an important matter to discuss."

"But Yosef is my guest as much as yours," Leyke replied. "What kind of secrets do you have with him?"

"Go out, I tell you!" shouted Meyshe Shneyur and glared at her.

Realizing there was no use in arguing, Leyke left the room, and Meyshe Shneyur closed the door.

"I asked you, Yosef, do you consider me a friend or not?"

"Meyshe Shneyur, I'm an open person, and I will tell you the truth: I don't really know you very well. You tell me that you believe in me. You ask what's wrong with me. But I'm never sure of your intent. If I'm afraid of you, Meyshe Shneyur, please don't take it the wrong way. All I know is that I'm alone here. I see things happening around me, but I can't find myself guilty of anything."

"A thief is afraid even when he's not guilty," said Meyshe Shneyur. "An inexperienced thief is afraid of the very thought of stealing. Which kind of thief are you?"

"Neither!" replied Yosef. "What are you saying? I've thought something was not quite right here."

"Believe me, Yosef, I swear by everything that is dear to me, I'm as loyal to you as a brother. No one here thinks you're dishonest. Although I can't speak for everyone, I certainly don't consider what you've done a crime. I've been in love, and I understand your situation. It's natural to be in love with Roza. How far have you gone with her? Tell the truth, have you grabbed and kissed her?"

"Heaven forbid, Meyshe Shneyur! Yes, I do love Roza, but I've not fallen into any sin."

"You're lying! You're telling me Roza has never talked to you and you've never declared your love to her? Yosef, like any good friend, I've been watching you. I can see you and Roza are in love. You don't have to pretend in front of me. That's what's brought on this storm and why I wrote you that note. To lead you away from the unhappiness that's tormenting you."

"Meyshe Shneyur," said Yosef, "do you believe there's a God in the world? I swear by Him that I am clean of any suspicion. Roza has not uttered a syllable about love to me. And I have not spoken a word to her or shown my feelings in any way!"

"I don't believe you!" exclaimed Meyshe Shneyur.

"What? What do you know?" asked Yosef.

"I know about the letters you've been writing to one another. How can you deny it?"

"Meyshe Shneyur, why are you interrogating me? What do you wish to uncover by this investigation? All I can say is that I am innocent. And nothing grieves me more than the belief that I am ungrateful to this family."

"Then what kind of trick is this?" said Meyshe Shneyur, holding up a crumpled piece of paper. "Do you recognize the handwriting? Isn't this Roza's letter to you in spite of all your protests?"

Yosef took the letter. The pieces had been torn and were pasted back together. Yosef read:

Beloved Yosef,

Take this letter, dear Yosef, the same way you have taken my heart. Yosef, I am ashamed of myself for writing this, but I cannot rest. I must tell you that I love you. Your voice and the way you read aloud are brilliant stars in my empty skies. Yosef, you alone are my sun. Oh, dear, why do I need this fancy writing? Why am I writing foreign words to you? Yosef, you are the whole of my thoughts. I love you!

I have written ten such letters to you and have torn them all to pieces. God only knows the crazy words I write for I am not in my right mind. I am mad and cannot speak my thoughts aloud. I want to explain the whole of my feelings to you, Yosef. I have been reborn since I have known you. Yosef, take my letter as you have taken my heart!

I'm afraid that this letter is not freeing me either. I wish that a breeze would come and snatch it from my hands and bring it to you. Then you could read it and spare me the first difficult words of introduction. How will I ever find someone who will take this letter from my hands and deliver it to you? But before I can send it off, my heart is filled again with new words to make you know of my love. Oh, what kind of fool am I that I go on and on like this?

Yosef could not read anymore. The paper was torn, and one could see there was something written about Meyshe Shneyur, but Yosef could not make it out. Tears filled his eyes, and he looked at Meyshe Shneyur in shock. "Perhaps you, Meyshe Shneyur, are the wind that Roza wished would send her letter to me. It sounds like her, but God is my witness, I don't know anything about it."

"I've had this letter for weeks already," said Meyshe Shneyur. "It's not possible that she hasn't written you since the day I found it. Can you swear that you haven't gotten a letter from her in the past few days?"

"Today I received a letter, but with an entirely different message. Not her words and not her style."

Yosef showed Meyshe Shneyur the letter.

"Look closely," said Meyshe Shneyur, "and you could hang them on a chain—a nice chain for your pocket watch! I see what the letter means. You said Roza told you she was going to a wedding with her mother, but they were actually heading off to arrange a marriage. They are negotiating with a potential groom, a simple youth, but he has three thousand rubles.

"Listen, Yosef, and understand what's happening. Roza is half crazy. You've only known her for a few weeks; I've known her for four years. You also know that matches have been discussed for her, but nothing has ever come of it. Whenever her mother tries to talk with her about it, Roza says she's not interested in matches and already has a bridegroom. Then she runs off crying. When her mother told me this and asked for my advice, I answered that you were as good a match as any and that they should act on it right away. I told Roza to hold on and went with Golde to explain everything to my father-in-law. We didn't tell him that Roza loved you but that we shouldn't keep looking for a match when we've already found such a good one right here in front of us. He went wild and shouted, 'How can you tell me this!' You know him when he gets angry. 'Hell will freeze over before I let that happen!' he yelled, even though his whole family and a lot of guests were in the house. I tell you, Yosef, you've made the best impression on everyone, but he swore that as long as he was alive and had any say over his own child, he would never allow such a match. So we stopped talking. Now they've made an agreement with one of Borekh Balshen's sons, and you know what a nobody he is. He's an empty dandy with three thousand rubles. Roza knows him and is finished with matches.

"Now she's embarrassed when reminded of her earlier talk. Believe me, the girl is empty-headed and as useful as a broken windmill. So thank God, Yosef, that He has saved you from this trouble."

"How did I not know about this?" asked Yosef. "How could I eat, drink, and live in this house and miss even a glimmer of what was going on here? It's like the intrigues in *The Count of Monte Cristo!* Yet how could Roza, who always seemed so quiet, innocent, and loyal to me, carry on behind such a fine silk mask? No, I don't believe it!"

"You have evidence in her letter today," said Meyshe Shneyur. "Each day she is different. You are lucky that my father-in-law had the presence of mind to ignore my advice. I wouldn't be doing my duty as a friend if I didn't tell you, especially seeing how torn apart you are by her. I hope that now, God willing, without her in your life, you will have some joy and will someday recall this talk with gratitude.

"Now my advice to you is this: swallow everything you know. My mother-in-law loves you like her own child, so tell her nothing. She made me promise not to tell you anything. You should settle into a position in the city and forget about Roza. She is not worth remembering. I meant to tell you in my letter that my father-in-law is angry with you, but I was afraid you'd consider me an enemy and not come to talk. My father-in-law doesn't know about the letter. I have kept everything to myself. No one searched your things. The letter was found, and I paid money for it. Obey me, Yosef. Your romance with Roza will have no good end. Find a situation and make a productive person of yourself."

As Yosef stood to go, Meyshe Shneyur said, "Wait a minute. I've just thought of a good place for you. Tomorrow I'll go into the city and check it out. Remain calm, Yosef. Don't be a child."

Suddenly, they heard the sound of a carriage on the street, and Meyshe Shneyur warned, "Mother-in-law is coming; everyone will be home soon. Go and don't let anyone know you were here with me tonight."

"I don't know how to thank you for setting me straight," said Yosef. "Good night, best friend!"

SEVEN

YOSEF AND ROZA

Yosef came into the corridor and saw Golde paying the coachman. "Oh, Yosef," said Golde when she spotted him, "it's so late. Why aren't you asleep yet?"

"How late is it?" asked Yosef.

"It's almost one o'clock. The in-laws held us up. They didn't want Roza to leave."

"Good evening, Yosef," said Roza standing just outside the door. "It's so dark. Please lend me a hand."

Without saying a word, Yosef gave her his hand and led her into the house. When Golde found Fridman waiting up for them, she told her husband how proud she was of Roza. Everyone, she said, including all the fine and educated people were impressed and delighted with their daughter.

Must I listen to this? Yosef thought. Don't these people have any human feelings? They act as though they don't know anything about Roza's treatment of me.

"Good evening again, Yosef," Roza said in a happy mood as she entered the room and interrupted his thoughts. "I'm sorry I had to run off so quickly. What was I telling you? Was it about the groom or the in-laws?"

"It's all the same to me," replied Yosef. "Good night, Roza. I still have much to do."

"Yosef, I won't let you get away so quickly. You have to hear what a good person the groom is. He's educated, he talked with me for quite a while, and I liked him very much. He's smart and fine and so much like you, Yosef. And the in-laws! It was a real pleasure to be in their company. I had such a good time—"

"Enough, Roza, don't exhaust me with all this talk. I don't want to hear about it."

"But Yosef, I have to describe the bride to you. I want to tell you how wonderful she is, and ask if you think there's anyone like her."

"You don't have to describe her to me, Roza. I know her. I know her better than you do."

"How do you know her?" Roza asked in surprise. "Do you know her from Kurland or from Mohilev?"

"I know her, I tell you. Leave me alone about this, Roza. Why are you doing this to me tonight?"

"And why are you in such a bad mood? I'm not letting you leave until you tell me how you know the bride."

"If you insist, I'll tell you. I was in her house once. I don't know how or why. Then I received several letters from her. God, what she wrote! How sweet and loving her letters were, letters she sent through an enemy of mine. And how cold and bitter was the letter she handed me herself. I didn't know her before, but that letter opened my eyes to the fact that my enemy was really my best friend. No, I don't dislike her. She's a decent girl, just not very smart. She wrote me such a long account about something a person could perceive in one wink. Now I know everything. So enough, Roza! You've made promises of friendship to me, but now stop talking and let me go."

"When did I make promises to you, Yosef? When did I talk to you about friendship? Perhaps you're confusing me with the bride! Mother, Yosef is not himself and won't talk to me."

Before Golde could reply, Roza said, "Fine, have it your way, Yosef. You'll remember me from this evening. Good night." She turned and walked away.

"What's wrong, Yosef?" asked Golde. "Why are you so anxious this evening? You look as though you went to sleep and woke up too soon. I know that feeling when you sleep for a few hours and wake up feeling chilled and sour. Here, drink some tea before the samovar gets cold. It will make you feel better."

"I did sleep, but not for very long. If I'm shivering, don't take it as a bad sign. Please don't worry about me. I promise to get some rest, but tonight I have something important to write."

"Yosef," said Golde, "Roza will have to settle accounts with you. It's a shame Rukhame is already asleep. If she were here, I know she would cheer you up. Roza and Rukhame are so alike but with different temperaments. Be kind to Roza, Yosef. What can you do with a young woman who is beside herself with happiness from the pleasure and honor of being in such refined company? Don't be angry with her. Defend her."

Without saying another word, Yosef headed to his room. Golde collected her things, read the nighttime prayers, and went off to bed.

Although the house was quiet, inside Yosef's brain a storm was raging. He sat for a long time, his head resting on his hands, then he reread the letter Roza had brought him and studied the words.

Is the Roza in this letter the same Roza who wrote the other letter? he wondered. It could be, but this just doesn't look like her handwriting. Yet how can I doubt that it came from her when she handed it to me herself? But the handwriting, and even more, the cold contents—this is not how Roza talks.

But isn't she foolish and even evil for pursuing such a game with me by pouring salt on my wounds? Is it right for her to go on and on about finding such a bridegroom for herself, and then irritate me by asking how I knew the bride? I wanted to say, "Roza, you're a decent girl, a goodhearted person. How can you be so cold-blooded in your disregard for my feelings?" Oh, Roza, do you have any idea how your words hurt me?

Be happy, Roza! That's what I want for you. And I forgive you—I forgive you with my whole heart! I've been such a fool. Really, what am I to you? If you were sold by your parents into a marriage—or even if you were a gift—you are free to do as you wish. I am vile for expressing my angry words to you this evening. What right do I have to these feelings? I'm just a teacher, an idler from the study house living in your home. Why wouldn't you be drawn to a rich, educated man with three thousand rubles?

You spoke to me like a smart, brave, experienced woman who knows and understands me. My character is weak, my wings are clipped, and I am bound by love to my parents and their wishes. But I will obey your decision and make a proper and useful human being of myself. Thank you, Roza. Tomorrow I will beg your pardon and ask for your advice. I will remain your proper brother, as I promised from the beginning.

As dawn broke, Yosef tried to sleep, but tears streamed from his eyes. How could his heart have suffered any more than it had already? He always knew the day would come when he would see Roza in a stranger's hands. He told himself again and again that he loved her only as a brother. But now, as his true feelings overflowed, he realized he had been fooling himself. If only he had swallowed it down without letting anyone know. But now he was choking on that hard, bitter bite. Everything was known, and Roza knew more than anyone else. It had been too difficult for him to be a *mentsh.* He was guilty and had not made his mask thick enough to keep people from seeing through it.

All these thoughts were still on his mind the next morning when Yosef got up, his eyes red and swollen from ceaseless tears and lack of sleep.

PART TWO

ONE

ROZA

Roza was happy with herself and the whole world when she arrived home from the wedding in Kurland. In contrast, Yosef felt the whole world standing against him. He struggled to forge his heart against her and restrain his feelings—feelings that were stronger than his own strength. Roza did not surrender to such thoughts; her heart was filled with love.

At the wedding for the daughter of a rich merchant that her father knew well through business, Roza had learned about a new type of person. All her life, she had only known suburban youths in whom she found no faults, but no great merits, either. But at the wedding, Roza had met and danced with several young men. She had held her own with them, yet her thoughts kept returning to Yosef. She found a certain emptiness in the men she encountered, and told herself, This one's too polite; he'll make problems for me. This one says he likes my face and hovers around giving me unwanted compliments. He's not embarrassed to look me in the eyes and say, "They're like two stars in the night sky." This one praises my hair, my fingers, my waist. God, how people flatter each other! No, Yosef wouldn't find two words to exchange with these people. All the men gather around the women, standing like soldiers before a general. And the women act like painted dolls without hands to serve themselves. Yosef wouldn't endure such "elevated people" for a moment. He'd say, "These women can't even pour themselves a cup of tea. At least they can drink the tea once it's poured, or they'd need their gentlemen to spoon it into their mouths." What Yosef told me is right: "It's understandable that men go after a pretty woman because of her looks, but a good woman is valued for her honor and worth." Oh, empty men, empty women! Yosef would never love you. You are not worthy of his love!

Even when Roza encountered a young man she liked, she found herself comparing him to Yosef. He's handsome, but not as handsome as Yosef, she told herself. Or, he speaks like Yosef, but Yosef is more refined and informed. As the evening progressed, she could clearly see there was only one Yosef.

She also felt uncomfortable with how the men presented themselves. One said his name was Moritz, and another said Peter. But Roza wondered, What are their Jewish names? Mordecai or Motke? Pinkhes or Peretz? Why do people think this is the thing to do? Silly, very silly! My Yosef is Yosef and will be called Yosef for as long as I am called Roza.

If Yosef were here with me, she thought, he'd show these foolish people how wrong it is to be embarrassed by their Jewishness. They'd fall in love with him, and come to know what it means to be a real Jew. These young women would quickly learn their idolizing gentlemen are empty and see there are better and more clever people in the world. I miss you, Yosef, and without you here my pleasure is reduced by half!

When Roza returned home from the wedding, she wanted to share her insights with Yosef. She felt delighted with herself, as the merry conversations had opened her heart. She was full of good feelings, and even Yosef's indifference did not lessen her pleasure. She had not felt any hidden meanings in his words and took them at face value. She did not know or try to guess what was hidden in his thoughts. Just as it is natural that one who is always full does not understand the sufferings of the hungry, so it is only natural that the truly good person cannot suspect another's dishonesty or guess their true intentions. The good-natured, happy one for whom the sun always shines, does not see those less-fortunate souls whose hearts are filled with worry and vexation.

That night, when Yosef was so sad and Roza in such a good mood, the two could not comprehend each other. But while Roza lay in bed unable to fall asleep from all the evening's excitement, her mood began to cool, and she started thinking about what Yosef had said. She reconsidered every word and felt he had not been speaking indifferently, but was unhappy and upset. She replayed the conversation over and over again in her mind.

He told me he wasn't interested in hearing about the wedding, but I didn't listen. He pushed me away with both hands like I was a frivolous little girl. No, Yosef, until now you've always encouraged me to talk with you. Have you finally had enough of me? Yosef, what's wrong? Why are you running away from me? What have I done?

Today you said you had something to tell me, but I was in such a hurry to get to the wedding I didn't want to hear it. What were you going to say? Were you going to tell me, "Roza, I love you! I am in love and in pain!" Were you angry and cold to me because I didn't want to hear it? Oh, Yosef, how happy those words would've made me feel if only I'd waited to hear them from you! You have the right to be angry, and I will punish myself all night with doubt. What did you want to tell me? Two people remain separate even when they share one heart and one soul. If a misunderstanding happens between them, they suffer for nothing. Oh, God, I know You have bound our hearts together. If only You had also given us the understanding of each other's thoughts, then Yosef would know what I'm thinking, and wouldn't treat me so badly. He'd love and comfort me. Dear Yosef, if I only knew what was tormenting you, I would heal you!

Tears spilled from Roza's eyes, and her whole body shivered from the cold. As hard as she tried, she could not sleep. She remembered Yosef saying he knew the bride and visited her house. He said the bride had sent him letters by way of a supposed enemy. He called her an innocent child and said she herself had put a letter into his hand that opened his eyes and revealed his enemy was really his best friend. Why did he say he already knew everything? Why didn't I ask him, "How do you know? What did she write? How did you answer her?" Did she ask for his love? Did he turn her down? Was he suffering because she was marrying another man? God, is this the Yosef that I thought I knew so well? Does his heart contain something that I don't know anything about? No, no, it cannot be! Why didn't I ask for details? Oh, it gives me a headache! This night is like a year!

Oh, Yosef, I am so miserable and have made you miserable, too. I feel so guilty for not sensing your sadness and cheering you up. Yosef, enough of this torture. Ten times already I have started letters to express my love for you, but I can't do it with a pen. How can a pen ever convey my feelings? Yosef, I swear to you, I will patiently wait out this night so I can explain everything in the morning. Oh, when will this night be over?

Roza's head burned with fire, and her body shook with cold. Although she dozed for a while, a noise in the house awakened her.

Still not day! she thought. Oh, my head hurts! How will I live until the sun comes up? I must see Yosef and tell him everything. I must not be shy. Mother and Father like Yosef; I will tell them, too. I love him, and I want to put an end to my pain. But there's still Meyshe Shneyur! Why does that man stand like a dark cloud over my bright future with Yosef? Please, dear God, let me live to see the light of day!

When Golde arose, she went to check on her daughter. Roza was feverish. Her breathing was heavy, and she tossed and turned in her sleep. Troubled, Golde covered Roza with several blankets and went off to do her housework.

When Roza awoke a few hours later, she called for her mother. Holding Golde's hand, she cried, "Mama, my head hurts. I don't feel well."

"My child," replied Golde, "I think you just caught a little chill from the wedding last night. Don't be afraid; you'll recover."

With all her heart, Roza wanted to tell her mother how she had spent the night, but she could not find the courage or words. Instead, she covered her mother's hand with kisses and tears.

"Roza, my dear daughter, don't worry. You'll be well soon," Golde said, trying to calm her. "Why are you so afraid?"

"Mama, are you truly loyal to me?" asked Roza.

"Roza, what kind of question is that? Don't you know me, dear daughter?"

"I know you, Mama, and so I ask you, 'Do you truly want me to be happy?'"

"Of course, my child! Would life be worth living if not for my beloved children?"

"Oh, dear faithful mother, will you listen to what's been causing me so much suffering?"

"Of course, dear child," Golde replied.

"Oh, Mama," Roza began, then shook her head. "No, I can't tell you now," she sighed.

"Rest, daughter. When you're well, you'll have plenty of time to tell me everything."

Comforted, Roza drifted off to sleep. As Golde left the room, she whispered, "Be well, my child; be happy. Your mother will not disrupt your happiness."

Although Golde did not believe in charms against the evil eye, when Sterne Gute came around with her tattered Yiddish prayer book under her arm, Golde admitted Roza was not well. Of course, Sterne Gute said it was the evil eye or the Jewish impulse to evil, which was even worse than the Gentile witchcraft, may it be cursed! Surely, it had come into Roza's room, laid its hands on her head and whispered in her ear. What it whispered, Sterne Gute did not know, but as they peeked in on Roza, they overheard her calling out in her sleep, "Yosef, come back! Don't blame me for the letter! Don't be angry with me; it's Meyshe Shneyur!"

"*Oy,*" said Sterne Gute, "that villain is in her mind even while she's sleeping! Don't wake her, Golde."

As Golde closed the door to Roza's room, Sterne Gute whispered, "It looks to me like an evil eye, may God send a cure. You should send Roza's handkerchief to Shmayahu the Talmudist who is good at removing evil eyes, may God grant him good health. He has never encountered anything he can't exorcise. Send for him, Golde, and, God willing, Roza will be well again. My husband says the Talmud tells us that ninety-nine die from the evil eye, but charity saves us from death. Today I'm collecting for the daughter of Khaym the tailor to buy her a ticket out of old-maidenhood. She's thirty years old already!"

Golde gave Sterne Gute a contribution, and also sent a message to Tevye the baker to allocate thirty pounds of flour to provide bread for the poor.

Before leaving the house, Sterne Gute set off to find Yosef. "Don't you know how to exorcise an evil eye?" she asked when she found him. "You're considered a fellow with many talents. Why don't you give it a try? My husband, Reuven, may God give him long life, is multi-talented. If you want to talk about exorcising an evil eye, even driving out a raging fever, may you never know from it, he can do it. Just listen to this: Before *Shabbes*, I went to pay my respects to our neighbor whose cow had worms. They had given her all kinds of remedies, but nothing helped. My Reuven took one look at the cow and came into the house. He said, 'What are they doing? They're telling you the cow has worms, but it's an evil eye!' Then he took a piece of rope and recited some verses over it. He said, 'Go tie this to the cow's left horn!' And what do you think happened? The ailment was gone in the wave of a hand. Now the cow's as healthy and lively as ever. The neighbor could've kissed my Reuven's hands and feet. He, of course, would not even take a thank you. Believe me, Yosef, if you're as good a friend to Roza as she is to you, take her handkerchief and carry it to Reuven so she can be healthy again."

"Who told you Roza's a good friend of mine?" Yosef asked.

"I just heard her talking in her sleep. She said, 'I like you so much, Yosef.' You know what they say, 'What you think by day, you dream by night!' But I must go now. When we see one another again, Yosef, I'll tell you what they're saying about you in town. I can tell you because we're relatives, although I'm not exactly sure of the lineage. Matters of kinship always confuse me. Have a good day, Yosef, and give a contribution, won't you? Today I'm collecting for two urgent causes that are both relevant to you. One: Khaym the tailor's daughter is getting married to Gavriel the idler. Two: Today is Thursday, and it's my *mitzvah* to collect bath money for the yeshiva boys."

Yosef gave her a contribution and walked away. Must I listen to this busybody? he asked himself angrily. I know Roza is ill, but what can I do? She wrote and asked that I leave her house. I will not disobey her wishes!

When Sterne Gute returned to Golde, she said, "*Oy*, how times have changed! Boys with girls—it was never meant to be! My husband didn't come to me for three years after our marriage, and still today he calls me by no other name than 'Listen.' They say in Messiah's time we will dance with the boys, but I don't believe it."

Once Sterne Gute was gone, Yosef urged Golde not to rely on the busybody's remedies for exorcising the evil eye. He insisted she call a doctor and Golde did not hesitate. Within half an hour the doctor arrived to examine Roza.

As the doctor was leaving, Golde anxiously asked about her daughter. The doctor smiled and whispered a secret: "She's not ill. She's just agitated—either by love or by a longing for someone. Don't worry, your daughter is quite healthy."

Surprised and greatly relieved, Golde asked Yosef if he would go to Roza and cheer her up. Putting his pain aside, Yosef obeyed, but he did not go alone. He took along Shimen and Rukhame, and it was a lively and merry visit.

Two

A STRANGE PRESCRIPTION

Roza swore to herself that she would tell Yosef everything the minute she saw him again, how she suffered day and night and longed for happiness. She even vowed to proclaim the words, "Yosef, I love you!" Yet whole days and weeks went by and the words never left her lips. It was not because her love had cooled, or that the words were not ripe for saying, or that she had lost her determination to say them. No, Roza had decided to tell Yosef with kisses and tears and to beg for his love with carefully chosen words. But time disrupted her plan. She lay in bed for several days, and when Yosef came in to read to her as Golde often asked him to do, he was never alone. Her brother and sister were always with him.

Yosef's hard night did not have a lasting effect on him, and he began to let go of his anger at Roza for writing her letter. Was it wrong for her to express her thoughts? he asked himself. She never said a word to me about her love, and she tore the letter up before sending it. How was she to know that I would read it? What has she done to make me act so unfriendly towards her? She is so much better and smarter than I. As difficult as it is, I must acknowledge her loyalty and honor her plea. Perhaps she is suffering, too, and trying faithfully to keep it to herself. Why should I now behave differently to her?

So Yosef went to see Roza as Golde requested. He presented himself with a loving and friendly manner and apologized for his cold treatment the night of the wedding. Hearing his words, Roza's heavy thoughts disappeared like dew in the morning sun. It was all just a terrible dream, she told herself. Why should yesterday's clouds make me shiver with cold when today is so sunny and bright? And she greeted Yosef cheerfully whenever she saw him.

One day she even asked who sent the letter she handed him on the day of the wedding, but Yosef answered with a smile, "Remember, you promised not to be so inquisitive? Today you'll have to honor my wish not to talk about it." And before Roza could make a reply, Yosef looked at his watch and remarked, "Be well, Roza. I must go now."

Roza could not answer. Her heart was so choked with feeling, she almost cried out, "Yosef have pity on me!" But Yosef was gone, and only Shimen remained to see her tears.

"Why are you crying, Roza?" Shimen asked sympathetically. "You know you can open your whole heart to me."

"Oh, dear brother," said Roza, hugging him. "My heart is so full. If only Yosef would stay with us forever, I would be so alive and young again!"

"Don't say such silly things," said Shimen, although his heart melted from her words. "The doctor says it's nothing."

"They say you can't live without lungs, Shimen, and without a heart, it's even harder! If you could look into my heart, dear brother, you would see how troubled it is."

Later that day, Shimen told his mother what Roza had said, and Golde recalled the doctor's words, "She's just agitated—either by love or by a longing for someone." The doctor, an old German, was a good man who knew and loved her children, so Golde hurried to seek his advice.

On his next visit, the doctor came while Shimen, Rukhame, and Yosef were sitting with Roza in her room. "How wonderful!" said the doctor. "I am pleased to see that my patient is being visited by so many young people. So what do you think, my child, how are you feeling today?"

"Doctor, tell me, will I die?"

"Die? Oh, yes, little Fräulein, naturally one day you will die. Like all mortals, my child, you must follow the course of life: marry, love, live, grow old, and die. But why be foolish and do it early? Do you think she's ready to go?" he asked the others.

"No!" answered Shimen.

"And who is this?" asked the doctor, indicating Yosef.

"He is our dear houseguest," replied Rukhame.

"I see," said the doctor as he noticed the depth of feeling between Roza and Yosef as they looked at each other. "Tell me this, little Fräulein, why would you let yourself die when you have such wonderful things to live for? Akh, my child, wouldn't this young man feel terrible if you should die? Look at him, how handsome he is, and how much he loves you. No, my dear patient, I am not giving you any more medicine. And I intend to tell your parents that everything is in order. My prescription: this is the best young man for you! Don't you see, dear boy, how charming and worthy your beloved is?

"Yes, dear children, I was once a young man myself, and my beloved got very sick. I was only a student at the time and knew very little about medicine, so this is the remedy I prepared for her: I said, 'Marie, I love you!' and she fell into my arms and gave me a long kiss. I carry that kiss on my lips to this very day. Oh, the happiness! It is the reward of life. My remedy worked, and my beloved was healed! Be happy, my children, that you are in love!" The doctor stroked both their hands with special meaning, then went out to report everything to Golde.

Roza was too bashful to look into Yosef's eyes, but Yosef felt only sadness. Soon the youthful company disbanded, and Roza was left alone with her mother.

THREE

YOSEF AND SHIMEN

From this day forward my foot will not cross her threshold, Yosef told himself. I'm too weak to remain cold-blooded through such an ordeal. Why do people act this way? Why would a doctor, a merry, straightforward old man with seemingly good intentions, pour salt on my wounds? It would be easier if I simply followed Roza's advice and left their house today. Oh, Roza, you are so good, clever, and honest. But I don't understand how you can love yourself so much that you would protect your good name from the smallest speck of gossip by permitting a whole mountain of it to fall on me. All I can do now is run away from all that makes me happy and face the suffering. How long shall I stay away, Roza? Until people stop talking? The people you're afraid of will never stop. Even if you're as proper as an angel, you'll never be free of their words. Sterne Gute wanted to protect you from the evil eye, but who will protect you from her evil mouth? Oh, dear, innocent Roza, I can't wait any longer. If you don't know what you're longing for, you won't have the heart to ask for it. Today, I will begin preparing for my journey. Yet how can I leave my little brother, Shimen, and the work we've begun?

Locating Shimen in the house, Yosef said, "Please come with me. I have something urgent to discuss with you."

Shimen followed Yosef to his room. As Yosef closed the door, Shimen said, "Yosef, before you start talking, please explain two things to me: First, for the last few weeks you've held yourself apart from the family. You've been preoccupied and pensive—things I've never noticed before in your personality. Yosef, are you getting tired of us? Do you regret coming here to live? Do you want to forget about me, Roza, Rukhame, and Mama?"

"No, Shimen," Yosef answered coldly. "How could I forget any of you?"

"If you don't want to explain it to me, that's all right," said Shimen. "I don't mean to embarrass you. But Yosef, I think you're running away from Roza, the one person who truly loves you, and falling into the hands of your enemy, Meyshe Shneyur, who is digging a hole for you. Yosef, I don't understand what's going on, and that's my second question: Are the two connected? I have tried to put the pieces together but fear I may be in error. It appears—and you probably knew this long before anyone else— that Roza loves you. But you think she's not worthy. You don't love her back because she's not educated enough. Yet I must tell you, Yosef, that you won't find another girl as educated as Roza, or as lovely, or with a soul as pure and honest. I'm her brother, and I'm talking about her merits the way I'd talk about my own beloved. You won't find another woman like Roza. You are worthy of her, and she is worthy of you. My mother is worthy of having you as a son-in-law, and I am worthy of being your brother-in-law.

"Yosef, please don't come up with a new plan for your life. Perhaps you have other hopes and dreams in your head that I don't know about. Perhaps you wish to return home and make a match with a rich family. But I say to you, Yosef, as your friend, as your

brother, you won't find another Roza out there. So stop tormenting yourself by trying to run away from us."

"Shimen, you are such a good friend! To begin with, I completely agree with you, so let's not talk about it anymore. Please
don't argue or question. Believe me, in time I will tell you everything. Roza sent me a letter in which she told me she loved me
but was convinced that nothing could come of her love. So she
asked me to withdraw gradually from your home. The letter disturbed me terribly, and I still suffer from it. But I'm determined
to fulfill her request. The question is, where do I go? That's why I
wanted to talk with you."

Shimen stared at Yosef in amazement. "What are you telling
me? Don't I know you, brother? And don't I know my own sister?
God, how could I have made such a terrible mistake?"

"Maybe you made a mistake with both of us," Yosef replied.
"Maybe in thinking that I was someone who held his ancestry in
high esteem; and with Roza, who has every right to improve her
status as the daughter of a rich family. Maybe now you can see it
differently, that Roza loves me but the situation, the relationship
between us, is not equal. I didn't ask you if she loved me, nor did I
tell you that I loved her. Shimen, I'm nothing to her, but believe me,
I would do nothing to harm her happiness."

"Do my parents know this?" asked Shimen.

"I don't know," replied Yosef. "But if they're not aware, I ask you
not to tell them. God knows what they'll think of me."

"So it comes to this," said Shimen, "that a brother who loves his
sister more than the world, has a sister who hasn't been truthful
with him! No, Yosef, I don't believe it. Roza is an honest child. She
wouldn't do such a thing. You did not get that letter from her!"

"From her own hand, Shimen! How can you really know what's
in another's heart? That night when everyone said she was going to
a wedding, she went to see a bridegroom. She herself told me how

handsome and clever he was, how the in-laws liked her, and how everyone accepted her. Shimen, there's nothing else to discuss. I beg you, let's talk about something more important."

"Oh, Roza, how did this happen?" said Shimen. "But Yosef, you must explain this to me: Why are you meeting with Meyshe Shneyur? Don't you know he's your enemy?"

"There's nothing to it," replied Yosef. "Meyshe Shneyur hasn't given me any reason to think he's a bad friend. In fact, he's done me a favor. He woke me out of my dream, and now I have eyes to look around and see where I stand. Do you think I only want to study and make do with being someone's exemplary son-in-law honored for his scholarship in the study house? No, Shimen, that's far from who I am. For years, I've been like a prisoner in a cell trying to escape my situation. My hands are empty and my feet are bound. That's why I came to your house to study with you, yet I've acquired very little towards my plan.

"In truth, out of respect, most of my earnings have gone into clothes so that Roza wouldn't be embarrassed going out walking with me. Now I'm resolved to carry out my plan. Shimen, here's what I want to say to you as a friend who loves you like a trusted brother: Look around at where you stand!"

"What do you mean, Yosef? What do I lack? Praise God, my father is rich and can afford a good match for me."

"Oh, Shimen, how can I explain this to you? Just listen with your head. You know Leyzer Zelig's son, Yankel, and you know how rich his father is. His father gave him fifteen thousand rubles upon his marriage. Everyone was envious. But listen to what happened to him. He ended his period of support as a new groom and went around with his pack of banknotes like someone fleeing from a flood. For six months he sought a business. He was offered a thousand businesses, but he was afraid to touch even one. Soon he had used up a thousand rubles and saw that his funds were getting smaller and smaller, so he decided to lend money at interest. For three years he exhausted himself running around all day dealing with one person after another. He earned a bad name for himself among good people because he sat at one shop for an hour, then another shop for another hour. And he couldn't find any rest at home because there was too much commotion going on and he had to keep his expenses low. His life turned bitter as people failed to pay back the money they owed him. So what is Yankel now? A pauper! He lives on a pension that is sent to him by kind people. He has five young children he can't educate, and he's not suited to any kind of work. He has nothing and no prospects. Tell me, isn't he the most unfortunate person?"

"Yosef, I know all this!" said Shimen.

"Good," said Yosef. "Now, let me tell you about Zalman the mechanic. Do you know him?"

"Yes, of course."

"Do you know he married with only a few groschen in his pocket? Zalman told me he comes from a very wealthy family. His father sent him off to study; but after a few years, Zalman announced that he wasn't any good at it and didn't want to study anymore. So his father turned him over to a machine manufacturer where he served five years as an apprentice. He learned the trade and now makes a good living. He got married and has a happy life. Everything about him is fine and alive. Name one rich person you know who lives such a satisfying life. I don't have to paint the whole picture for you, Shimen. I can take you to meet him; and if you have eyes to see what an honest life looks like, you'll feel the same way I do. Tell me, dear Shimen, wouldn't it have been better if Leyzer Zelig, instead of giving his son Yankel fifteen thousand rubles, had done what Zalman's father did?

"Let's not fool ourselves about what will become of us. There's nothing to say about me; I don't need to talk about myself. But what will become of you, Shimen? Will you let yourself fall into a life of speculation with a pack of banknotes in your hand? You are young. You haven't acquired a lot of knowledge yet, but you can go to school and complete a course of study. Rouse yourself, brother, don't wait until the difficulties of life befall you. We've studied a few things together, but they're fleeting. Although they can help us out of a difficult situation, they can't move us into a different one. We are left between heaven and earth without a footing. The science that we are learning—history today, geography tomorrow, all the seven wisdoms in all the seven worlds—is a taste of the Tree of Knowledge.

"Shimen, do you know what it means to eat from the Tree of Knowledge? It brings death! The little science that I know has opened my eyes to see my surroundings and what lies ahead for me. I see people living and being happy, but they're not searching for any knowledge. To know something from the Tree of Knowledge and not eat fully of it is the curse that drives people from their Garden of Eden! If you don't make use of what you know, you have nothing. Shimen, I'm as unfortunate as Adam was when he found out he was naked. I'm not ashamed before the Jews of Mohilev; there's nothing to be ashamed of. Adam wasn't ashamed before the animals and the beasts of the field; he was ashamed of himself. And I'm ashamed of myself. Roza loves me; let her keep loving me. But I wouldn't make her happy if I married her in my current situation. I must have the ability to put bread on the table! I will not squander my strength on a thousand different things anymore; I will only focus on that which will help me succeed. If I succeed at the study of Talmud, fine. It will not be based on the opinion of some educated scholar, but because I'm more adept at studying than anything else. The only worthy person is the one who succeeds, who has talent and cultivates it. If I don't succeed, I'm prepared to learn a profession.

"My advice, Shimen, is that you begin to think about yourself while you still have a little time. Soon your head will be turned around. After Roza's marriage, you will become a bridegroom yourself. Jewish matchmakers are all hungry. Even with smart parents, it's dangerous to be a bachelor with so many sharp teeth around. If you're good at studying and inclined to do it, I advise you to continue. But if it's too hard for you or too distant, then learn a profession or specialty at which you can earn a living wherever you go."

"I know you're right, Yosef," said Shimen, "but my parents would never allow it."

"Maybe not in one or two days, but you can repeat my words to your mother. She's a clever woman and will understand. I'll give you some excerpts from my diary. Better for you to steep yourself in my words before saying anything. For now, look around at the people you live with and see if this is how you want to spend the rest of your life. It's getting late. I'll get you the pages; read them and tell me your decision. I want to know before I leave. I can't stay here much longer. Brother, let this be the one favor I can do for you. You have been so good to me, and I can only say that I hold no one in my heart as deeply as you!"

Yosef and Shimen hugged, kissed, and both men parted with tears in their eyes.

FOUR

THE DIARY

After Yosef handed him the pages from his diary, Shimen left in a bitter mood. He felt that Yosef had meant well, but wondered if his thoughts about Roza were right.

How did Roza fool me so completely? Shimen asked himself. Should I go ask her myself? Should I tell mother about it? Roza tells Yosef to leave our house but speaks to him in such a friendly manner. What cute faces she showed with the doctor. I can't conceive of such dishonesty.

Poor, lonely Yosef. Why do you think so little of yourself? How can you say all your scholarship is not worth a piece of bread? Is the world so mean that man really does live by bread alone? No, Yosef, all you're learning is precious and worth the effort!

Shimen began reading Yosef's diary:

2 Cheshvan 5630

I've been here for several weeks now and feel as though I am nowhere. Some call me "idler," as people often do. Some pay me honor and are shy in front of me. Some praise me for my diligence, but I am diligent because I have no one to speak with, and can't sleep. What should I do with my time if not study diligently?

My cousin who gives me books asks if I have gotten anything from them. He wants to know if I have grasped the authors' intentions, and what remains of each author when I have finished reading his book. The questions are strange, but they force me to penetrate more deeply into what I am reading.

He says, "No one writes a story for its own sake. The author is called by a certain cause to eliminate evil and encourage good." That made me consider which of the books reflected my own ways of thinking. Often I found one of my own thoughts in a sentence or idea, but not in the whole story. In one novel, the character was the son of a German nobleman; in another, the son of a rich merchant. Their lives were so different from mine that at first I could not see how they could serve as examples for me.

But then, since I know a little about German and Russian life, I could see that beyond people like Shmuel Yose the schoolteacher, Yude the *shammes*, and Gasan's sons-in-law, there are people out there who live differently and have a better grasp of the world. But these people are far away. First of all, they are not Jews, so how can we imitate them? Secondly, we are shown finished, ready-made people—the educated are already educated, and the happy are already happy. But how did they get that way? The authors do not tell us. Or is the process such a small detail it's not worth talking about?

* * * * *

17 Cheshvan, evening

What is my cousin's motive? Is he doing me a favor by revealing the truth about my life, or is he so unhappy with his own life that he's simply trying to tell me I'm not so bad off? "What will become of you?" he asks. "Do you want to be unhappy like me, a lowly schoolteacher? If I were where you are now, I could still amount to something. I would not have to suffer the desolation of my poor, naked children and hungry household. I would not have on my conscience how unhappy I have made my wife. But now, how can I leave them in a splintered ship on a stormy sea while I swim to shore to save myself?

"You ask me why authors write only about finished people. I can't tell you. The question that plagues me is why our Jewish authors don't write stories from life that can show us a better way. Even when our writers set out to address the latest questions about religion or the problems of bread for the hungry and the first steps young people must take to live their lives, they are only able to write from their own experiences which are limited by their narrow, troubled lives.

"In my time, I have come to understand from books that there is a world beyond the Talmud. But when I go out searching for something comparable to it, as you are searching today, I grow angry at all the Jewish writers who are blind to what is needed.

"Today, I give myself to you as a book, Yosef; read as much as you want. Look on my troubles and know that the world kept me happy for a long time before I began to expand my horizons. So, Yosef, here are my papers; I give them to you with God's help. I have not buried anything.

They have cost me sweat and blood. You will find your whole generation in it and see what can become of a person."

As I read my cousin's papers, I recognized him and myself. He depicted himself as a real person, not as the hero in a novel. Because a person cannot take the advice of another, the author needs only to provide a true portrait. My cousin has helped me see that I am different and must decide for myself what goals to seek.

Shimen read a few excerpts and saw this for himself. But we must not make our readers weary with extraneous talk and let Shimen get back to reading the final pages of Yosef's diary which are closer to our story:

Did R have an effect on me, or are my eyes open due to my conviction to more clearly see the environment in which I live? Oh, it is terrible to see how my years are passing by. Like a machine, I get up from my bed and run to the study house to pray. Don't I already find God in myself? Aren't my thoughts the best prayer? I find it so hard to flatter people, and even more so, to fool God with sugar-sweet phrases. You hear my prayers and thoughts at all times, God; my praying is only for people. I don't go to the study house to search for You. There, I only see people who do not know You and commit all kinds of sins, all kinds of crimes in Your name.

* * * * *

Borekh the blacksmith had a *yortsayt* last night, and I know he had no dinner because he had to spend twenty-five groschen for the whiskey. Today he brought in a half measure of brandy, but they still took his prayer shawl until he provided enough brandy for the whole *minyan*. As a pledge, he had to give the tavern keeper his hammer and other tools which he needs for a day's work. They recited a blessing for the whiskey and forgot about Borekh's soul!

* * * * *

Yekusiel the tailor took the gold watch the bride had sent the groom. The groom, Sore the widow's son, Aron, had given the tailor a vest to mend and had forgotten to remove the watch from the pocket. When Yekusiel gave him back the vest, the watch was gone. Aron started shouting, "Where is my watch?"

"Hoodlum!" shouted Yekusiel. "You lost your watch in some whore house, and you're trying to put it on me?"

The next day, out of the clear blue sky, Yekusiel was seen buying whiskey. The bride knew the groom to be an honest person, and loved him; but when her father heard all the talk about Aron, he broke off the engagement.

Today the truth came out that Yekusiel had sold the watch. But Yekusiel is a Chassid, and among Chassidim there is unity. The rabbi said a special blessing, and after several servings of Passover spirits with marmalade, the rabbi had to be led home by the arm.

* * * * *

I haven't written for a while. I really wanted to stop writing altogether because my diary is so full of bitterness it fills me with shame. What remains for me to write are things I would rather not think about. What I see and hear in the light are so sad. What goes on in the dark must be even worse! But mysteries are for God; figuring them out is for us. I have to write what I hear and see. I don't know what drives me to it, but I must.

*   *   *   *   *

More than anything else, I grieve for the poor woman. A lonely young widow had to take a job as a maid. She worked for Dovid the miller and became pregnant by him. Dovid's wife noticed and drove the poor woman away, beating her with her fists. She was ashamed but did not say a word and tried to earn her bite of bread by carrying chickens or bags of beans for people. No one knew of her misfortune. One day, she was found half-frozen to death in a cellar clutching the newborn baby to her breast. They sent her to the poorhouse where madwomen ran around cursing and swearing at her.

Oh, people, why do you swear at her? Do you not feel her pain? Is it nothing to her that her child was born in a cellar where she lay alone for three days? She said she didn't come out for fear that God might punish her further. Could she have gotten any harsher punishment than to fall into your hands?

Golde knew about the situation and tried to help the young widow, but she is, it seems to me, too cautious. She is afraid, she says, that people will talk, and she must protect the honor of her own children.

Today Shmuel the porter and Avreml the tinsmith drove the young woman all over the city shouting, "Charity saves from death!" She sat in the wagon with the child in her arms. A corpse could not have looked worse. Everyone with legs came running to the study house where the *bris* was done. The rabbi was the circumciser, an official from the burial society held the child, and Gad sopped up the blood. Oh, you leeches, did you for one moment consider that unfortunate mother who made your faces twinkle with such joy and pleasure today?

The good Jew who performed the circumcision gave the child the name Yokushn. "Why Yokushn?" I asked the rabbi. He answered, "Because he is a son of a concubine, and Jews should know he is not a kosher child. Wherever he goes, when he says his name is Yokushn, no one will give him a Jewish daughter to wed." Now you can see what kind of Jew the good rabbi is.

"Rabbi," I said, "this child is certainly not a bastard. He is a kosher child according to the Law." Perhaps the rabbi knew the boy was a bastard because he replied, "One must not question the character of a saint!"

Oh, Jews, don't you realize what will happen when this child grows up and finally has the sense to understand the cruel sentence you have placed upon him because his mother was an honest Jewess who did not want to toss her child into a foundling home as so many rich and pious people do. Instead, she accepted the shame and suffering so her child would remain with her and remain a Jew. When he feels the hateful stamp you have placed upon him, his anger and despair will make him a blind enemy to you and his people. Then you will answer to God and these unfortunate souls!

Shimen continued to read the entries in Yosef's diary until daylight. Finally, he came to the place where Yosef wrote about himself:

I have kept this diary to see myself reflected in the company I keep and what it would be like if I spent my whole life here among these people. Oh, God, what would a reader say if he found this book of troubles? What I wrote in these pages, I must bear again and again, over and over.

I see that I cannot stay here any longer. The one who held me here like a magnet is now pushing me away. I will go and take her image with me in my heart. I will carry her dear mother's love and loyalty in my soul. But how can I leave Shimen? I still want to be his brother and teacher. And dear Rukhame, only you still consider me a friend. Bright child, today I love you without resentment or reproach. Enough! I will not stay here any longer. Another life beckons me.

I am with you, Yosef! thought Shimen. I am finding such a life wearisome as well.

FIVE

YOSEF AND ROZA

Several days passed before Shimen could discuss his thoughts with Yosef. In the meantime, he could not make sense of the story about Roza's letter. He talked quietly with his mother who sensed that Roza was in love with someone else.

Shimen was angry with Roza, yet he struggled with his feelings. What right do I have to be angry with her? he asked himself. What sin has she committed if she honestly loves someone other than Yosef? Competing thoughts between love and rage caused him to weep, and he stopped talking to Roza altogether.

Yosef stopped visiting her too and began spending whole evenings with Meyshe Shneyur. Sometimes Shimen accompanied him, and poor Rukhame, sensing Yosef's withdrawal, stopped eating and drinking.

Once Roza was fully recovered, she found herself alone. No one came to see her or invited her out on walks, and she could no longer ask Yosef to explain himself. In her loneliness, she wrote Yosef a few words and handed the note to him herself.

Dear Yosef,

You once said you had something to tell me, but I was foolish and did not want to hear it. I ask you now, please, give me a little time and listen to what I have to say. My heart is weak, and I cannot keep silent any more. Yosef, I must tell you something. I am crying as I write this.

Roza

Yosef put the letter aside and answered that until he was able to leave, he wished she would do him the favor of not writing or speaking of things he did not want to hear.

In the days that followed, the Dark Young Man kept his eye on Roza and reinforced his power over the family. Roza was abandoned by everyone and wept alone in her room. Yosef felt her sadness, but based on what Meyshe Shneyur had told him, thought it was due to the marriage proposal taking longer than expected. The Dark One had an explanation for everything and, out of spite, even praised Yosef to his father-in-law in front of Roza.

What has become of me? Roza asked herself one *Shabbes* afternoon when she saw Meyshe Shneyur, Rukhame, and Shimen going out for a walk. What has my brother-in-law done to soil my name that everyone is running away from me? Today will be the end of it! Where is Yosef? I must find him. After looking through the house, Roza went to the garden where Yosef was sitting with his head propped on his hands, looking deep in thought.

Yosef knew his life was in turmoil and he vowed to leave by morning. He told himself, Now that Meyshe Shneyur has paid my expenses, I must go. Oh, how painful it is to think about leaving this beautiful place. Is not every tree, every leaf, holy? Oh, God, You alone can feel my torment. How can I tear the image of Roza out of my heart? Even the birds seem to feel my heartache with their sad, mournful songs. Be well all you sweet little hiding places. You've heard my sighs and felt my tears. Oh, Roza, I leave with a wounded heart, but also with faithfulness and friendship to you forever. You are not guilty that fate brought you into my life.

As tears fell from Yosef's eyes, Roza approached him quietly. "Yosef, are you crying?"

Startled, Yosef stood up and caught his hand on a twig which tore his skin. Alarmed, Roza took off her shawl and said, "Yosef, excuse me, I didn't mean to interrupt your thoughts. Please, let me bind your hand to stop the bleeding."

Roza tied her shawl around his hand and thought, Oh, dear friend, I would gladly bind all your wounds and heal all your pains if only you would let me.

"Thank you," Yosef said and began to walk away.

"No, Yosef, I don't accept your thanks. Now you must listen to everything I have to say to you."

"Roza, can't we leave this for another time?" Yosef asked.

"No, I can't be patient anymore. Yosef, don't you know how dangerous it is to play with a snake, to make friends with a snake? I beg you, for your own happiness, which is as dear to me as life itself, and for my own health if you value it at all, run away from Meyshe Shneyur!"

Yosef stiffened but remained silent.

"I'm not blind. I see that something is going on around me," said Roza. "I see that you are different towards me. You've become completely different! Oh, Yosef, I don't deserve this. This misunderstanding makes me so unhappy. I have three words to say to you. I've tried to write them in letters—so many letters that I've written and torn up. I'm not an educated Jewish girl. I can't match your learning. But I ask you to listen to my words and know there is nothing else that remains in my heart. Yosef, I love you! I love you, and I'm sorry!"

Roza burst into tears, and her trembling, pleading voice robbed Yosef of all words. At first, he considered saying, "It's too late!" but her tears brought tears to his eyes, too.

"Be well, Yosef," said Roza. "There's nothing more to say."

"Roza, I beg you, hear me out," said Yosef. "Tell me, what will become of your letter now?"

"What letter, Yosef?"

"Don't you remember the letter you delivered to me on that evening when you were supposedly going to a wedding? I learned later you were actually meeting with a prospective bridegroom. Roza, you are lovable, and I tell you if you hadn't handed the letter to me yourself, perhaps I could believe you now."

"I don't know what you're talking about, Yosef."

Yosef removed the letter from his pocket. "Here, were these not your true feelings?"

Yosef handed Roza the letter. She looked at it and turned pale. Suddenly, she cried out, "Yosef, have mercy! Where did you get this disgraceful thing?"

Roza pushed the letter back into Yosef's hands. "Now everything is clear to me," she wept. "Dear Yosef, I am innocent! I don't know what to say about this letter. It was given to me, and I was asked to take it to you. I would never do anything to hurt you. Oh, that Meyshe Shneyur! What does he have against me? See my tears, Yosef? I know I can't get your love by begging, but I beg you, run away from that snake!"

"Dear Roza, innocent messenger," Yosef said gently. "You have suffered so much to win my favor. I love you, sweet Roza!" Taking Roza into his arms, Yosef kissed her.

"First, Roza, I was the poorest man in the world. My only hope was in Meyshe Shneyur who lent me a few rubles so I could leave this house. Now, thank God, I am happy with my dear, sweet Roza!"

"Oh, Yosef," sighed Roza. "With tears, with sacred prayers, I begged God for you! Now I am the richest woman! Our parents won't hold us back. My mother knows your true worth. I am so happy, Yosef! I've carried so many images of our life together, but they've all flown from my mind. All I can think of saying is, 'My Yosef! My dear, sweet Yosef! I love you!'"

As tears streamed down Yosef's face, Roza saw a troubled look in his eyes. "What is it?" she asked.

"Oh, God, must I see a dark storm on my brightest day? Must the name Meyshe Shneyur lay like a heavy stone on my heart? Roza, what will Meyshe Shneyur say?"

"He does not own me," Roza answered. "You needn't worry about his intrigues anymore. I am honest and happy and have only one heart. Today and for all time it belongs only to you. I am yours, Yosef, yours. God made me for you!"

"Dear God, why did You create Your Paradise with snakes?" asked Yosef. "I heard the snake, and he poisoned me! Roza, dear angel, Meyshe Shneyur embittered my life, and I almost lost you. Now I have you back, and I am yours. My heart and my life are yours. I am no longer afraid of snakes and will, as the Torah says, trample him underfoot. Roza, give me your hand. We will swear before God who sees our tears and knows our hearts and minds. God, be our witness! Be our helper!"

Yosef and Roza kissed again and left the garden. In the house, they found Meyshe Shneyur drinking tea with the family. Roza's father was in his chair studying a book of commentaries. When Fridman saw Yosef, he said, "Without you, dear Yosef, it's like being without glasses. Come here and explain this commentary to me."

Yosef went over and explained the passage to Fridman who reacted gratefully. The exchange filled Yosef with happiness, and he left the room knowing he had Fridman's respect.

Roza was also happy and wanted to make peace with everyone. That evening at the dinner table she smiled and laughed, and Shimen noticed that she and Yosef were conversing again. For Shimen, not talking to Roza had been harder than not drinking water when thirsty, and so at the first opportunity, he went to see his sister.

Roza told Shimen that she had resolved her differences with Yosef, but refrained from mentioning their declarations of love. She then related how Meyshe Shneyur had poisoned Yosef with her letter. Shimen's anger quickly turned to hatred, and if it were not for Roza and Yosef asking him to keep silent, he would have taken his revenge on the Dark One.

That evening, when Meyshe Shneyur invited Yosef to join him, Yosef said, "You have no reason to be my enemy, Meyshe Shneyur. I have tried to be a good friend to you, and now I ask that you respect my wishes and let me go my own way. I'm an honest man, and you'll do better with me using honesty than intrigues. I'm not giving you a lecture. Just remember: one good friend is better than ten false friends."

"I was trying to do you a favor," Meyshe Shneyur replied.

"Thank you, but I don't need your favors anymore," said Yosef, offering his hand. "Good evening!"

Later that night, Golde lay awake in bed. Guests were coming, she thought, and the greatest guest was the holiday of Shavuos.

Yosef could not sleep either. He had so many things to do to accomplish his plan which the declarations of love had interrupted. He knew his happiness would only be realized if he could provide Roza with all her needs. She doesn't want luxuries, he told himself, but for us to live an ordinary life I must earn a decent living. To become educated, I must attend a university. But I don't need to study just to be an honest, happy person who provides for himself and his family. The world is mine. I still have time and can learn a profession. I will be happy with my Roza, and she will be happy, too! With these thoughts, Yosef fell asleep, but his sleep came with a difficult dream.

Unable to sleep, Golde, who perhaps loved Roza a little more than her other children, rose from her bed and went to check on her daughter who seemed to have finally returned to good health. Golde sat on the edge of Roza's bed and gazed at her lovely child. Roza's black curly locks lay across her pure white throat as she breathed lightly, and a sweet smile played on her face. Her lips were closed and seemed to move slightly as though kissing someone in a dream. Golde could not tear herself away. Such a sweet picture, she thought. God, am I the only one who thinks she's the most beautiful girl in the world, or do others see it as well?

Roza turned in her sleep and said with a sweet smile, "Yosef, I love you. I love you, dear Yosef!"

"Oh, I know that smile, dear child," Golde said quietly. "I still remember those sweet dreams in which my lips spoke words to my beloved. How lovely the world was back then. If only our whole lives could be lived in such sweet dreams. Be happy, Roza. It is better to live in the dream of sleep than to be envied by people during the day. In our dreams, we are free and can take off our masks. In dreams, we speak easily of things we tremble to think of by day. Sleep, my dear heart, your mother's faithful eye watches over you. You have enemies, dear child. Meyshe Shneyur cooks up plots against you. He begrudges you your Yosef and says you love someone else, but your mother knows the truth now and calls on God for help!"

Golde repeated the words three times, "He who watches over us neither slumbers nor sleeps," then kissed Roza's forehead, and left to check on Yosef.

She found him asleep in a feverish state. "Meyshe Shneyur," he called out, "I give you everything. I only ask that you do not harm my Roza. She is innocent as an angel. Oh, don't tear out my heart!"

Frightened and with tears falling from her eyes, Golde woke Yosef who could barely catch his breath. "You were having a nightmare," she said. "You were holding your hands over your heart."

"Thank you, dear mother! Only you would save me in the middle of the night from a bad dream after all the goodness you've shown me during the day. I was being tormented, and I cried out. An enemy was chasing me, and, if you hadn't awakened me, I would not have had the strength to resist him."

"Spit three times, Yosef, then say the nighttime blessings again. A dream is nothing. Say it to yourself: 'A dream is nothing.' Good night, Yosefke. Be calm. Your enemies will, God willing, become your friends and see only your joy and happiness!"

Golde kissed the *mezuzah* as she left the room. God knows, she wondered, if the *mezuzahs* in this house have, God forbid, been damaged. How did such a dream get into Yosef's sleep? Tomorrow, without fail, I will call the scribe to examine all the *mezuzahs*.

Back in bed, Golde could not sleep. Her heart told her that the Dark One, whom she hated more than ever, was thinking something evil about her children. Tonight, the words Yosef expressed in his dream convinced her there was something to worry about. A *mezuzah*, she knew, could not drive out a snake. He would have to be dealt with in another way. "God, help my poor children," she prayed. "Protect them while awake and asleep."

Six

GOD SENT HIM

The sun emerged bright and beautiful on the morning after the couple resolved their conflict. The nightingale in Roza's room sang, and Roza had time to fantasize. With her wounds healed and her torments forgotten, she sat in bed feeling calm and happy. She had decided to tell her mother everything and to reveal the truth that she could not live without Yosef. When she heard Yosef go downstairs, she got up and followed after him.

Golde sat at the table surrounded by her children. Everyone was drinking tea, and it was a happy scene. It was evident in Roza's and Yosef's eyes that they were different this morning. Fridman sat with the family, too, but did not take part in the conversation. He was busy pursuing two things at once. In one hand he held a porcelain teacup; in the other, he held his scriptural study guide. He always read his daily inspiration before beginning his business day.

In addition to the tasks he had assigned to Yosef, such as book-keeping and writing letters which had become more difficult for him in his elder years, Fridman delighted in having Yosef around to interpret passages from the Talmud or certain commentaries which he studied during his free hours. Yosef often spent long periods of time with Fridman pondering spiritual concepts. They also talked about world news, Nature, and Jews in general. As the days passed, Fridman began to regard Yosef so highly that he turned to him for advice, and Yosef soon learned everything about the business.

At first, Fridman was a little concerned at how strongly his children clung to Yosef, but he trusted their instincts. He was especially pleased that Rukhame was doing so well with her lessons. When the Dark One came with a negative report, Fridman, who already questioned his truthfulness, said, "Don't begrudge another person's life. My children are certainly as honest as you are, and you don't come close to Yosef!"

"It's not me that's saying it," replied the Dark One. "People are talking!"

But Fridman responded angrily, "Get out of my sight. Don't come to me again with such gossip!"

That was when Meyshe Shneyur had begun to weave his intrigues and had the letter written by a forger who was known for his talent in copying other people's handwriting. Then he had the letter sent by an accomplice so it could be delivered to Yosef by Roza's hand.

As Fridman finished reciting the morning prayers, he turned to Yosef and said, "Today, you should go to Reb Leyzer the tailor and get a suit of clothes for the holidays. That's my advice. God willing, if business stays good for me, I will, with God's help, make someone else happy. So don't skimp; get the best. You understand me? Golde, do me a favor and go with him to the city today."

While Fridman was speaking, a mail wagon came to the door, and a tall, heavyset Jew got out and came into the house with a merry, "Good morning!"

"Reb Itsik, as I live and breathe!" shouted Fridman. "What a guest, and so unexpected. I'm so happy to see you!"

The guest took off his coat in the anteroom and headed for the samovar. "Wait," he called out, "I have to see which of your children I can recognize. Look at these young people. In only a few years the whole group has grown up! This must be Rukhame! Golde, what a lovely young woman she's become. She will be asking for a husband soon! Come over here, Rukhame, do you remember me?"

"Why shouldn't I remember you?" replied Rukhame with a laugh. "Aren't you one of us? You know what they say, as a young person gets older and wiser, an older person gets younger and more foolish. I also remember a spanking you once gave me, and now I can take my revenge!"

"Bravo!" shouted the guest. "May God give you more and better! And Shimen! You were just a child the last time I saw you. And Roza—oh my—how beautiful you are! Tell me, is this handsome young man your fiancé who has been invited for the holiday? I may be getting younger and more foolish as Rukhame says, but I still know what's good! Bravo, Roza, you have chosen like an expert! And bravo to you, young man. You have chosen a bride whose equal you won't find anywhere else in the world! *Mazel tov*, Roza. *Mazel tov*, groom. *Mazel tov*, in-laws. *Mazel tov* to all of us! Now, where's my cake!"

Everyone laughed, and the guest noticed how the two lovers blushed with a glorious color. Golde, who had also taken pleasure from Reb Itsik's words but wanted to relieve the children of their embarrassment, said, "Good luck never hurt anyone! And as long as we're giving *mazel tovs*, Reb Itsik, my daughter Leyke just had another son!"

"*Mazel tov* for that too!" proclaimed Reb Itsik. "But tell me, who is this young man here?"

"You don't recognize me, Reb Itsik?" asked Yosef. "I recognized you right away."

The guest came closer for a better look, and Yosef pursed his lips and opened his eyes wide. Roza's heart pounded, full of anticipation, and almost shouted, This is my beloved Yosef! Who could not recognize him?

"Yosefke, how did you get here?" asked Reb Itsik. "I will pay the fine, whatever it cost! How could I ever forget my Yosefke?" And Reb Itsik fell on Yosef's neck, kissing and pressing him to his heart until Yosef groaned from the squeezing.

"It's been eight years since the last time I saw you, Yosefke. Akh, how you have changed! You were already a fine young man equal to any other, and now you're even finer. And such wise eyes! You know, if you hadn't made that face, biting your upper lip and looking at me so sternly, I never would've recognized you. Oh, what a gem of a child you were! Your picture has been hanging in my office for ten years now. My wife is completely in love with you, and it's a good thing I'm not a woman, because the way you look, I would fall in love with you myself!"

"Thank you for such a compliment, Reb Itsik," said Yosef, "but praising one to his face is not a virtue. And I remember you used to call me a little scoundrel. I was always arguing with you about it; so now, you'll have to pay the penalty."

"Well isn't he a scoundrel?" shouted the guest. "Say so, everyone. Golde? Roza? Rukhame, you believe in telling the truth to someone's face. Say it!"

"If you want, I will say it," answered Rukhame, who had not taken her eyes off Yosef and Roza. "But I will only do it because you've asked me to. And this is what I say to your face, Reb Itsik: he's more handsome than you. Not just one time more, but a thousand times more!"

"Akh, you little hooligan!" shouted Reb Itsik. "For that, you will not get the gift I've brought for you. Not even a little taste of it!"

"Excuse me, Reb Itsik," Rukhame replied defending herself. "You asked me directly. Should I have disobeyed you?"

"Never!" laughed Reb Itsik, and from his pocket, he took out two beautiful silk scarves which he gave to Rukhame and Roza. For Golde, he brought fancy napkins and other household items, and for Fridman, an expensive box of cigars and bottle of port wine.

"Shimen, you'll come with me, and I'll buy something for you. And Yosef, since I must pay you a fine, I'll take care of you too. We'll all go into the city after prayers."

The door opened, and Meyshe Shneyur came into the room. "Meyshe Shneyur!" shouted the guest. "I swear, you look seven times darker."

Meyshe Shneyur greeted Reb Itsik with a forced smile, but his blood boiled when he saw Roza and Yosef sitting together. Yesterday, he surmised that Yosef had learned the truth, and now he threw a poisonous look at the handsome young couple. Seeing his eyes, Roza suddenly felt ill, and cried out, "Mother help me! Oh, save me!"

Yosef felt it, too, and wanted to comfort Roza, but thought, "What will people think?" and remained silent.

"What's wrong, Roza?" Golde asked in alarm. "Look how pale you've become!"

"Excuse me, dear Mother; excuse me, Reb Itsik. I thought there was a spider on my neck."

"A spider?" said Reb Itsik who was clever enough to realize what was going on. "Don't get excited. What can a spider do, children? But what startled you, Yosef?"

"I once felt a spider crawling on my neck. I know how frightening it can be," Yosef replied, looking at Roza.

Roza's heart said to her, Is he an angel, a prophet, or do we just have one heart? He knows who the spider is. Oh, Yosef, you suffer the same as I do. Why shouldn't we be completely happy together? God, have we sinned against You in some way that You would throw this spider into our wine?

"Oh, the things that brides say!" said Reb Itsik with a sigh. "One dead fly ruins the best olive oil! Look how that cursed spider made everyone so sad. Ay! Here's what to do: take that spider and stomp on him with your foot. Then everything will be happy like before."

"You can't always stomp him," answered Yosef. "Sometimes he runs away before you can even scream. And sometimes a fly spoils the best oil without even touching it."

"You're right, dear Yosef," said the guest. "Nevertheless, don't be a child. And I'm talking to you, too, Roza. Don't be children. Don't be afraid of spiders. Come on, be happy and lively as before!"

"It's time to pray," said Fridman, who was seeing things he had not noticed before.

"I'm a guest," said Reb Itsik. "I'll pray as soon as I get home. I still have time. God is not going anywhere."

Fridman nodded and headed to his office to pray.

"Yosef," said Golde, "don't forget to send the scribe from the study house to examine all our *mezuzahs*."

"I won't forget," Yosef replied. "Are you coming, Shimen? It's getting late."

Yosef glanced at Roza, and she returned his gaze. As Yosef and Shimen left the house, she went to the window and watched until they turned and headed down the street to the study house.

Roza, Rukhame, and Meyshe Shneyur left the room. Golde stood by Reb Itsik near the samovar. "How did he come here?" asked the guest.

"He came—or God sent him—to teach our children. We thought he had relatives, but he came without any. Like people say: you're a relative as long as you're rich; but, heaven forbid, if you're poor, you keep turning to a richer relative until you run out. He was wise to teach here rather than in the city, and I'm very happy God sent him to my home. Who knows, maybe this was predestined. I know you, Reb Itsik, you laugh at everything. So if I tell you it was predestined by God, you'll think I'm just a superstitious woman. But it really was predestined. Somehow my Shimen became attached to Yosef and almost dragged him here against his will. I had wanted Shimen to find a friend who would study with him, but soon I liked Yosef so much, I couldn't let him go. I tell you, Reb Itsik, it cost me some effort before he agreed to stay with us. And now, thank God, he's been here more than a year, and neither the children nor I can live without him. He's baked into our hearts! How, I wonder, can a mother let such a dear child go? Do you know his mother, Reb Itsik?"

"Like I know myself, Golde. Thirty years is not a day!" answered the guest. "I was in their home for thirty years. His father was once an important merchant who owned property and orchards, but he was brought down by a slanderer. I don't know how he's doing now, but it must be bad if his dear child had to leave home to wander as a poor Talmud student. And now he's here with you in a suburb of Mohilev. This explains the changes that have taken place in just a few years. It seems like only yesterday that Yosef was a child. If you had told me then that this boy, who was treated like the Messiah being born, would one day wander all alone in the world, I would not have believed you. Dear Golde, his mother is a warm, dear, and clever woman. It melts my heart when I remember those happy days when Yosef came home from *cheder*. How each person hugged and kissed him. And now? Here he is all alone in the world."

"But is he all alone living here?" Golde asked. "How could I be more true to my own children than I am to him? Is he not as happy with the person who's looking after him as he was with his own mother? Isn't he like a brother to my children? It's no surprise that Shimen can't live without him, but even Rukhame calls him 'my Yosefke!' And as you can see, Roza has her eye on him. What do you say, Reb Itsik? Doesn't this look like something that was predestined?"

"Golde, do you have any doubt that Roza loves him and that he loves her? Even a blind man could see their embarrassment when I unwittingly called everyone's attention to them. Take it from me, Roza will never look at another match. But why take it from me when she can tell you with her own mouth? Here's hoping that my journey here is not for nothing and, God willing, I will see this match carried out!"

"We will see," said Golde happily.

"The holiday is almost upon us," said Reb Itsik. "I'll have to get something new for myself. I danced at your Zelda's wedding and at your Leyke's wedding, and, God willing, at Roza and Yosef's. I'll be part of both families! You must accept the biggest and best wedding gift from me since he was practically raised on my knee. And if God allows me to live and is generous, I will offer the boy what his father once did for me. He helped me out of a great misfortune. How could I ever forget and keep a distance now? I will tell you more about this later, but now I must go pray."

As Golde began clearing the table, she thought, God brought Reb Itsik here. What is hard for me to say, Reb Itsik has no trouble expressing. Dear God, what else do I need from You? Do I need You to come from heaven and say, "This is your daughter's predestined one"? Haven't I already been given a hundred signs? God makes the poor rich and the crooked straight. If Yosef's parents had not come upon hard times, he would never have come to our city. And if God were not sincere, Yosef would never have found our door. It seems as though God Himself is our matchmaker, and the experts are the happy couple themselves. May God give them good health and good fortune, amen!

SEVEN

THOUGHTS WHILE PRAYING

When is there a better time to think clearly about matters—especially household matters—than while standing for the Eighteen Benedictions? In truth, the Eighteen Benedictions is a bit of good luck for any burdened person because he must recite it at least three times a day. And certainly God—who does not consider us slaves under His yoke, but as beloved children who obey and love His name—would not consider it a sin if we found ourselves absorbed in our own thoughts while praying to Him. Perhaps we just think more agreeably about God during this time when our minds are free of base and corrupt thoughts.

And what do we pray for in the Eighteen Benedictions? We ask God for health, a good livelihood, and to have mercy on us. We ask Him to rescue us from every evil hand, to free us from every heavy yoke, and to provide us with everything we need. And what comes to mind during that moment when, deep in thought, we no longer hear ourselves praying? We think about the joys our children bring us, how well our businesses are doing, and a thousand other

122 / J<small>ACOB</small> D<small>INEZON</small>

happy events. And dear God hears our hearts that are so full of joy and thanks even though our lips are reciting other words.

We also think about unhappy events, heaven forbid. About household difficulties, trouble with children, businesses that are failing, meager livelihoods, poor health, and every other difficulty that presses on our hearts. And God hears and feels our sufferings.

God is good and all-knowing. He knows our flaws and weaknesses and that as people we are not angels. We do not have the ability to talk with Him the way the angels do. He gave us the speech in our mouths so we can understand, in our limited sense and wisdom, what is said to us, and so that we can make ourselves understood in our feelings, wants, and needs.

But God, who is kindly and examines each person's heart, mind, and body, understands the speech of our hearts and does not need to hear the words of our tongues. He hears more clearly than the one who tries to fool himself or others by assailing the heavens with his showy devotions, word repetitions, and snapping of fingers while praying. So we should take it neither as a sin nor as a model when we relate that Fridman—a truly pious Jew—was standing for the silent Eighteen Benedictions and thinking about his home, his wife, and his children whom he loved deeply.

I am as fond of Yosef as I am of my own children, he thought. So why wouldn't he be worthy? I know that Roza would not reject him, but these days it's not appropriate to make such a match. On the other hand, my business is, thank God, getting better. My credit is also good. So why do I need to worry about breeding to get a higher status? The world doesn't look twice at the child of a bankrupt father who borrows money with his own blood to pay for a dowry. But everyone wants to believe that a rich man who carries a letter of pedigree from some so and so is somehow more important than a good businessman who lives a quiet life, and has no intentions of eating off another person's plate.

Still, my own capital can't cover my growing business, and I must rely on credit. What will the lenders say? "Fridman took a poor boy. That's a sign things aren't going so well for him." Gossips are like dogs! It will be a miracle if people don't talk.

A person can't just live as he likes. Of course, we want a good son-in-law for our daughter. But if you must deal with people, sometimes you have to give in to them. Anyway, it's not settled yet. As Golde always says, "What is predestined will be!" Better to let God handle it and be happy! In the meantime, I'll dismiss all the matchmakers for a few months until I can work out something with Yosef. Then we'll see!

EIGHT

DEVOTIONS ON SHAVUOS

Yosef was happy. He had a friend and supporter in Reb Itsik and hoped that through him he would achieve his goals. He knew that if Reb Itsik approved, his parents would not be opposed to his love for Roza.

On the day before Shavuos, the weather was rainy, and Yosef remained in the house with Fridman, helping to put things in order before the holiday. At sunset, the rain began to pour down, flooding the muddy streets. Lights could be seen in homes across the way, and the sounds of praying could be heard as people recited words and sang melodies in a sleepy tone.

The poor spent most of the day hurrying around to get what they needed. Shoemakers and tailors, who got little sleep during the week before the holiday, now praised God in their clean and festive rooms, reciting the devotional prayers even though they hardly understood any of the words. A Jew must have a little pleasure before falling on his face or closing his eyes to sleep.

Even more merriment was heard in the building closest to the study house. There you could not differentiate the voices because the reciting was mixed with so much laughter. "Bombs"—wet hand towels twisted into knots—flew from every corner. In the place of honor sat Gad Hillel Zebuluns, Shmuel Yose the schoolteacher, Heshl the liquor dealer, Yekusiel the tailor, and Gasan's two sons-in-law. Nearby stood Fayvish the milk deliveryman reporting the news. Everyone was laughing and he, not knowing why, laughed along with them.

Gad, who was holding on to a little cushion instead of a twisted hand towel, threw it at a young man who was entering the door, catching him square in the face. He, in turn, grabbed the cushion, stuffed it with a clay candlestick, and tossed it back, missing Gad and hitting Shmaye the idler, who was trying to convince people he could bring the Messiah. Shmaye used to sit on the ice with his bare buttocks in the freezing cold, and more than once left pieces of skin and flesh when he got up. In the summer, when there was no ice to sit on, he would hire the *shammes* to whip him a few nights a week. Although the *shammes* resented him for not letting him sleep, he prepared the best switches during the day and whipped Shmaye at night for the few groschen he earned. Shmaye would grit his teeth and grumble, "This is nothing compared to the beatings in hell," which made the *shammes* hit him even harder. One day, Shmaye lost heart and cried out, "*Oy*, you are a demon!" and fainted.

The cushion bounced off Shmaye's head and landed on the man sitting opposite him: Mordecai, Shmuel Yose the schoolteacher's father. Mordecai was a mean, old-fashioned Jew, who did not approve of the Chassidim in the study house. He was just falling asleep when the cushion startled him. Infuriated, he stood up and asked, "Who threw the pillow?" Everyone shouted, "Shmaye!"

Mordecai was already angry with Shmaye for stealing two of his students, so he was happy to take his revenge. He went over to the young man and slapped his cheeks. Then he called over his son, Shmuel Yose, and told him to set Shmaye on the table so they could skin him alive. Or, as the Chassidim say, "Uncork him."

In a second, Shmaye was on the table, and the whole study house was pinching and hitting him. One with a tin candlestick, another with a board, and a third with his Shavuos prayer book. Shmaye did not struggle hard and was probably happy to get this punishment without paying any money for it.

In the meantime, one of Gasan's sons-in-law, who had incited Shmaye's undeserved blows, went over to Tevele the ale man, took him by the arm, and said, "So, are you coming, brother?"

"Where?" asked Tevele.

"To Reb Leyb's."

"And what will we do there? Is there a card game? Or perhaps we'll study the Shavuos prayer book all night?" Tevele laughed.

"You'll find everything you want there, and I'll provide the whiskey if you'll just give me a little good advice."

"Of course," replied Tevele. "Whatever you ask!"

The two left the noisy study house and walked through the rain to the lodgings of Reb Leyb, who was known as a fugitive soldier, a Petersburger, and a general rogue. He lived in a new house, and when the young men arrived, they knocked on a shutter.

"Who's there?" called a voice in Russian from inside the house.

"Your friends!" shouted Tevele.

"Tevele? I swear! And who else?" asked the voice in the house.

"Another friend. Open up!"

Eventually, the door opened, and the two men entered the house.

"A blessing on those who have come, Meyshe Shneyur!" said Reb Leyb. "Do you know Tevele the ale man?"

"Of course, I know him," the Dark One replied.

"A happy holiday, Sorele!" shouted the new arrivals to Leyb's wife. Sorele was one of those women whose name no respectable person could mention without contempt; the kind of woman that a man like her husband would pick from thousands to assist his business. It was obvious she was Leyb's helpmate since, as we see, the city's scoundrels often called her by name. Smoking a cigarette, she sat in a white blouse with her hair disheveled.

"I swear, it looks like a Gentile's house in here," laughed Tevele. "Where are your holiday candles, Sorele? We must praise our wives for sitting at home and blessing us as we go off to recite prayers all night in the study house. Right, Meyshe Shneyur?"

"Sure," answered the Dark One. "Why shouldn't they bless us? I hear people blessing you all the time, Reb Tevele! 'Maybe he's a little airheaded,' they say, 'but look what he does for the community! He collects matzo for the poor and gives boots to the Talmud-Torah children.' But, Reb Leyb, what if they knew what we know? They would curse themselves for ever blessing him!"

"They'll never know!" replied Tevele. "And how do you get by, Meyshe Shneyur? Everyone knows you're a big man in your father-in-law's house. Even if you did something wrong, they'd say, 'Since Meyshe Shneyur did it, it must be right.' You're lucky! God blessed you with the face of one who fears heaven. People think you only live on Psalms and midnight study.

"I, on the other hand, have the misfortune of a homely face, and although I work to make myself look pious, it doesn't help. But my father-in-law knows who I am, and you know why? Because he's no better. His head still works, and he goes for every idea I come up with. Thank God for that! But among the public, I must appear righteous. That's why I collect for the Talmud-Torah and do all those other things."

"You're the lucky one," said Meyshe Shneyur. "If my father-in-law was like yours, I could have my way. But the devil take him, he is a genuinely pious Jew who I can't get my hands on. It's pure luck if you can get your father-in-law into your trap!"

"What do you mean luck?" interrupted Tevele. "Do you know how it was in the beginning? Soon after I came into his house as a bridegroom, my father-in-law began bringing me into his business. That's when I saw what was possible. One time my father-in-law discovered me in a very compromising situation and volunteered to give me a good thrashing. Since I wasn't going to stand for it, I smashed the glasses, the dishes, and broke the big mirror hanging on the wall. I screamed, 'Look here father-in-law, this is how I will answer you every time you dare to say a word to me!' He rolled up his sleeves and intended to hit me in the jaw, but I'm no slouch as a fighter. Then I noticed him looking around at what I'd done. He trembled, and I discovered a treasure in his trembling. He was hoping no one overheard what had happened, because if they found out, how could he keep his trusteeship in the burial society?

"So, Meyshe Shneyur, why are you falling behind? Aren't you getting enough money? Perhaps you should disguise yourself a little. Just so long as you're leading them around by the nose and not the other way around!"

"No, brother," answered the Dark One, "everything that glitters is not gold. But what are we doing here? The tired-out honor of sitting? We came here to discuss improvements, and the lady of the house needs to help out her guests and not kill them from hunger. Now listen, I'll give you half a dozen bottles of port wine if you'll hear my story, and give me your advice on how to extract myself. And if your advice pleases me, I'll make a new holiday for our Chassidim."

"Very good!" said everyone, and soon there were cards on the table and plenty of whiskey. The players paired up and Tevele, who had no money, partnered with Meyshe Shneyur. Their agreement was Meyshe Shneyur's money and Tevele's brains. And in truth, Tevele was more than clever. He understood the winks Reb Leyb's wife gave him and quickly disposed of Meyshe Shneyur's money. Toasts of "*L'chaim!*" came from all sides of the table, and when Meyshe Shneyur's pockets were empty, he began to relate his story.

"Brothers, do you know the 'Laws and Customs of the Son-in-law'?" asked the Dark One.

"Of course, we know!" the others called out. "You're supposed to like the in-laws even more than the wife herself."

"And what else?"

"You must keep track of everything they do," said Tevele. "If they do well, you should jump in with both feet. But be careful not to ruin your stomach! If they have children, and if they're boys, they must be sent off to study in Volozhin or Mir, so they can grow up to be good yeshiva boys. But if they're girls, you do what you can to keep them under your thumb. At least that's what you do if you're as skillful as Yidl Hirshelikh's son-in-law. He put his eye on his sister-in-law—that's how nobly he paid back his father-in-law! I tell you, whomever God helps will be successful. That's the best advice, and then you don't have to worry about your brother-in-law!"

"If I could do that I wouldn't need your advice," said Meyshe Shneyur. "But I'm not a handsome guy like Yidl. Why would my sister-in-law even look at me? Better for her to find someone else. Besides, you don't know her. She's a perfectly modest woman, may she drop off the face of the earth! Once I sent her a Petersburg dandy, but she cut him off so sharply he couldn't look her in the eye afterward."

"So listen," continued Tevele, "and don't beat me up for saying it. If God doesn't help you in the way He helped Yidl, you'll have to help yourself. My advice: you must find her a groom who's a complete idiot. A brother-in-law who's a fool is a piece of luck! He can be very useful. Once you get your hands on him, you can lead him by the nose wherever you want. Who could wish for anything better? Even in the best situation, you shouldn't let them take in a brother-in-law who needs to be supported by the family or comes from the same town. It's a terrible misfortune to end up with in-laws who are aligned with your mother- and father-in-law! The first and best rule is this: you must always remain the gem. That is the central tenet we must follow as long as the in-laws are alive. Then, when they finally close their eyes, we inherit everything! After that, there's no need to worry about keeping the father-in-law's books or counting the money the way he did. That's the short version of the 'Laws of the Son-in-law.' It may be enough for a young boy to pass the exams, but not for us. And since such details aren't recorded in any books, you must become a learned expert in these matters on your own. So what do you say?" asked Tevele.

"You are quite the fellow!" shouted everyone. "You could be the devil's own son-in-law and help him out quite a bit!"

"But tell me, dear advisors," said Meyshe Shneyur, "what do you do with someone who is handsome, clever, an excellent student, and also of the best breeding? And if that's not enough, the father-in-law admires him, and the mother-in-law dotes on him like a firstborn son. Tell me, what do you do when everyone is infatuated with him? Even my own wife has asked me to let Roza be his bride. What do you do when you're expected to answer with an enthusiastic 'Amen,' hand over the books, cede the house, and humbly stand beneath him? Because who are we fooling? The in-laws already like him better than me, and Roza herself is ready to lay down her life for him. So, brothers, be good fellows and advise me. How do I get rid of him so I can follow the 'Laws of the Son-in-law' according to our kind?"

"You must know, Meyshe Shneyur," began Reb Leyb, "there's no matter that can't be managed. If you're not a coward, you can play the same game on your in-laws that Yidl played on his. Is there a maid in the house? Fix it so he's got to take her. You understand what I mean?"

"I understand very well, but the maid is already married and a very proud woman. No one would believe it. Do you think Roza is blind or crazy? Help me, brothers!" Meyshe Shneyur shouted as the whiskey loosened his temper. "I tell you, it'll be disastrous for us all if we can't get this young man out of our territory!"

"The devil!" said Tevele. "Do you know the bride, Reb Leyb? So tender and lovely. She's a queen of hearts, a true princess! Someone like that needs a husband who's a scourge and plague!"

"But where will I find one?" asked Meyshe Shneyur.

"Listen to my advice," said Tevele. "First, soil your potential groom's good name a little. And here's how: You know we have people in the city who believe everything we say. And if nobody believes us, we can always say we caught him with a woman and brought her to the rabbi. You know people will talk about this, which doesn't hurt our plan. If you want, I can tip the rabbi off in advance. I can tell him what people are saying about Yosef, and our wise rabbi, who is a master in such matters, will undoubtedly call him to the study house. I can also remind people in a sermon tomorrow that the Messiah can't come while young men are out strolling with young women like the Fridman daughters. That will certainly make your father-in-law angry with Yosef. What do you say?"

"Small potatoes!" said Meyshe Shneyur. "If he wants to stay, I can master him and rake him out like a leaf. I'll have a forger send another letter to him, which just missed getting the job done the first time. The problem is that a guest has arrived who wants to take Yosef to Petersburg. I admit I'm partly to blame. I told Yosef that his sitting around would never help him achieve his goals. Somehow, he convinced my father-in-law to send him off to Petersburg with merchandise on commission. So you see, there's something to worry about, and you'd have to have Samson's strength to break the chains that now bind him to my father-in-law's house."

"True," answered Reb Leyb. "But don't you know that Samson was overpowered by a woman? We should keep that in mind as we devise our plan."

"I'll tell you what, Meyshe Shneyur," said Reb Leyb's wife. "I'm available for the guest if you need me. Whether he's young or old, just bring him here, and I'll manage him very well."

"I'll try," replied Meyshe Shneyur before turning back to the others. "What's your advice, Reb Leyb?"

"My advice? This can't be done with your bare hands. Maybe around here you can get something done for a thank you, but in Petersburg even water costs money. Do this right, and he'll be out of your house before the rooster crows."

"How much money are we talking about?" asked Meyshe Shneyur, his eyes full of joy.

"The two of us will have to talk about it. Reb Tevele here will sign on as a silent partner. He's good for it and will make everything right and proper. We'll all meet again to agree on the contract. Tevele, do your part and set off the alarm about Yosef to our people. I'll send my donation: a less-than-modest girl who'll go to Fridman's house and know what to say about Yosef. I'll talk to the rabbi myself. In short, it's all coming together so let's not ruin our plan.

"I like you, Meyshe Shneyur. You're not a fool, and you're not shy with me like the others. You should know, even among thieves and murderers, there are clever ones and foolish ones. At one time, I was not so clever and had to catch up quickly. But enough! We'll use whatever tricks are necessary. I know the apprentice is not shy with the master and always thinks he can do it better. Be patient, Meyshe Shneyur, you're still new at this. You'll pass the master soon enough, but you won't forget him! Now, a drink of whiskey, and a good *l'chaim,* brothers. May we say *l'chaim* again next year when everything is concluded!"

"To a good life and to peace!" said Meyshe Shneyur. "Let us drink that our Roza will take an ill-bred boor for a husband!"

"Let's drink that my Elke may pass on, and I can take her sister Dvorah," said Tevele.

"Whoever doesn't wish that for you will never have it for himself," said Meyshe Shneyur. "But Roza would never have me. If I'd been born as smart as you, Tevele, I wouldn't have all these problems!"

"*L'chaim!*" shouted Sorele with a big glass of whiskey in her hand. "I would like to say to my dear guests that we should all drink to our prayers being heard! *L'chaim!* Next year in Jerusalem—or if not—in Makaria at the fair!"

"Amen!" answered her husband and the guests.

From behind the wall came a heavy, bitter whine.

"The devil, who is that?" asked Tevele. "I swear someone is listening!"

"Not likely," said Leyb. "That's my old mother-in-law, the witch, lying in her bed snoring for all she's worth. She's sick and will soon be telling the angels her secrets."

"Don't worry about her," added Sorele. "She's already so dotty if you pissed on her head it wouldn't bother her."

"I wouldn't mind wishing that on my mother-in-law," said Meyshe Shneyur.

"And on my father-in-law," added Tevele. "Anyway, we must not teach our teacher. He knows that walls have ears, so if he has spoken, he probably knows there's nothing to fear."

"We'll begin soon," said Meyshe Shneyur, "but now it's time to go home. What the devil! I can hardly lift my feet, and my head is spinning. Too much to drink. No matter, my wife will think I'm tired from praying."

"When will we meet again?" asked Tevele as he stood up from the table.

"Tomorrow for coffee and rolls," said the woman. "I'll be waiting for you. You must come. Do you hear what I'm saying?"

"Everything you've said!" said the Dark One. "Are we finished?"

"Yes," said Reb Leyb. "Everything is ready now. Go home in good health. And remember my blessing: May God give us victory, and your Roza a stroke of very bad luck!"

"A real field marshal!" said Meyshe Shneyur as he headed to the door.

"Wait, my son," said Reb Leyb. "I have something else to tell you. You should send the letter carrier to me right away. He can be our eyes. And you must undertake the work of the letter carrier with anything that Roza, your father-in-law, or other members of the household send out. All posts and packages of money must go through our hands. You hear me?"

The group drank another round of whiskey, kissed one another in friendship, and left for home.

NINE

A FEW DAYS BEFORE THE JOURNEY

The Shavuos holiday was a merry one. In the study house and in many homes where there was a company of Chassidim—and where Tevele was never missing—Yosef's scandalous activities were discussed. Even the women in the study house were hissing like geese as they related what was going on with the new teacher in Golde's house.

In the little corner where Dvorah Basye the tavern keeper prayed, the buzzing was so loud, they did not hear the start of the holy *Kedushah,* and only near the end did they manage to rise up on their toes. During the Torah reading, there was so much commotion in the women's section that the men clapped, banged the walls, and slapped their prayer books for the women to be quiet. But nothing helped. The names of Golde, Fridman, and their daughters were whispered and repeated over and over.

A big gathering of half-drunken Chassidim at Khaym Gutman's house turned over the slop bucket and started sliding around in it. Khaym's wife cursed and begged her husband not to ruin her holiday, but Khaym could not force his uninvited guests to leave. So his wife went out and brought back her father-in-law, Avrom Gut-man. Avrom was an old Jew, tall and severe, but with a calm character. He went into the house and found Gad, Meyshe Shneyur, Tevele, Shmuel Yose the schoolteacher, Yude the *shammes*, and several others. More than shame before the old man, they felt fear and sat like millstones as they exchanged news. They asked Meyshe Shneyur if he would be insulted if the news included one of his father-in-law's children.

"It's all right with me," said Meyshe Shneyur. "One can tell the truth even about one's own father. Say what you know, and I'll tell you whether it's true or not."

Tevele, using lots of Chassidic euphemisms and coarse talk, re-lated what he had heard about Yosef and the kind of justice that should be done to such a young scoundrel who had no trace of God in his heart. "Shouldn't he be driven out of town or at least brought before a rabbinical court?" asked Tevele.

Avrom Gutman listened with pursed lips, and when Tevele was finished he stood up and shouted angrily, "Akh, you scoundrel! You swindler, rogue, heretic, slanderer! You dare to talk about Yosef when all of you put together are not worth the scrapings from un-der his fingernails? Scoundrels, get out of here! Out, you drunkards and convicts! I'll show you what happens when someone slanders the name of an honest Jewish son or daughter in my house!"

The old man grabbed Tevele by the collar and threw him out the door. The other Chassidim fled through the windows. Singing and dancing, they hurried off down the street.

There was also joy in the Fridman household, although it was displayed in a completely different way. The children were happy, and their parents were delighted as well. Yosef was honored above all the guests for the holiday. There are times when the heart is full, and we feel so happy that every word we say seems purer and sweeter, and Yosef hit the mark with everything he said. The guests treated him royally and drank a toast to his health.

Reb Itsik lifted his glass to Yosef and Roza, spoke warmly at some length about the young couple, and suggested they drink a toast to each other. This gave everyone the impression that the engagement was a fact, and Fridman put his arms around Yosef and kissed him tearfully, then did the same with Roza. During the meal, Fridman sat at the head of the table with Yosef next to him. Rukhame, who insisted on sitting beside Yosef, watched intently as he put each bite of food into his mouth. All the guests pointed out that she was not a little girl anymore, and that such openness with Yosef was inappropriate. But Rukhame would not listen. She loved Yosef as a brother and asked why she should be embarrassed to show it.

A little later, Yosef and Roza had time to talk together. They described their sufferings and came to an understanding with each other. "We should tell our parents everything," said Yosef. "It'll be better than trying to hide our feelings from them. That was the worst part for me."

That evening, Yosef's wish was fulfilled. Reb Itsik had prepared him earlier by saying that Golde had an important matter to discuss with him. Soon after, Golde approached Yosef and took him out to the orchard beyond the garden. She told him with tenderness and wisdom that she knew everything and that she considered it the greatest luck that Roza had fallen in love with him because she herself would have chosen him out of thousands.

"From today on you are my child!" Golde said and kissed him like a mother. "Be an honorable child to me, Yosef, in this world and the next!"

Yosef was speechless. He could only lift his beautiful eyes, full of tears, to heaven. Golde felt his enormous gratitude and said, "Ask God for me, dear child, to preserve me for you!"

Yosef took her hand and kissed it.

"One more thing, my child," Golde said. "We want you to be-gin traveling with Reb Itsik. There's no future for you here in the suburbs. What can you learn here? Believe me, it'll be hard for us to part with you even for a short time. And poor Roza will cer-tainly suffer. Like any faithful mother, I'd like the pleasure of seeing you both happy. But you are still young, and you can't go to Peters-burg for the first time by yourself. Prepare yourself for the trip. Reb Itsik will be leaving in a few days. Now, my son, go to your Roza and tell her. I wish you well in your happy news!"

"Good evening, dear Yosef," Roza said when Yosef found her in the garden. "What have you brought me? I can see you have some-thing to tell me."

"I have much to tell you, dear Roza, and I don't know where to start."

"So tell me everything at once," she said eagerly.

"Our love is indestructible, Roza."

"I've never doubted that, Yosef. That's not news to me."

"Well, I told you I didn't know where to start. But it's news that our love has received the consent of your parents. Your dear mother talked with me and then sent me here to tell you."

"That mother of mine!" said Roza. "Who has a more under-standing mother? Come, let's go thank her."

"Roza, we can thank her in our hearts. But now I have to deliver some other news. For a long time now, I've been mixed up in my head, spending all my energies on things that are not important. That is, not obtaining the knowledge I need to help me achieve a good career in the world. I've studied history and the natural sciences, but these offer nothing that can help me earn my bread. So once and for all, I must take up some specialty that will permit me to make a living. Now it turns out that I can get a position where

I can learn a business. Reb Itsik wants to take me to Petersburg with him. There, in his office, I can learn all aspects of bookkeeping, and then I'll have no worries about getting a position. But before I give him my decision, I wanted to talk with you."

"Yosef," said Roza as tears welled up in her eyes.

"Be strong, Roza. Please think about it. I don't want to do anything against your will."

"Yosef," replied Roza, taking his hand. "If you're giving me the right to tell you how I feel, then I say, 'Please don't leave!' I tremble at the thought. Can we talk about this later?"

"Roza, we must talk about this now and come to an agreement. Reb Itsik will be leaving in a few days, and you know I must go with him. Enough of being childish, Roza."

"Childish? Is it childish to want to enjoy the spring breezes and the warmth of summer? This is our spring, Yosef. You know I want to be worthy of you and seek only to please you. I appreciate your earnest and philosophical side. But everything has its time. Yes, Yosef, we only live once and must prepare for the future, but your seriousness will make you old before your time!"

"To the contrary, dear Roza. Our ancestors acted like children into old age, and like children, they never had any proper concept of life. We must shorten our childhood a little to lengthen our lives. What will we do when it comes time to run our own little world? I will not lend out money for interest, so how will I make a living? Roza, do I have the right to take your freedom before I'm an independent person? I know it will be hard for us to part, but a person's whole life is a series of oppressions and deprivations. God grant us, dear Roza, that this will be the hardest and final deprivation in our lifetime. We live in a time when we must start doing things differently from our parents. They used to say, 'Don't obligate yourself,' but one must make a commitment or nothing works.

"I'm determined to make that commitment today, dear Roza, and you must commit to being separated from me for a short time as we prepare for our future. Some people comfort themselves with simple sayings like 'Distance makes love grow stronger.' Oh, beloved Roza, our love can't be any stronger than it is already!"

Roza fell on his shoulder and wept bitterly. "Dear Yosef, do you know how many tears and sighs you've cost me? Oh, God, what is love? Is it really a flower that only grows on tears and pain? No, Yosef, I can't let you go. But I know we live in a time when one must be strong. We must put on a smiling face even if our heart is breaking. Go, dear Yosef, if you must, and come back to your Roza!"

As Yosef held Roza, he began to cry, too. *Should I go and leave such an angel in tears and pain?* he asked himself. *Or should I stay knowing that someday tears will flow that I'll never be able to dry? Oh, Fate, what assignment have you given me today?*

"Yosef," said Roza, moved by his tears. "You told me yourself that terrible angels with swords stand at the gates of the Garden of Eden. And this shows us no happiness can come without bitterness and torment."

"Yes, dear one," answered Yosef. "Many thorns grow along the road to happiness, and we can't touch the happiness without our hands being pricked. But that makes the happiness even greater! Nothing good comes easily, Roza. I hope the rivers that flow between us and our happiness are not so wide as those blocking other journeys on the path of life. And I do not see any high mountains or deep valleys before us. The path is short, and with God's help, we'll soon be happy again. Don't worry, Roza. You're like a shining lantern guiding my way, and thanks to you I'll not wander from my path. May God send you strength and patience as we get through this painful time. I know you must remain here with

Meyshe Shneyur who pursues and punishes us for no reason. Roza, don't be afraid of him. God will not forsake us. Meyshe Shneyur will see how good we are, and he will be good to us in return. He's really not as bad as he appears."

"No, dear Yosef, he is bad. He is terrible! My heart can't conceive of anything good in him," said Roza. "I take comfort only in the fact that I'm staying here with my parents. Oh, there's never good without bad! Don't worry, Yosef; this evening we'll be happy again. Go to Petersburg; our troubles are not so difficult. There's only a small cloud in our clear, shining blue sky. Now I'm at peace, dear Yosef, and will learn to live without you for a short time. It's not even a separation. Our hearts will always remain as one! Give me your hand and tell me you'll not forget me for one minute as I'll not forget you!"

Yosef gave her his hand just as Golde came into the garden. "My children!" she cried, unable to hide her feelings after overhearing the last part of their conversation. "Dear children, be as happy forever as you are now. I pray that God will preserve me and allow me to see your happiness with my own eyes. Don't be shy, children. When I was your age, I longed to be happy, too. But those were different times, and my parents didn't understand. So instead of the happiness I wanted then, God has repaid me with my children's happiness."

Golde embraced the children and kissed them. The children stood silently without words to express their gratitude.

"Forgive us, dear Mother," Roza finally said, kissing her mother's hand. "We didn't know about your faithfulness and didn't expect so much from you. God has brought us together, but until now we felt guilty and thought we had to hide our happiness."

"See how a mother's heart is a prophet?" Golde replied. "It feels and knows what its children are thinking and dreaming. Now that you know my loyalty, dear Yosef, don't be shy with your mother. I want this for both of you."

Yosef swore to be true to Roza as long as he lived.

"Now I'm completely happy," said Golde, "I don't long for anything else from You, dear God. You've granted the happiness I've always wished for my children. I thank You! Preserve me for their sake, Eternal One!"

"Oh, Mother, I must go thank Father for his blessing," said Roza.

"No, dear child, you must thank him only in your heart. You know your father is an old-fashioned man and would think it odd if you thanked him for Yosef. And we mustn't hold it against him that he doesn't feel the same way we do. You know our parents lived like that for many generations. It's only now that there are millions of people to whom it seems strange and incomprehensible. This is not the time to thank him. But you can thank him, Yosef, for the loving-kindness he's shown and for his willingness to help you become a *mentsh*. I'm sure he'd like to speak to you, dear child, so go see him. Tomorrow you'll be leaving. You know Reb Itsik can't wait any longer."

"Oh, Mother, why does he have to leave so soon? Why wasn't I told about this earlier?"

"Dear Roza, we didn't know your happiness had returned. But don't worry. With God's help, Yosef won't be gone for long. God willing, he'll be back in time for Sukkos. Now come back into the house, children. And Roza, you must learn to act like a grownup and contain yourself."

Golde took Roza and Yosef into the house and left them at the big round table where Fridman and his guest were sitting. Reb Itsik was being witty, and the whole family was rolling with laughter. Fridman handed Yosef a glass of tea and pulled him to his side.

Only Rukhame sat with a sad-looking face. Not only was Yosef leaving, but Shimen, too, was preparing for a trip. Yosef and Reb Itsik had prevailed upon Fridman to send Shimen to a commercial school to further his education.

Fridman took Yosef into his office and talked to him for several hours. He instructed him on all the rules he would need to follow in the big city. He also told Yosef that, God willing, the engagement would be announced when he returned home for Sukkos.

Golde did what every good mother does, and put Yosef's things in order. As a surprise, she packed a new suit of clothes she had a tailor make for him so he could move among his peers as an equal.

She then headed to the kitchen to have food prepared for Yosef and Reb Itsik's trip. But when she arrived, Golde found the kitchen in chaos. There were broken pots on the floor, overturned chairs, and the maid sat with a distraught look on her face. Her hair was disheveled, and she was weeping and cursing. No matter how many times Golde asked her to tell her what happened, the maid could not stop crying. Finally, Golde prevailed, and the maid blurted out: "Leye Sherke's maid came over and told me about our Yosef," sobbed the maid. "And when I couldn't listen anymore, I grabbed the new *cholent* pot and hit her in the head with it. But that didn't stop her, so I grabbed her by the hair and began beating her. Her screams brought in Meyshe Shneyur who pulled us apart. If it hadn't been for him, that slanderer wouldn't have gotten away alive!"

"But why are you still crying?" Golde asked. "Silly girl, when dogs bark, we can't always close their mouths. Let them say what they want; they will not dissuade us. Any ill that Yosef has done to them, the Eternal should do to me!"

"But it upsets me so," said the maid who continued to sob. "Why did Meyshe Shneyur call me a hussy? How could he sling such dirt and mud at me after everything I've done for him?"

"You probably shocked him with your curses, so he became angry with you," said Golde.

"No, I know why he acted that way," said the maid. "Perhaps you should know, too."

"I don't want to know," Golde said. "What business is it of mine? I beg you Rishke, let's not talk about this anymore. For Reb Itsik's trip, please make some plank bread, olive-oil rolls, a few almond biscuits, and a *bobke*—all the wonderful things you made for the holiday."

As Golde left the kitchen, the faithful mother said to herself, To spite my enemies, dear God, may my Yosef eat in good health and with an even better appetite!

Golde knew the Dark One was out to get Yosef, but she consoled herself with the thought that God always sends the cure before the plague. The dogs may bark now, she told herself, but Yosef is going away, and they'll splinter their teeth and stop. God will bring him back, and our enemies will see our happiness! Returning to her family, Golde sent all the children off to bed.

But Roza could not sleep. Her heart raced, and she struggled to grasp all that had taken place. She thought, Oh, God, today I poured out my heart to someone. Tomorrow, I'll be all alone again. How painful it is to separate! Why is the world so cruel? Why must Yosef leave? Is it possible he's really not mine? God, where do such dark thoughts come from? Yosef, don't be afraid because we're not officially engaged. Your first kiss was the strongest contract. I'm yours, Yosef. We have sworn before God, and He is our witness. He answered "Amen" to our vows. I'm no longer afraid of my dark brother-in-law. He can burst chains, break walls, employ the torturing angels of hell, but he can't touch my heart and innocent soul. God dwells there; God is my protector!

Roza lay thinking and dreaming. She wanted to sleep so she would be strong for tomorrow's parting. Tossing and turning, she buried her head in the pillow, her heart so full she did not realize her tears were flowing like a river. Getting up with the dawn, she frantically started working on the watch holder she had begun sewing for Yosef and had put aside for the holiday. She wanted to finish it before he left, but when Golde came in and saw her red, swollen eyes, she took the piece from her hands. Then Yosef came in, and when Golde told him what she was doing, he asked that she not let it grieve her. Rather, he said, he would not be bothered knowing that Roza owed him something.

"Yes, you know how faithfully I pay my debts," Roza said. "How could I ever rest if I knew you were expecting something from me?"

"Good, then I'll have something to look forward to when I return," Yosef said with a smile. "But tell me, dear Roza, are you rested? Can I remind you that I'm leaving in less than an hour? They've already sent for the horses!"

"Be at ease, dear Yosef, I'm quite calm. Last night I figured out everything. Let me get dressed, and I'll see you for tea in just a moment."

Roza went into her dressing room and cried again, this time not so hard, and in ten minutes she was walking downstairs where Yosef was waiting. Everything was ready for the trip. Fridman had given him a sum of money. His travel pack, bought on Reb Itsik's orders, was stuffed with good things. Soon a bell was heard outside the window, and Roza felt her heart tear at the sound.

The wagon has arrived to take my Yosef away, she told herself. How welcome will be the wagon that brings him back home again.

"To the journey!" commanded Reb Itsik.

Golde, always the faithful mother, urged Yosef to put on his heavy overcoat to ward off the cold wind. Although a little overheated, Yosef stood with his face shining so brightly with love that Meyshe Shneyur could barely look at him without asking forgiveness for his dreadful conduct. A thought flashed through the Dark One's mind: *How much better things would be for me if I were as fine as Yosef.*

Shimen watched in quiet confusion. He tried to imagine how he would manage with Yosef so far away. Rukhame sobbed and followed Yosef around at every turn. Only Roza swallowed her tears. She looked at her beloved Yosef; how handsome and loving he was. She stood like a statue, her heart pounding in her chest. *Oh, I'm not going to make it,* she thought when the moment of separation arrived.

Reb Itsik stretched out his hand to Fridman and shouted, "Be well, my friend!"

"Good health!" answered Fridman, and the two men kissed as was the style.

Then came Yosef's turn. Fridman embraced him warmly, kissed him, and said, "Go in good health, dear child, and return in good health. Don't forget, dear boy, you're traveling to Petersburg. It's a different world there with a different way of life. Be a *mentsh* and don't let yourself be led astray. Bring back the honest heart you're taking with you. As for the business, I'll write everything out so you'll know what to do."

Then he turned Yosef over to Golde, who spilled tears on him. She pressed him to her heart and said in a loving voice, "Yosef, honest people live in Petersburg, too. The same God that knows everyone's hearts and thoughts here knows everyone's hearts and thoughts there. May God protect you, my child."

"That's enough!" Rukhame cried out. "Leave him alone, or you'll wear him out. Yosef, you won't forget me, will you? Travel in good health for me. See, I am already different than I was before."

They kissed in front of the whole household, and no one said a word. Yet Rukhame felt embarrassed when Yosef pulled his lips away. He had given her a new feeling with his kiss, and at that moment she became even sadder than before.

"Roza, be well," said Yosef in a tender voice.

"Yosef, I'm coming with you as you start your trip," replied Roza. "I've asked for a carriage, and Rukhame and Shimen are coming with me. We'll have a little more time to take our leave."

"Goodbye, everyone," Yosef called out. "Don't forget to write. Be well, my dear ones!"

Reb Itsik and Shimen rode in the wagon. In the carriage that followed, Roza and Rukhame sat on one side and Yosef on the other. The driver touched the horses with his whip, and the journey began. Fridman, Golde, Zelda, Gavriel, Leyke, Meyshe Shneyur, and the whole household stood in the doorway waving their hands and sending blessings for good health.

Once outside the city, Yosef and Roza got out of the carriage and stood together for a moment. Roza cried, swallowed her tears, and took off her white silk scarf which she placed around Yosef's neck. "Travel in good health, my beloved Yosef. I can't go any farther. Will you write to me?"

"Yes, as often as possible," Yosef answered tearfully.

They kissed and their tears mixed together.

"Don't worry, dear Roza. I'll be home soon."

Shimen climbed out of the wagon, and Yosef got in beside Reb Itsik. The driver urged the horses on, and the distance grew quickly between the two young lovers.

"Travel in good health!" called out Rukhame and Shimen. Roza remained silent, but her lips whispered, "Amen."

PART THREE

ONE

THE LETTERS

Yosef sat alone in his room until late at night. He had no interest in listening to the piano music coming from downstairs or attending the theater, going for a walk, or visiting friends. He was preoccupied with only one thought: Why had he not received a letter from Roza?

Two months had flown by since he had arrived in the city, and he had already completed everything that Fridman had requested. Shapiro, the bookkeeper at Reb Itsik's office, treated Yosef like a brother and gave him more work to do. Not to make his life more miserable, but to distract his young friend from the lack of news from Roza. Shapiro thought the extra work would leave him little time to think about her, but Roza never left Yosef's thoughts.

Even while they took a break and walked through the noisy streets of Petersburg, Roza was on Yosef's mind. No matter where the bookkeeper took him, Yosef kept asking, "Why hasn't she written?" And Shapiro had no words to console him.

In the evening, Yosef would escape to his room and write. Neither the piano from below, the tumult in the streets, nor the frequent knocking at his door could tear him away from his writing. He sat and wrote, and tears streamed from his eyes. His whole pure heart was visible on his face, and he poured out all his bitter feelings in his letters.

Yosef wrote until the piano was silent and the streets deserted. Then he stood up, gathered the pages together, arranged them by number, and began to read:

Dearest Mother,

Oh, how I wish to be with you now, sitting in our little home by your side, telling you my troubles, and seeking your advice. It seems as though everything around me is a dream, and that I am living in an imaginary world. But not like those childish fantasies and puzzles I used to enjoy that left me feeling happy and alive. No, these are different and more difficult to interpret and solve. I feel like I am dreaming and a riddle has been proposed to me; but no matter how hard I try to figure it out, it can only be solved with another dream or riddle.

If only I were with you now to hear your opinion about my new direction and activities. Perhaps your words would awaken me from this deep sleep, and bring me into life again. Oh, Mother, why are you silent? Your child is lost and suffering.

How many times as a child did you lighten my heart by telling me I was having a bad dream? Waking and sleeping, you always kept your eye on me. Now, Mother, I sit here with such a heavy heart. I am tormented in a bitter dream, yet you keep your distance. I cannot cry out. I blink my eyes and wave my hands to tell you of my pain, but you do not understand. Are you no longer the same mother, or am I no longer the same son?

No, Mother, I have no right to speak this way. I have sinned against you! In my good times, when I was happy, I was silent and did not tell you how happy I was. Now, when I am so lonely, and my heart is so full of sadness, I want to run to you, confess everything, fall on your neck and cry out, "Take me back and let me be free!" I need your comfort, Mother. Why won't you write what I want to hear?

For the longest time, my thoughts have been all mixed up and without direction. Often I sit doing my work, writing long columns of numbers while my mind is thinking of other things. Suddenly, as if awakening from a deep sleep, I become aware of what I have written and wonder how I added or subtracted correctly without paying attention. My senses sleep at work, and my eyes are closed to the whole outside world. I live in a dream, do my work without mistakes, and wonder how it is possible. Only now, as I write to you in this letter, am I fully awake.

Yesterday, I went walking by myself in the wide streets of Petersburg. In the middle of these streets are rivers that split off in different directions. As I walked along, deep in thought, I noticed how all the small streams spilled into the great Neva river. Until that moment, each stream had gone on its own separate course; but when it reached the river, it was swallowed up and dragged away. Mother, I see my own situation in that river!

I remember as a child standing beside a little stream that flowed between two green fields covered with flowers. Where, I wondered, was the water going? Once, when the other boys were swimming, I tried to find out where the water was coming from. How amazed I was to see a little rise in the ground that divided the stream in two. One stream went smoothly on its way; the other picked up a faster current. A little farther on that stream fell into a little river that swallowed it up and carried it away. No matter how hard it tried, the water could never return to its original source.

Mother, I am like that little stream, swallowed up by a larger family, and moving farther and farther away from you and Father. Now I am flowing with them and unable to follow my own course.

The reason is Roza, their lovely daughter who is living the life I wish to live, too. Mother, I love her with all my heart.

Surely, Reb Itsik Vilner has told you how I came to Petersburg, so now I can tell you that my second parents are very pleased with me and want me to be happy with their daughter. That is why they have sent me here to learn a profession. I admit this is my goal. My eyes have been opened, and I have seen how naked and unarmed I am on this endless battlefield where people quarrel over a piece of bread. I am afraid you will have to give up your hope of seeing me become a rabbi.

Mother, I know you always wished for my happiness. Perhaps God will provide happiness in the Next World, but I must make my own happiness in this world. All I want in this world is to find happiness with my Roza.

Be well, good Mother. Say hello to everyone, and pray to God for my Roza as you pray for me.

Your Yosef

Yosef folded the pages and looked at them with tears in his eyes. Then he began to reread a packet of letters he had written to Roza over the past several days.

New Moon of Av, 1840

Dear, sweet Roza!

My thoughts leave me no rest. I must write again today even though I just sent you a long letter and have not heard anything back from you. I find joy in writing about our hours of happiness together before my trip to Petersburg, but in writing one becomes engrossed in oneself and I must guard against being childish or sentimental.

You once told me, "I would like to be a child again and enjoy our springtime without worrying about the rainstorms that come in summer." At the time, I did not pay much attention to your words. I did not know that someday I would understand them.

Roza, I have made myself so serious and old. If I were not afraid, I would be a child again, throw aside my office, and come running home to you. In your arms I would have a good cry, unburden my bitter heart, and become human again. Then I could come back to Petersburg and do my work like everyone else. But for now, I have drawn the bitterness of life to myself, and cannot heal.

2nd Av 1840

Writing has become more important to me than talking. Love makes one vulnerable, and writing helps me the way moaning helps a sick person and tears lessen the pain of someone who grieves. If only I could just keep everything inside me, but my heart is not made of iron, and is breaking under the burden. How could you not write to me? Or is it possible someone is keeping your letters from me? When I search for reasons for your silence, I feel a dark confusion.

Many questions race through my mind, and a dark doubt seizes me: "What am I doing here? Is this my Siberia where I am paying for my terrible sin of loving Roza?" Oh, dear Roza, you must know how I suffer. How can you leave me in such torment? I cannot write anymore. Tears pour from my eyes, and my heart is breaking.

6th Av

Roza, seeing you now would make me so happy. I could tell you all about my life here in Petersburg. Oh, how many tears have I added to the river of tears that pour through the streets of this city? How many sighs have I added to the eternal sounds of weeping that never end day or night? How many lonely people do I see every day wandering the streets lost, abandoned, and bereaved? Oh, God, You made your world good, but the people in it have been made so lonely and oppressed. How does one who is unfortunate conceive of the misfortune of others? How does a person born in prison know the pleasure of freedom? What did I know of the world when I lived in Mohilev? I found no great happiness there, but now I see my misfortunes were not so terrible either. Here, I see so many who are bright as the sun and dark as the night! From rich people with lavish homes and fancy coaches to poor people who drag their bootless feet over burning stones and wither away from lack of bread and water.

Oh, what an inconceivable world! Who arranged it this way? My heart is weighted down with bitter thoughts which I have not expressed to anyone and should not be writing to you, dear Roza. Whenever I see someone's happiness, my heart weeps from anger and grief. Everything seems to hurt me. Each wound stings more than the next, and new wounds appear every day to replace the old ones.

8th Av

Today I will stop writing about myself and tell you a little about current events. You know, dear Roza, that my love for our Jewish nation is unlimited, and I rejoice like a little child whenever I see that people are beginning to appreciate the Jews. Here I see Jewish doctors, merchants, and geniuses of all kinds. God grant that our enemies, the begrudgers, will come to understand our progress and stop speaking ill of us. The government knows the truth but has remained silent until now. Soon, only unscrupulous newspaper writers, writing for their own ends or a small fee, will continue to speak against us. Their conscience is so corrupt they do not realize how great their crime is!

Do you remember, dear Roza, when you once asked me why our enemies search for such terrible things to say about us? Why, if one Jew commits an injustice, tells a falsehood, or steals something, they blame us all? When you asked this question, I wanted to answer you with kisses. But then your dark brother-in-law came in and directed our conversation to another topic. Now that I remember, I will answer your question with the reasoning my teacher once gave me. He was more particular about my sins than any of the other *cheder* boys who were always in trouble for playing jokes. I told him I had not done anything worse than the other students, and that I was only a small boy. I promised that when I got older, I would be more careful and not do such things anymore.

"Listen, my dear little Yosef," said my teacher. "The other boys are rough and make their mistakes. But you, my child, are not like them. You are a nice boy, and you have a completely different nature. For you, even a small error is unsuitable."

Perhaps this can be an answer to your question, dear Roza. My teacher spoke to me this way because he looked at me more closely than the others. He had higher expectations for me. I did not fully understand him then since I was only a child and committed childish sins. But when I got older and wiser, I came to understand my foolishness.

The people who speak against Jews, who are more particular about us than they are about other peoples, do not judge us with a test for lead, but with a test for gold. The finer the nature, the more it must be refined. As we become more refined, our mistakes become more visible.

When my teacher talked with me, I gave the excuse I was only a small child. Is this not similar to our situation today? In our current condition are Jews not like children? How long have we wallowed in the muck of the ghetto where no beam of light was permitted to reach us? We are weak, just out of a sickbed, and it is hard to be a whole person. In such a short time, how can they expect us to be perfect in every way?

9th Av (Tishah b'Av)

Today I went to the cemetery. Although I did not want to go, I did my duty and will describe the graves to you—the dungeons of the Jews where our peoples' misfortunes lie buried, and where I stood lamenting and fasting. Oh, the whole ruined Temple! Among the general population at the time was a rabbi who diverted the people from their pure Jewishness. They became wild; women and children suffered, men became drunkards, robbers, and thieves. But as we look back on it, we were not so guilty. Had the Jews been an autonomous people, or if at least the government had paid any attention to our religious leaders, we would not have seen a new sect arise that grieved the entire Jewish people. A few young, ignorant, and uneducated ruffians would not have become their leaders, and the people would not have followed them like a flock of sheep.

Are we not seeing this again today as the government stands at a distance, and our own educated people have no power to forbid the rule of corrupt Jews who have swept like a plague through our communities? Our brothers fall, and we cannot help them. The populace is still wild and without the sense to understand what is good and pious. Even when they are told that God wills them to do something, thousands disobey. Even when ten smart people shout, "God does not require this of you. This is not piety!" no one listens.

How many of our sages have sacrificed their lives for our people? How many have written with their heart's blood to show the right way? How many have waged war with their pens against the lawbreakers and false leaders?

Oh, Roza, how do we rescue our people from all the worthless ideas that lead them astray? This alone would make us into the nation we desire but cannot envision for ourselves. Instead, we leave progress in dead hands that are powerless to lead us forward.

Even our pens are unable to fight against this. Oh, when I think about Jewish writers my heart weeps! So many talented authors languish in chains; so many poets walk among us without bread. This is our greatest shame. Jews are always showing their gratitude to the Gentiles for any favor they receive. Yet we do not show the same gratitude to our own Jewish writers and activists. This neglect has led more than one to leave our people. Why do we not realize their love for us? They rarely make any money from their writings, so it is not about making a living. All they want is to see their works in print. But older Jews want nothing to do with such works, and younger Jews are even worse. Because of their ignorance, they are embarrassed to hold a Yiddish book in their hands.

You know, dear Roza, that I am a child of my people. If I thought that I could help them with my flesh and blood, I would let it out drop by drop for their cure. But who will listen to me? If, as so many others have done, I wrote another edict or prohibition, perhaps then they would obey me. But if I tried to quell the fire in my heart by writing a book that points out their errors, how unfortunate I would be! I would not mind my misfortune if I could be certain that my efforts would help a few people. But I know that publishers would never print it, and if they did, it would soon be burned. Those who would read it would say, "What kind of villain is he? What kind of heretic?"

So I write these words to you, dear Roza. You are the only one who understands me. God has made us different, and someday we will both be of service to our people.

10th Av

Roza, it is already morning, and once again there is light coming through the window to reveal the troubles of a new day. Why am I so different from other people? Does the dear sun not bring comfort and hope to the miserable? Does it not pour healing balm onto the wounds of the suffering? Why, then, does it stick me with a spear and pour poison on my wounds?

Every day I have waited for the letter carrier and each minute has seemed like an eternity. Yesterday, when he arrived, he said he had a letter for me. I went pale as a corpse. My hands shook, and I could barely take it from him. The envelope had a heavy seal that I had to tear through to get to the written words. I was almost blinded by excitement and did not see that it was only two sheets of paper. On one there were just two lines from your father. The paper was stained, and the ink was smudged. I could not make sense of it and quickly turned the page. I wanted to read the rest of the letter, but the whole sheet was empty. Not one word was written on it!

The blood pounded in my head. I bit my lips. I was in terrible pain. I wanted to cry out. People looked at me and shrugged their shoulders. They asked me questions that I did not hear. I know I answered them, but I do not know what I said.

Oh, Roza, what does your father's smudged and torn letter mean? What does the empty page indicate? I suspect someone has done this to make me suffer. How could a person be so terrible? No, it must be a mistake. Instead of picking up the letter, your father must have grabbed an empty sheet of paper. Yes, I believe that is what happened.

Roza, write me! Do not let me suffer anymore. But do not suffer yourself. The wounds in my heart have not healed, but they are familiar; I can withstand them. Do not suffer; I will suffer for you.

Your Yosef

Yosef stopped writing. Daylight filled the room. If Roza could just read this one letter, he thought, then she would know not to suffer. God, punish me for her; punish me more. With these words, Yosef fell asleep.

Two

DAWN

"Have you talked with him?" the short man asked the door-man at Reb Itsik's office where Yosef worked.

"No, Leyzer," the doorman answered. "I went by there yester-day evening. I knocked on the door ten times for sure. Of course, I couldn't knock very hard. I didn't want him to be afraid I was coming after him."

"You're right, brother. We have to be careful not to leave a trace and keep things nice and clean like before. But we're going to have to move a little faster. Did you see the dispatch from Leyb today?"

"No," replied the doorman.

The short man took out a piece of paper and read:

> Try to secure the merchandise quickly.
> The principle may be lost today.
> Leyb Sorkin

"So, what do you say?" asked the short one.

"It will happen today," said the doorman. "I'll go to him soon. We may have to change our plans. He asked me to go to the bath-house with him at eight o'clock. Instead, I'll go at seven and say

163

that something has come up and I need to do it earlier. You take the coat with you. The watchman at the bathhouse is one of us. Give him a wink, and he'll exchange Yosef's coat for yours. It will go quickly, and he won't even realize what happened. Do you understand what I'm saying? Send Reb Gruneman to old man Savitske, and we're all set!"

"Good, that feels better than switching the coats in his room," said the short man. "He won't notice a thing. What time is it now?"

"Six-thirty," said the doorman. "I'll go get him, and you get everything ready."

"You don't need to instruct me," said the short man resentfully. "I've done plenty of difficult jobs in my time. Do you have any coins with you? You know Savitske won't touch it without a bribe. My advice to you: don't come out of the bathhouse with him. It's no good if he figures it out. Anyway, how long are we supposed to take care of him? In a year, once the engagement happens, the match will be off, right?"

"What's right is right," said the doorman. "Wait here; this is where he lives. Don't forget, check his number, his name, and his appearance. Don't get mixed up!"

The short man stayed outside as the doorman went into Yosef's building and knocked loudly on the door. The door did not open, so he knocked again even harder.

Yosef, who had not been asleep for long, was startled by the knocking and went to the door.

"Who is it?" he called out.

"I!" answered the doorman.

"Khaym," said Yosef, "do you have a letter?"

"No, I came to call you to the bathhouse," replied the doorman. "Remember, you invited me to go with you this morning."

"Is it already eight o'clock? I just got to sleep."

"What's wrong with you, Yosef?" asked the doorman. "Let me see how you look. Are you sick? Let me see your eyes."

Yosef opened the door. "I didn't sleep. I spent most of the night writing."

"Do you have the letters?" asked the doorman. "I can mail them for you."

"No, I'll mail them myself," said Yosef. "Thank you, but you know I don't like to make others do things I can do for myself. But I'm not going to the bath today. Dear Khaym, don't take it badly that you came here for nothing."

"It doesn't bother me," said the doorman, "but it worries me that you'd let such a nice day get away from you. Come, Yosef. If you won't go to the bathhouse, the doctor wants to see you again."

"So now the doctor considers me his patient? All he told me was that bathing is good for frayed nerves."

"That's what he told you, but he told me, 'Pay attention to your friend. He should go to the baths every day.' If you want to go, we must go now, Yosef. The choice is yours."

"I need a little more sleep," Yosef begged.

"But I won't have any time later to come back," answered the doorman. "Come, Yosef. A young man like you shouldn't go around smelling bad. Suppose you have to attend an important business meeting today. It's also important for your health, dear friend."

"All right, I'll go," said Yosef. "But wait a minute, I have to address my letters. Later, I'll go by the post office and drop them off myself."

As he addressed the letters to his mother and Roza, the doorman brushed off Yosef's summer coat and brought it to him. "Now we are ready," Khaym said. "Come along! And if you get a letter today, you will buy me a vodka tomorrow!"

"All I want is one letter, and I will buy you whatever you want!"

"My heart tells me that I will bring you a letter today," said the doorman. "I'll go ask at the post office as soon as we've finished bathing. But hurry up!"

They left the building and stopped by the post office on their way to the bathhouse. Although Yosef wanted to put the letters into the mailbox with his own hands, they arrived too early to buy stamps, so he placed the letters in his coat pocket until he could mail them later. The doorman smiled to himself as he realized that in addition to the coat, he would also get his hands on Yosef's letters.

Less than an hour passed while they bathed, and when they were done, the doorman handed Yosef his coat. He quickly ushered Yosef out before he had time to check if the two letters were still in the breast pocket where he placed them.

Outside the bathhouse, a horse-drawn cab was waiting, and the doorman said, "Yosef, take a seat. Don't worry, it won't cost you much. I know the driver."

Yosef did not hesitate and got into the cab. He directed the driver to the post office, but the driver acted as if he did not hear and turned down a side street. When Yosef persisted, the driver turned around and headed to the post office. The doorman leaped out of the cab and said, "Yosef, give me your letters. I'll stick stamps on them and throw them in the box."

"No," said Yosef in annoyance. "Get the stamps, and I'll put them in the box myself."

The doorman ran inside but quickly returned. "It's still too early," he said as he climbed back into the cab. "There's no one here yet." Without waiting, the driver headed off to Reb Itsik's building.

As they entered Yosef's office, the doorman tried to help Yosef remove his coat. Yosef refused, and as he took it off himself, he was shocked to find that his letters had been exchanged for two others. Blind with fury, he shouted, "God, where are my letters? I have lost my letters! Someone has taken them from my pocket!"

"No, Reb Yosef," said the doorman calmly, "there are no thieves in the bathhouse. Think about it carefully. Perhaps you were given the wrong coat by accident."

"You're right, Khaym," said Yosef, trying to calm himself. "Do you know the men who were bathing with us this morning?"

"I know them all," said the doorman. "They're all honest men. Open the letters. Perhaps you can see who signed them; then you'll know who has your coat."

Yosef opened the envelopes, but the names were unknown to him. He hurried back to the bathhouse and posted his address, sure that the person would inquire about his lost coat and letters. He could not believe that someone had done this willfully and hoped his letters would be returned quickly.

Instead of returning to the office, he went home, a thousand thoughts mixed up in his head. Sad and agitated, he took up a piece of paper and began to write:

Dear, good Roza!

I am in great distress, and because my hands are not tied up with office matters, I look for no other consolation than to write to you. It is the only thing that holds my broken heart together.

I spent the whole night writing a letter to you and felt so happy knowing you would read it. But a bizarre accident has befallen me. This morning when I planned on sending you the letter, I awoke too early. No, if I tell it correctly, someone woke me up. I tried to buy stamps but there was no one at the post office, so I put yours and another letter into my coat pocket. Now hear and be astonished. Somehow at the bathhouse, someone switched my coat for his, and took my letters with him! Could this be an accident? Or is it possible, dear Roza, that our enemies are pursuing me here with no other intention than to snatch my letters and cause me more pain? I am becoming suspicious of the doorman at my office. Today he tried to get hold of my letters to mail them. He has been acting strangely, and I am beginning to suspect his motives. Perhaps he is the one keeping your letters from getting through to me.

Suddenly, Yosef was startled by heavy footsteps outside his room. Leaving the letter on the table, he opened the door and was stunned to find a Russian police inspector and two uniformed policemen standing in the hallway.

"Are you Yosef Rozenberg?" asked the inspector in Russian.

"I am," replied Yosef.

"Show us your documents," said the inspector.

Yosef showed the policemen his papers and the certificate that permitted him to reside in Petersburg.

"Is this your money?" the inspector asked, showing him a paper ruble.

"No," answered Yosef.

"You took a cab today?"

"Yes."

"The cab driver who brought this money to the police station said you gave it to him. It's counterfeit. He said he asked you to exchange it, but you refused. According to the law, we must conduct an investigation. If we don't find anything suspicious, you will be set free."

The policemen searched through Yosef's room without leaving any corner untouched. When they found nothing, they picked up his coat and started looking through it. "That's not my coat," Yosef said. "Today it was switched at the bathhouse. I have witnesses. Whatever is there, I don't know anything about it!"

"That's not my concern," said the inspector as he began looking through the pockets and examining the lining. Hearing the rustle of something sewn into the collar, he ripped open the coat and removed a sealed envelope with Yosef's address written on the front.

"Is this your address?" asked the inspector.

"Yes," answered Yosef as he recognized Roza's handwriting. Struggling to remain calm, he opened the envelope, but instead of a letter, he found a stack of Russian currency.

"These are counterfeit!" exclaimed the inspector, examining the money. But before he could say another word, Yosef, in shocked confusion, lost his balance and fainted.

Only later when he regained consciousness did Yosef grasp what had been done to him. He awoke in a dark room with the door locked. As he thought about his situation, pieces of the puzzle began to fall into place. Roza had indeed written to him, but the doorman had taken the letters. Then the thief threw him into a pit and buried him by planting counterfeit money in the switched coat. He suspected the doorman had been bribed.

As Yosef looked around the room, a shudder went through him: no more than four walls, a concrete floor, and a mattress. So this is where I'll spend the rest of my days and nights, he thought. Oh, God, why do You punish me so harshly? I know that my heart and hands are clean. All I ask is that You protect my Roza so she doesn't know about this. Don't let her suffer! God, You showed me Your light for one brief minute. I enjoyed it for one blink of an eye, and now You repay me with such misery and suffering. But please protect my Roza!

Yosef wept bitterly. He put his hot forehead against the cold, wet wall, and lost himself in his dark, confused thoughts.

The inspector had taken all of his papers, including the letter he had just begun to Roza, added an official stamp, and sent everything off with his report to the Minister of Police. That day in the office, people wondered why Yosef had not come to work. That night, Shapiro the bookkeeper went to his residence and was told by the landlady that Yosef had been arrested and taken to the police station.

At the police station, Shapiro learned that Yosef had been moved to another location, but no matter how much money he offered, he could not find out where. He informed the office of what had happened and wrote to Reb Itsik about the events. Each person he talked with sent him on to someone else, and when the bookkeeper pressed hard on an official to tell him where Yosef was, he was told that it would be much better for him to stop his inquiry. Yosef was being held in a very serious matter, and suspicion could fall on those who had dealings with him. So our unfortunate Yosef sat, and no one knew where he was.

THREE

UNTIL LATE AT NIGHT

On the same evening that Yosef was thrown into a dark cell in the Petersburg jail, lights glowed in the Fridman house in the suburb of Mohilev. A passerby looking through the window could see Fridman sitting at the table smoking a cigar. Across from him sat a heavyset Jew in a short frock coat who was drumming his fingers on the table. Two other Jews stood nearby talking loudly. One was short and had a big nose. The other, who was thin and emaciated, stomped his feet and waved his hands. Someone from out of town might have thought that a crazy person had broken into Fridman's house and was behaving like a lunatic, but a local would quickly realize that Meyshe the Madman was presenting a marriage proposal. Seeing his gestures, the experienced person would understand his meaning, but anyone overhearing his words would be at a complete loss. The other matchmaker tried to interrupt and talk over him.

Outside the house, a man crouched beneath the window trying to overhear the conversation. When Kuzmo the butler discovered him, he asked to see Meyshe Shneyur.

Meyshe Shneyur left Fridman with the matchmakers and found Leyb Sorkin waiting in the shadows. "What's new?" the Dark One asked.

"We couldn't have wished for better," answered Leyb. "Come see me at home or the brewery."

"Home is better," said Meyshe Shneyur.

An hour later, the two men were sitting in Leyb's house. Leyb took out a telegram and handed it to Meyshe Shneyur. The Dark One struggled with the Russian letters but managed to figure out the words:

> The merchandise is safe and has been placed in secure hands.
> The expenses were seven hundred rubles. Send money now.
> We don't want to redeem the merchandise too soon.
>
> Khaym and Company

Meyshe Shneyur understood the meaning, and his heart stopped.

"Why are you so shocked?" asked Leyb. "What did you expect when you asked me to get rid of him?"

"I'm not shocked, but I'm a little afraid. You shouldn't send him to hard labor forever," said Meyshe Shneyur.

"You're such a child! Don't be afraid. We don't have to do anything now. Wait and see. Let him rot for a couple of years. And even if they do transport him somewhere else, why should you worry? Are you that eager to have him back again?"

"As far as I'm concerned, he can drop dead," replied Meyshe Shneyur. "But what do we do now?"

"How are your in-laws doing?" asked Leyb.

"My mother-in-law's sick to death. My father-in-law's cold and distant. But I think he's ready to discuss another marriage now that Yosef has disappeared. What can I say? He's angry about the missing thousand rubles he requested Yosef to send him from the business. He got a letter from his office saying the draft had been paid, but he received no indication from Yosef. I spelled out my opinion of Yosef, and I think he's beginning to believe what others are saying as well.

And the letter that came from Yosef made him so furious that, at my suggestion, he opened Yosef's chest. There he found several incriminating things that disturbed him: a letter from his mother in which she wrote that he must not forget the folks at home and advised him not to rely solely on his father-in-law's inheritance; and letters to and from Roza in which he talked about every evil impulse and mocked her parents. My father-in-law was so livid he could've killed Yosef himself. Now, I think he's ready to reject him as a bridegroom.

"This may be the best time for Golde, too. She's been ill, and people have been told not to worry her with problems. Even so, my plan is to make her think Yosef is dead. But you know, Leyb, the whole thing hinges on Roza. She still loves him. When she saw the letters, she tore them up and shouted they were fakes. She swore that she would rather do herself in before she ever stopped loving him. Believe me, sometimes my heart almost melts. She's so good to everyone—even to my children and me. She never goes out anymore and keeps saying she's waiting for the miracle when God takes her from this world. Here, you can read one of her letters."

Meyshe Shneyur took an envelope from his pocket and handed it to Leyb. "It cost me a pretty penny to get my hands on this. It was nearly impossible to get it out of the mail."

After Leyb finished reading Roza's words, he handed the letter back to Meyshe Shneyur. "Yes, I see how you can melt from pity. But don't forget, pity can also damage you. It's of no use! What's done is done. To slaughter and not kill is cruel; to kill completely is kind. I prefer to be a master of kindness in such cases."

"But what now?" asked Meyshe Shneyur.

"We'll be guided when the time comes," answered Leyb. "In this hot minute, I can tell you nothing. But we can write an answer to Roza's last letter and have Yosef ask her for his freedom. Can you find someone who can imitate his handwriting?"

"I have someone who helped me before. If I hadn't been so foolish, I would've had Yosef write it himself. Now I'm involved in this whole business."

"*Nu*, what can you do?" said Leyb. "When the letter is ready, give it to me, and I'll mail it from Petersburg. By the way, do you have the rest of the funds? I have no money for the trip."

"No, I don't have a groschen on me," answered the Dark One. "I'll bring you something in the morning."

"I need it now, Meyshe Shneyur. They're writing from Petersburg that I should send something right away. If not, they say they'll release the merchandise. Brother, once you crawl in, you can't crawl out."

Meyshe Shneyur pulled out a hundred ruble note and laid it on the table.

"And how about giving me an I.O.U. for another three hundred?" asked Leyb.

"That's enough for now."

"Meyshe Shneyur, I tell you it's just business. Sign this paper, and don't worry; nothing's going on."

Meyshe Shneyur signed the note but wondered if having Yosef as a brother-in-law would be better than doling out money to these crooks. But does a thief have any sense? Sense would show that it pays better to be honest in one's dealings with others, but Meyshe Shneyur was too poor a mathematician to figure out what was in his best interest.

"What will be, will be," the Dark One finally said. "Now, let me tell you what I've done to ensnare the princess. Soon she'll be buried completely. What use do I have for her lovely face or fine education? My wife is a simple housewife. They gave me the worst daughter and offered the best one to that ingrate. No, I'll push Roza until she comes to me begging for a piece of bread. Then, when she considers me her provider, my Leyke can go off to sleep and never wake up again, and 'the spider' will become Roza's husband who she must kiss and obey. It will happen as soon as I've destroyed my father-in-law's business and ruined his household. Good night, Leyb. Do what you can. I won't get in your way."

"You're too excitable, Meyshe Shneyur," said Leyb. "Make it a rule to stay cool at all times and with every person. If it were up to me, I'd fix it so Roza didn't live long enough to see her Yosef again, and I'd make sure Yosef didn't live to see Roza. Your whole wish, brother, was to see that Yosef and Roza were separated, and, thank God, that's already been accomplished. You're a clever fellow with influence over your father-in-law. You're no youngster. Go home and make your situation better. Be cold-blooded and wait until God sends you a groom who can't count to two. Try being good to Roza and act like a wonderful brother-in-law as you use your expertise to arrange a marriage for her."

"Where's Sorele?" asked Meyshe Shneyur.

"Does she ask where I go?" asked Leyb. "Go home. Write out the letter for the forger and see that it's properly prepared."

Later that evening, as Meyshe Shneyur entered the house, his angry, cruel heart was filled with dark thoughts about Yosef and Roza. Closing the door to his study, he took out a packet of letters that Yosef had written to Roza and had unexpectedly fallen into his hands. His spirits lifted as he began to write in Yosef's voice. First, he reminded her of all the plans they had made before his trip to Petersburg. Then he pulled out Yosef's sweet, loving words and poured poison into them to rip Roza's heart away from him.

Opening Roza's letters, he poured himself a large glass of whiskey and drank it to the bottom. Since his youth, he was accustomed to drinking. His father had worked in the liquor business, and, as a pious Chassid, had wanted his only son to develop a proper taste for whiskey at an early age. Now that he was married, it was a *mitzvah* to drink to the state of the world. His wife often begged him tearfully not to drink so much, but he just answered her with curses and told her to mind her own business. Even before he put down the glass, he was startled by a commotion outside. Leyke pushed open the door. "Meyshe Shneyur, what do you know about this?" she demanded.

"Know about what?" he asked.

"About what happened to Yosef! Thief, my heart tells me you're responsible for this. Have mercy! What have you done to him?"

"What are you talking about, Leyke?" said Meyshe Shneyur with a pious look on his face. "I swear, I don't know anything. Tell me what you've heard."

"Yosef's in jail in Petersburg! A telegram just arrived and said no one knows why it happened. How could Yosef have any enemies? Who would want to hurt him? You might convince some people that you don't know anything about this, but not me. How could you take such a dear child and throw him into a pit of vipers the way Yosef's brothers did in the bible? Oh, you scoundrel! Now, with a telegram, you have the nerve to bring home the bloody shirt you've stained with your own hands and say that a wild beast attacked him! Oh, Husband! No wild beast would do what you've done! Have pity on him, on Roza, and on my mother who has never done you any harm!"

"Your stupid thoughts are addling your brain!" shouted Meyshe Shneyur as he refilled his glass with whiskey. "What a performance! Do you have any idea what a pain it is to have an idiot for a wife! Listen carefully, Leyke: If I hear this kind of talk from you again you'll stay a grass widow for eternity!"

"My God!" shrieked Leyke. "Have you forgotten that He sees and knows everything? He waits long and pays fast. And don't forget that I know who you're in business with—with Leyb Sorkin! Meyshe Shneyur, have pity on your children and fear God. He will repay you measure for measure!"

FOUR

PITY FROM A WOLF

Meyshe Shneyur gritted his teeth and grabbed a candlestick to throw at his wife's head, but before he could pour out his rage on her, the door opened, and Roza entered the study. She was white as a sheet, and her eyes were red from weeping. Her terrified expression was enough to melt the hardest heart. Even more remarkable was her coming so late at night, especially since she had not visited for nearly half a year. Leyke was shocked at her appearance, and Meyshe Shneyur grabbed at the scattered papers on his desk.

"I know everything now!" Roza cried out. "You don't need to hide anything from me."

Leyke ran from the room in tears as Roza implored Meyshe Shneyur: "Brother-in-law, have mercy! Not on me, on Yosef! Do whatever you want to me, but don't hurt him. He's completely innocent. He was silent about his love for me until I forced him to reveal it. Take your vengeance out on me for being one of Fridman's children. I won't touch any of your precious possessions or interfere with your plans. Just leave Yosef alone. Meyshe Shneyur, he's not guilty. I alone am the criminal. Take out your vengeance on me!"

"Roza," said Meyshe Shneyur coldly, "what do you want from me? What you're saying makes no sense. How can I talk to you while you're acting like this?"

"Meyshe Shneyur, you're a human being. You weren't born among wolves! You know the difference between guilt and innocence. You're not a stone; you feel pain. Feel my pain and have pity on me!"

"Roza, calm yourself. I'll talk with you if you'll just understand I'm not your enemy. Listen to me, and then you can say what you want."

"No, Meyshe Shneyur, see my tears. I have made someone miserable. For some reason, you have cast him aside because of me, and now that dear person sits in a Petersburg prison! Just tell me what you've accused him of? What have you invented against him? I ask you for nothing else!"

"Roza, I have no intention of listening to this kind of talk from you. Were I not who I am, I would throw you out for accusing me of things that only a dead soul would do! But because I respect you, Roza, and because I know you have deep feelings for Yosef—feelings which I encouraged here in this house—I will show you that I have no fewer feelings for him than you do. Once I tried to help him because I thought he was a worthy person. In fact, I not only valued him, I valued you as well, and have been your friend even though you curse and spit on me. You think Yosef is in jail? God forbid! If only he were, you wouldn't feel as unhappy as you do now."

"What are you saying?" Roza shrieked with a trembling voice. "What's happened to him?"

"Hear me out completely, Roza, and don't interrupt. What did Yosef write to you? Search through his letters, and you'll know where he is now."

"He hasn't written to me! Or do you have his letters? Give them to me, Meyshe Shneyur! Have mercy. Give me his letters!"

"Don't get wild, Roza! You're acting like you've lost your mind."

"Oh, Meyshe Shneyur, I'm not far from it, but I'm thinking clearly now. You say Yosef's not in prison, but what about the telegram?"

"Roza, I beg you, listen to my whole explanation. Then you'll change the way you're talking to me."

"Talk, talk! I know who I'm talking to, Meyshe Shneyur. But remember, besides me, God is also listening. Do you believe in Him, Meyshe Shneyur? Oh, God, I call upon You as my witness!"

"Listen, Roza, you're in love. Love makes the smartest person blind, and when love is destroyed, it can make a person wild and crazy. Roza, I know what love is, and I have sympathy for you. I understand what you're going through and will tell you what I know. I'm afraid you never saw how untrue Yosef was to you. Even while he was here, he was laughing at you."

Then Meyshe Shneyur went on to tell Roza many shameful things about Yosef. When he was done, he said, "Now you understand, the telegram is only a trick. Reb Itsik fired Yosef from his office, and now he's out on his own. He wants to marry a Christian woman but needs a birth certificate to be baptized. So he's trying to scare us by writing that he's in jail. Roza, I don't need to explain this to you. Your father is certainly loyal to you. Ask him, and I'm sure he'll tell you everything. This is why I don't excuse myself for wanting to take revenge."

"Meyshe Shneyur, you're a liar and a murderer! You're cruel and have no human feelings! I came to ask for your help, and what have I accomplished? Oh, dear God, You've created so many poisonous snakes in Your world, and to each You've given its own assignment: the deceiver, the man-eater, the blood-sucker! Even this Moor who is my brother-in-law is no better than a snake. He accuses Yosef! Why does he poison and vex us?"

"This is how you talk to me?" asked Meyshe Shneyur in a cold-blooded tone. "Fine, Roza, but I won't carry a grudge against you. You're ill and speak from a fever. Two weeks from now you'll speak differently, I promise you that. Then you'll say, 'This Moor saved me from death and showed me what was true and false.' But now, in your troubled state, you can't understand anything!"

"No, what I can't understand is how a wild wolf has suddenly decided to save my life. But I can tell you this, Meyshe Shneyur: In two weeks I will speak differently to you. That's when you and I will make an appearance before God so you can answer to Him for the injustices you've caused!"

Before Meyshe Shneyur could reply, Roza dashed out the door.

A few moments later, still trembling from her encounter with the Dark One, Roza entered Rukhame's room. She found her sister sitting on the bed writing a letter. "What are you writing?" she asked.

"Wait," said Rukhame, "I'm almost finished." Putting down the pen, she handed the letter to Roza.

My dear Yosef!

I am sure that the dispatch we have just received—and which has made your Roza deathly ill—is something faked by your enemies. They did this, it seems to me, because tomorrow the family of a prospective groom is coming to see your Roza. Father is angry with you, and Mother is sick, may God protect her.

So, Yosef, if you had nothing to do with this terrible fakery that Meyshe Shneyur told Father, please telegraph us right away and put us at ease. If you have, indeed, forgotten us as they say, then write from Petersburg. But before you do, remind yourself of my devotion to you and how unhappy you have made my dear sister. She only prays that God may forgive you. God may forgive you for forgetting us, dear Yosef, but not for forgetting your Jewishness!

So I remain your faithful sister as ever. Be faithful to your God and your people even if you are not true to those who love you. But if you change your faith, as they say, I will erase the words I have always signed to you:

Your Rukhame

"Oh, dear sister, you are my last consolation in life!" cried Roza as she threw herself on Rukhame's neck and hugged her.

"I love Yosef as much as you do," Rukhame said. "I asked Father to go to Petersburg to find out what's really going on. I asked him to telegraph Reb Itsik. But he was so angry he refused. He said he already knew everything and had always expected something like this would happen. I don't believe it, and you mustn't believe it either, Roza! We know Yosef wouldn't do anything bad, and we mustn't believe the things his enemies have invented about him."

Seeing the desperate look in Roza's eyes, Rukhame asked, "What's wrong, sister?"

"Dear Rukhame, my heart is faint. My head hurts, and I can hardly breathe. God in heaven, have pity on me! My heart tells me Yosef is in jail and doesn't know why. He's suffering from cold and hunger. He weeps and worries because he doesn't know what's happening to me. And here I am, free but bound by my own family, and have no way to help him. Oh, my head spins when I think there are people in the world who could do such awful things!"

"Roza, stop crying, or you'll make yourself sick," said Rukhame. "You must stay healthy. God only knows how this will all end. I swear to you that Yosef will come back and that he will always remain the same to you forever. Just stay true to him, Roza, and stay true to yourself!"

"But what if I lose my mind, dear Rukhame?" Roza asked, putting her arms around her sister. "What if I stop feeling? What will happen to me then? I'm afraid that no one will ever take me as their wife. That thought alone makes me crazy!"

"Sha," Rukhame said trying to comfort her, but Roza just wept.

Five

A MOTHER AND HER DAUGHTER

Roza and Rukhame went through several bitter weeks after the arrival of the telegram about Yosef. The Dark One carried out his business, and a constant procession of matchmakers entered the house. Each related the latest rumor about Yosef. Some said he had already been baptized; others said he had robbed a nunnery and had been sent to Siberia for twenty-five years of hard labor. All cursed and berated Yosef as they extolled the virtues of their prospective bridegrooms for Roza.

On her side, Roza did all she could to bear up. As hard as Fridman tried to make her forget Yosef by sternly scolding her for not dressing up for the prospective in-laws, his words had no effect. Roza resisted with all her strength.

Over time, Roza's mother, Golde, was told everything. Although she found it difficult to believe all the evil things people said about Yosef, her confidence waned when Reb Itsik's letter arrived. Reb Itsik described what a ne'er-do-well Yosef had become. He thanked God there had not been a formal engagement and that Roza was still free. If she had married Yosef, he said, her whole life would have been ruined. At least now she had a chance for happiness. He advised Roza to forget about Yosef and suggested her parents arrange a match as quickly as possible.

The letter arrived from Vilna with a guest who also brought a letter from Roza's younger brother, Shimen. No one suspected that this was all the work of Meyshe Shneyur who had forged Reb Itsik's letter and put it together with a letter from Shimen that had been stolen out of the mailbox. The two letters were delivered by a thug from Vilna, a student in Leyb Sorkin's school for criminals.

The letter worked so well that Golde, who had always been on Yosef's side, now stopped defending him and agreed to negotiate a match for Roza with the head of the community council's son. This marriage had been discussed two years earlier but only found favor now because the matchmaker declared the head of the community council had all the wealthy families under his thumb after seeing the new conscription list of boys over twenty-one destined to serve in the military.

Dear God, I don't want to sell one child to protect my other children, Golde told herself, because what happens to the individual Jew is what will happen to the whole Jewish community. I don't believe that the children of Judah should be soldiers. Let that matchmaker say what he wants about the groom; if he's not like Yosef, I won't accept him. Please give me strength, dear God. How else can I answer my dear lonely child?

Golde asked herself this question several times each day as she noticed Roza becoming more and more depressed. At times she worried her daughter was going deaf because she had to repeat herself so often before Roza understood or responded. As the days passed, Rosa stopped mentioning Yosef and became angry if anyone talked about him. Golde's heart mourned when she recalled that it was her advice that sent Yosef to Petersburg. She suspected that Roza still loved him deeply, and would have gladly approved the match if Yosef turned away from the terrible path he was on. Golde was willing to pay any cost to bring this about but knew Yosef was in jail for a criminal act, and that ransoming him would be impossible. She also knew that her husband had the right to choose the groom now. Her error in recommending Yosef had cost him a great deal, and now she had to hand over the reins and let him drive as best he could. She had always believed in *basherts*—heavenly-decreed marriage companions—and wondered if God was now punishing her for wanting Yosef instead of Roza's true intended, the head of the community council's son. Or was it still possible that Yosef was really Roza's *besherter* and that God would soon release him to come home?

Such are the thoughts of a perplexed person who cannot think of anything better to do than fold their hands and let things take their course by trusting in the empty, meaningless word *"bashert."* At first, Golde could not think of Yosef as anything but Roza's predestined one; but now that he was gone, she was considering someone else. How many thousands of such "predestines" are in the world?

"Mother!" cried Roza when Golde entered her room. "What news do you bring? Is there a letter from Petersburg?"

"That's enough about Petersburg, dear Roza," replied Golde as she caressed her daughter's cheek. "Better that you'd never heard the name of that city and been spared so much pain and trouble."

"I'd be happy now, Mama, if you and Father had not wanted Yosef to be a Petersburg merchant. We are all responsible for his misfortune. I don't believe he's guilty, Mama. He's in jail for nothing; for some libel put on him by some enemy. And because of me, he's stuck in a dark hole someplace. He's suffering because I love him and because you considered him your child. I won't believe anything in the world that anyone says until my ears hear it from Yosef's own mouth!"

"No, Roza, Yosef can't come and tell you anything. He's in jail, or God knows where. You saw what Reb Itsik wrote. Although he was the author of the whole plan and loved Yosef like his own child, he warned us to protect you from this poisonous viper. The guest from Vilna took the letter from Reb Itsik's own hand. What more proof do you need? Yosef has made you so unhappy, my dear. We can't ask God to repay him measure for measure, but we can ask Him to help us forget him quickly. We can ask God to steer Yosef on a better path so he returns to himself and his parents. And we can ask that He send you your true intended bridegroom so you can live out your years in joy and contentment."

"Oh, Mama, stop talking; I can't listen anymore. How can you ask me to forget Yosef? How can you let yourself be fooled? Don't you understand this is all the work of Meyshe Shneyur? And isn't it obvious there's a whole network of intrigue mixed up in this? No! My heart is still tied to Yosef, and I feel this misfortune has befallen him because of me. I have sworn to him, and how shall I answer for that vow? What right do I have to break my vow before I've heard one word from him?"

"Please, daughter," said Golde, "don't speak with such intensity. It'll only damage your health. Yosef has already broken his vow to you. He turned from you when he abandoned God in his heart. You are no longer a child, Roza, and you can't get away with accusing Meyshe Shneyur of things that only a highway robber would do. No, my child, it's time for you to see how Yosef led us astray and to understand where you are in the world. You know I'm not the kind of mother who wants to live out her own ambitions through her children or wants to buy into a family with a noble heritage. All I want is for my children to be happy—for you to be happy. When I saw how happy you were with Yosef, I was over-joyed, and I did everything possible to ensure your father would give his permission. But then we sent him to Petersburg where he met rogues who led him into evils ways. So it was just not meant to be, Roza. You must believe me when I say that if I had even a shred of hope for him, I would wait and risk your health and mine until God relents and returns him to us. But now, since it's clear as day that Yosef is lost forever, and you, my child, are nineteen years old already—may you live to be a hundred and twenty—we must move forward. You know your father can't work as hard as he used to, and I am not well. So, tell me, daughter, how would you end it?"

"Oh, Mama," cried Roza, "I would end it with my life! But as long as I still have control, I am still Yosef's. If I ever lose possession of myself, then you can do whatever you want with me!"

Roza threw herself on her mother and wept. "Oh, Mama, hold me; don't take your watchful eyes off me. I have no strength left. Just remember that I vowed to Yosef, and Yosef vowed to me, and he has not broken his vow. Let me rest, Mama. My mind has not been at peace for so long!"

As Roza wept, Golde whispered, "Be well, my child. May God have pity on you and heal your wounds."

When Golde left the room, Roza picked up her diary and began to write. As her tears spilled onto the page, she asked herself, How will this end? Like everything, it must end, and I cannot die until I know the outcome. I must see Yosef again, and show him I've been faithful to him.

She wanted to write down her thoughts, but her head began to spin, and she lay there in despair until Rukhame came in to console her.

Six

THE LAST ATTEMPT

The morning sun shone bright and clear as Roza lay in bed and thought, How many bright mornings have I missed, and how many more has poor Yosef? Can he even see the sun in the prison where he sits? For some, the sun brings light, warmth, and freedom. For me, it brings only sadness.

When Rukhame awoke, she dressed and went downstairs to send Kuzmo the butler to the post office. The Gentile returned with two letters, but neither was from Petersburg. A half-hour later, the mail carrier arrived and asked for Roza Fridman. Rukhame took him straight to Roza's room, where he handed her a registered letter that bore the order "hand-deliver."

"This is from Yosef," Roza cried. "This is his handwriting!"

She signed for the letter, and with trembling hands tore open the envelope.

Petersburg, the 20th

Dear lonely and unhappy Roza!

The first words of my letter confirm the bad news that you are alone and unhappy. I, the one who is writing this to you, am responsible. As painful as this is to write, I can no longer put it off.

Someone once told me that there is no sweeter task than writing to a dear friend and pouring out your troubled heart. And what friend is dearer to me than you, poor unhappy Roza? And so writing to you now is bitter, bitter as death.

If only I could die now, death would free me from a terrible future. But I am alive, and the world holds me fast, bound to life with chains. One lives unwillingly, and death comes when it wants and not when one wishes.

If only someone had warned me on that day when your tears penetrated my dark heart and pulled forth the words, "Roza, I love you!" Or when your sweet lips touched mine for the first time. If someone had told me, "Yosef, beware! One day you will be different, and your beloved Roza will curse your name," I would have considered that person my worst enemy. Now, I am the one who is saying my name should be cursed!

Roza, I have fallen! The world has turned its entire fury on me. But just one spark in my heart has not gone out, and that is the image of your loveliness, which still lives inside of me. So I beg you to hear me out, and only afterward to curse me. I do not justify myself; I only want to show you what can become of a person when he loses his balance.

Once in Mohilev, Roza, we watched an acrobat walk along a rope. Do you remember what I said then? That each person treads the path of life on a thin rope and uses his reason and integrity for balance. If he loses that balance, he falls, and the more elevated he is, the harder he lands. I have lost both my reason and integrity and can no longer balance. I fall with every step I take.

I believe you were not responsible for that letter you brought me that caused me so much pain, but it reminded me that I was doing nothing but wasting my time studying. Someone wrote to me in your name that you did not like the purpose that brought me into your home. Satan is clever and sows his poisonous seeds in good advice. Meyshe Shneyur sowed his seeds very widely and, like an evil spirit, put into my head the thought, "What will become of you here?" So I traveled to the big city of Petersburg without ever knowing that evil demons were drawing me there. Meyshe Shneyur knew my character and what Petersburg would make of me. He is the cause of my misfortune!

Roza, I do not want to recount all the terrible places I have been. I hardly remember them all myself. At first, I let myself do what was not permitted, then later, what was forbidden. I lost all shame and did things in broad daylight with witnesses watching. Reb Itsik threw me out of his office, people stopped respecting me, and that is when I first understood why a drunkard does not stop drinking even when he loses his whole human worth because of it. I could not stop. Just the opposite; I made it worse! I sought out Reb Itsik to abuse him, and my joy increased when I saw that people were afraid of me. Then God sent me an actress from the theater who enticed me. She fell in love with me, and while I was in need and without good judgment, she offered to rescue me if I would be baptized and marry her.

I know you loved me, too, Roza, but it was because I was handsome, innocent, and seemed worthy of love. Your love was really a kind of self-love because you wanted someone handsome and smart to show off to people. But my present love loved me in that instant when I was an outcast being swept away on a great current of sin, and she did everything to save me. For this reason, I am taking the leap and moving into another faith. Oh, God, I cannot do it! My people are as precious to me as life itself!

But what can I do, Roza? My enemies cooked up a plot to destroy me; and before I could denounce them, they planted counterfeit money on me. Now I am stuck in a dark hole. If it were not for my lover, I would have long since died of hunger, cold, and discouragement. But she has done everything a person can do for another, and if I live, it will be for her alone. I hope her plan will work out, and it will be better for me to convert than to stay in this prison or spend the rest of my life doing hard labor.

Roza, I once told you that I would rather stretch out my neck to the slaughterer's knife than to abandon my faith or deny my people. What I did not know then was the meaning of eternal filth, eternal hunger, and eternal hard labor!

I am still young, Roza. A whole new life lies before me. Perhaps it will bring me some happiness. Without any hope of my return, why should you be chained to me forever? I have made my decision. Tomorrow I will give my answer to the authorities and be free.

Please give my greetings to your mother and give her my little book of Psalms in which my poor heart found consolation. I am ashamed that I am no longer worthy of that little prayer book.

Be happy and healthy, Roza, and forget me as I will soon be forgotten by my people. Tomorrow I will be named "Osip," but today I am still

Your Yosef

With her heart heavy as a stone, Roza read the letter again. She did not feel the rush of blood to her face or the flood of tears to her eyes. She read the letter to the end and kissed it. "Oh, Yosef, Yosef!" she cried out. "This is your letter, and you're more miserable than any person in the world. But I'm even more miserable than you. I'm miserable because the first cause of your misery is me!"

When she raised her eyes from the letter, Roza could not see anything. The room with all its windows spun around, and unable to bear any more, she gave out a bitter cry and fell to the floor.

Rukhame tried to revive her, but nothing helped. Roza clutched the letter tightly to her heart and lay in a faint. Rukhame shouted, "Roza, this is not Yosef's letter!" but her sister did not hear. She cried out, "I swear to you, Roza, this is not from Yosef. Yosef wouldn't forget me! I know this even though he hasn't written a single word to me. This letter is as fake as all the other fakes that have been put on him. Don't believe it, Roza!"

But Rukhame's words were futile. Roza's senses, so weakened by her sleepless nights and worry about Yosef, were shattered by the contents of the letter. Her consciousness, which had already been hanging by a thread, left her completely.

Rukhame found her mother, and together they put Roza to bed. The good and modest Golde could not bear to see her daughter's suffering and uttered her first curse against Yosef.

"Don't curse him, Mama!" Rukhame pleaded. "He's not guilty. What can he do if people invent all kinds of terrible things about him? I believe that Yosef's in jail and can't tell us that he's the victim of these terrible libels."

"Hush, Rukhame!" shouted her mother. "You must never mention his name to me again!"

"No, I will never forget you, Yosef," Rukhame said quietly after her mother left the room. "Even if Roza and the whole world forget you, I will remember your name in loyalty and pain. Oh, Yosef, you may be alone, but there is still one person who is yours for as long as you live, and who will never belong to anyone else even after you're dead. And that is your loving Rukhame."

Roza spent the entire day in bed. A doctor was called to examine her, and after prescribing several medicines, told Golde to bring in another doctor. Overhearing them, Roza thought, What good are doctors? If my mother knew the extent of my wounds, she'd bring the slaughterer to end my life. My mother wants me to live, but God has forsaken me. Meyshe Shneyur, have pity on me and end my suffering in this world.

When Golde came in with the medicine, Roza sat still as a stone. "Is that poison, Mama?" she asked.

"Dear child, what are you saying? This is medicine to make you healthy again, may God have mercy."

"May His mercy take me from this world!" Roza whispered under her breath. "Mama, why do you give me medicine? So I will live on and be tormented forever? I won't take your medicine. Give me poison if you want to be good to me, Mama."

Golde hurried from the room with tears in her eyes. Dear child, she sobbed, the person who should be poisoned is the one who poisoned you with that letter! This is how he repays our family? May Yosef know nothing good for what he's done. Dear God, why are you visiting this suffering on me and my family? Have I been so sinful in Your eyes?

When her mother was gone, Roza got out of bed and reread Yosef's letter. Taking out a sheet of paper, she began to write, "Dear unfortunate Yosef!"

A river of tears flowed from her eyes and poured onto the paper. It seemed as if the whole world was drowning in a sea of tears. Her heart was broken, and her body ached with grief, yet she wanted to collect her thoughts and write. As hard as she tried, no words came from her muddled brain and empty heart. Oh, this is the moment I've dreaded most, she thought. I can no longer think or write. I've lost my mind! Don't lower Your eyes from me, dear God. If You've taken away my senses, please take all of me. Don't leave me up for grabs.

These were the last words that went through Roza's mind before she sank into a deep depression.

SEVEN

AS SOME SAY

Good! Even better than I'd hoped, thought Meyshe Shneyur when he saw the effects his letter had on Roza and the family. I just have to be sure the letter isn't left with Roza. Who knows what could happen if she re-examines it and realizes this is all my doing? It's a wonder it hasn't occurred to her that it's a forgery. But accusing myself was a clever touch. Oh, you have to be smart to be deceitful! You have to be careful where you step to avoid falling into the hole you've dug for someone else. Thank God, my goal is in sight. Now I must make certain the match is made and sealed. My father-in-law is ready to move forward. The groom is an idiot; he can't write three words without his teacher. The only problem is Roza. She's still sick and won't come out of her room. But no matter. It doesn't pay to get impatient. I haven't spared any money or effort, and now it's up to God. Soon I'll be in control again, and then I'll have a little treat for all my troubles.

What I need is a doctor who'll advise that Roza should be married before she's lost in depression forever. Shleyme is my father-in-law's friend. His son is a doctor. Now that he's married and no longer a potential bridegroom, maybe I should have a word with him. Fridman is certain to believe him.

Such were the thoughts of the dark, despicable man who was so engrossed in his own deceptions that no ray of truth could penetrate his criminal heart. It never occurred to him that truth always prevails. Although it may be wrapped up in the most abominable lies and treachery, truth is like the sun shining in the sky. A lie is no more than a cloud that hides the light for awhile, but the truth will always break through the darkest clouds that cover it. The problem is that we do not always see the sun through the darkness, and often the sky must clear completely before the sun reveals itself again. The truth is like that, too. It is never lost, but may not reveal itself at the right time.

What if someone had asked Meyshe Shneyur, "Why are you doing this to Yosef who is so pure and innocent? Surely one day your lies will be chased off by the truth." Perhaps then the unworthy man would have felt a sense of regret and turned away from his devious plan. But no one tried to discourage him, and he never read any books that provided a good example. All the deceitful things the young criminal had done during his time as a son-in-law in the Fridman house had been successful, so what did he have to fear? He rarely saw any examples to show him that the truth is always revealed in the end. But he had plenty of opportunities to see how deceit could make him happy, and he envisioned himself like Leyb Sorkin, a murderer and crook who had spilled blood and had no other business in the world than to steal and kill. Leyb lived like a prince. He took cabs everywhere, paying a ruble an hour, so he never had to walk. He lived a good life drinking wine and enjoying pleasures like a wealthy man. It was always a holiday at his house, and he feared no one. He did what he wanted, and in public, he was given more respect than the finest proprietor, because his ruble was well-received everywhere. So what if the moment he left a place, everyone cursed his name and said how much they hated him? Or complained how he used people, and how every ruble was covered with someone's blood?

Was there anything to show our Dark Young Man that being a crook was bad? As a child on his father's knee or as a son-in-law in the study house, had he not heard fine people being ridiculed? Had he not seen with his own eyes how happy and lucky everyone seemed in his circle of crooks, and how anything could be bought with money? So why should he be afraid? Why should he care if after his death, or after Roza's death, it came out that Yosef had suffered at his hand? Today it was enough to satisfy his revenge on Roza for being smarter than his wife and to bury Yosef for being more handsome and lovable. His plan was succeeding, and this made him happy.

Only a few weeks passed before the Fridman household began to dress up for the guest that Meyshe Shneyur awaited with joy and Golde anticipated with dread. Angry with Yosef and doubtful about Roza's new groom, she still hoped for someone better. She faced the day of the engagement party with despair because she knew it would destroy any possibility of finding another Yosef for her Roza.

Golde did not show her feelings, and although she had ordered that Yosef's name never be mentioned in the house again, she often spoke of him and wept over his misfortune. When guests came to visit and began talking about Torah or other learned matters, she always felt something was missing, an absent contributor to the conversation who should have been there. Then she would sigh a bitter sigh, and her heart would cry out inside her, Yosef! Yosef!

When she saw a young married couple on the street walking side-by-side, she remembered how happy she had been when she saw Roza and Yosef walking together. She felt his loss most deeply while sitting at the table with Rukhame who was always chattering about something. Yosef was never out of Rukhame's mind, and when she would slip and mention his name, she would stop in mid-sentence knowing her mother's prohibition. Golde often left the table and cried alone in her room.

Only Fridman acted as if Yosef never existed. He never talked about him or was tempted to do so. He was an old-fashioned man and showed little affection towards his wife, although he never had any trouble giving in to one of his children. If one of his daughters said she was in love, he told himself, What girl doesn't like a boy, and what boy doesn't like a girl? But Jews can't have anything to do with falling in love. This is just another way for young Jews to follow lockstep after the Christians. Once Gentile ladies started strolling about with parasols, Jewish women wanted to do it, too. When Christians started walking in pairs, male and female, Jews started doing it, too. The Christians have their custom of letting the groom choose his bride without a matchmaker, but at least we don't do that, thank God! And to think my own dear daughter almost introduced this fashion into our household. Soon they'll want to allow men and women to dance together at weddings the way Christians do. *Nu,* Master of the Universe, can anything good come of all this?

Meyshe Shneyur also continued to tell his father-in-law tales of Yosef's immoral deeds, which angered Fridman even more because the Dark One had not warned him earlier of Yosef's criminal character. By the evening of the engagement ceremony, Fridman looked sad and weary from all the grief and troubles he had suffered during the time spent discussing another groom for Roza.

What did Roza say? How did she anticipate the day of the engagement? We can glean her feelings from the way she spent her time holding on to Yosef's letter and treating everything with cold indifference. She only took medicine or ate food when someone brought it to her; otherwise, she made no effort to do anything for herself. If someone asked her a question, she answered with a "Yes" or "No"; to everything else, she was oblivious. Eventually, her misery became so deep she no longer knew what was happening to her. Often she would awaken with a start and ask tearfully, "Rukhame, am I a bride yet? Have they sold me yet? Oh, please don't let them sell me."

Golde sympathized with her child and wept quietly, but she was a mother and took pains to keep others from knowing that Roza had lost her mind. The household and staff were all loyal, and not even the smallest report was carried outside the house. If the doctor had not advised that Roza be married off quickly, or that the match was with the son of the head of the community council of whom Golde was greatly afraid, she would have postponed the marriage and waited until her daughter was well again. She would have talked with the groom to see if her child would be happy with him. She would have waited a little longer for Yosef's return. But what could she do? How could she go against her husband who insisted that Roza was this groom's predestined and that this marriage was made in heaven? The Dark One also set to work to confuse her, and by the time he was done, Golde hardly knew her own mind and was left with no more time to intervene. After a good cry alone in her room, hidden by the walls that had seen her in this condition so many times before, she went to see Roza.

Roza was sitting with her head in her hands. Rukhame sat beside her on the bed sewing.

"Why are you spending the whole day in here?" Golde asked Rukhame. "Everyone in the house is busy, and the in-laws will be here soon. The house is not even cleaned properly, and here you sit sewing? Go get dressed and go help the others with what they're doing."

"I will not get dressed," Rukhame answered, "and I will not go to the engagement party seeing how unhappy it makes my sister!"

"Mind your words, Rukhame!" Golde ordered.

"It doesn't matter, Mama. You can say whatever you want in front of her. She doesn't understand a thing. I doubt even Meyshe Shneyur the Moor knows what's going on inside her head."

At the mention of Meyshe Shneyur's name, Roza opened her eyes. A heavy, bitter sigh tore from her lips.

"Be well, dear sister," said Rukhame with tears in her eyes. "God will see your loneliness and give you back what He has taken from you. You still have the strength to refuse to be sold, Roza, and if not, may God protect you!"

Rukhame pressed a warm kiss to her sister's lips and went out. Roza tried to return the kiss, but her lips stayed pressed together as tightly as her lonely heart.

"Roza, my child," said Golde gently as she tried to control herself. "Get dressed, dear daughter."

"Mama," Roza said in a heavy voice.

"What is it, my precious child?" Golde asked as a sea of tears burst from her eyes.

"Oh, Mama," sighed Roza, and covered her mother's hands with hot tears. Golde wanted to tear herself away, but Roza would not let her go. "Mama, Mama!" cried Roza.

When Golde finally broke free, she ran to her room, threw herself on the bed, and wept in sorrow for her beloved daughter.

Observing everything, and fearing his mother-in-law's interference, Meyshe Shneyur began hurrying things along to prevent the engagement from being delayed another day. He sent for the rabbi, Yude the *shammes,* Gasan and his sons-in-law, and Tevele. He sent a second *shammes* for the in-laws and told them to come a little early with the justification that Fridman was going away later in the day.

EIGHT

THE ENGAGEMENT CONTRACT

The clock struck four, and guests began to arrive. Golde's pleas not to sign the contract today were of no use. As the clock struck five, the in-laws arrived, and Yude the *shammes* called out, "Welcome, mother-in-law! Welcome, father-in-law! Welcome, groom!"

A stout, well-fed woman entered the house, followed by the groom who walked with his head down and eyes lowered as if he were holding on to his mother's apron strings. Meyshe Shneyur took him to the seat of honor, and the mother-in-law fussed that Golde had not come outside to greet her. The groom glanced around the room as though he were searching for something. The famous matchmakers, Shleyme the cantor and Meyshe the Madman, set up a storm of questions: "Where's the bride? Why aren't you showing her?"

That was when Fridman suddenly realized Roza was missing. He had not noticed this earlier in his desire to forget she wanted nothing to do with the engagement. "Wife, go get her," ordered Fridman. "Tell her she must come now. It's an insult to the in-laws and the groom!"

"I'm not feeling well," answered Golde. "I asked that the engagement be postponed until tomorrow or the next day. But no one listened. Now do what suits you. I have no strength."

Fridman hurried out to get Roza. He found her on her knees on the bedroom floor, her head buried in a pillow. "Get up, my little princess!" he shouted. "Stand up, I say! Get dressed and go meet your groom. Do you hear me, Roza?"

Roza stared at him and remained mute.

"Help her get dressed!" Fridman ordered Rivke the maid, who came in with a tray of cookies she was trying to keep away from the matchmakers until the engagement ceremony was over. "Hurry!" Fridman commanded as he left the room.

Rivke brought Roza her best clothes and helped her dress. Then she gently led her to the large room where the guests were waiting.

"Bless the one who comes!" shouted Shleyme the cantor.

"Welcome, bride!" exclaimed Yude the *shammes*.

Dressed in her finest clothes, Roza looked beautiful. Her black hair fell against her marble-white throat on which she wore a velvet ribbon hung with a medallion that Yosef had given her. Her lovely, confused appearance made everyone look at her in wonder. She kept her eyes lowered, and her cheeks glowed like two red roses. In her left hand she held a fan, but in her right hand, she clutched the medallion that was her last connection to the lost love who still lived in her heart.

The carefully arranged room and nicely dressed guests awakened Roza who looked around to see where she was. She searched for someone to focus on, but could not find her mother or sister. She felt lost and alone in the crowd of people, some of whom she knew and others who were complete strangers. She wanted to run, but Meyshe the Madman took hold of her arm and led her to the father-in-law. "So how do you like this merchandise?" asked the matchmaker. "I swear, if my wife would give me a divorce, I would leave matchmaking and take this one exactly as she is right now."

"Go to hell!" shouted Shleyme the cantor. "It's time for you to stop with your cute little jokes. This is a man who's already had eight wives in his life, and now he wants a ninth?"

"Turkey! If I want a little something extra and can get a new wife every year with a hundred rubles, how can I lose?"

Everyone laughed but the groom, who was dumbfounded by the bride's beauty. He sat silently without even a smile. Roza began to sense how she was being seen, but her courage was broken and her head too unclear to think of something to say. She recognized the two matchmakers who had always frightened her, but now she could not get free by scolding them for their coarse talk. Her weapon, her tongue, was silent. Her hands were tied, and she was drowning in the middle of an ocean with no ship, no shore, and no rescuer in sight. Her dying heart screamed, I'm lost, lost, lost! But no human ear could hear it. Only God in heaven received it, but He gave no consoling answer in return.

"What a shy couple this is," remarked Gasan. "As if they're both from the old world. Fridman, I've always said your Roza belongs to the old order, but your Rukhame belongs to the new. You know, one time Rukhame answered me, and it took me an hour to realize what she meant. I'm embarrassed to admit that if she had answered me well, I would've grabbed her off the steps and said *mazel tov!*"

"Where is she?" asked the mother-in-law. "Why hasn't she come to see us? Is this really the bride or the bride's sister?"

"The bride's sister is a little angry with her mother and doesn't want to be at the engagement," explained Meyshe Shneyur. "Listen, folks, it appears that both the bride and groom are of the old world, but here in the new world, we must do what's in style today. Let's give the bride and groom a little time to discuss things on their own. Of course, it's not so comfortable for them in front of us, so let's leave them alone for awhile. It's not such a long time since I was a bridegroom, and I remember how it was."

"Can't we move things along a little more quickly?" asked Fridman. "I love to spin out the whole Passover Haggadah, but when it comes to the horseradish and bitter herbs, I prefer to get through it quickly. We should follow that style here, or we'll never get done."

Everyone chuckled at Fridman's comparison, and the mother-in-law took the bride by the hand and led her to a side room. She then returned for the shy groom, whispered in his ear that he should be a good person and not talk foolishness, and closed the door behind her.

The couple sat for a long time. The groom's heart trembled and his teeth chattered as he waited for Roza to say something. But she sat quietly staring through the window that looked out into the garden. Rukhame, who was walking outside, saw her older sister and was drawn to her. She came into the house and hurried to the room where Roza was sitting, but Gasan was standing by the door trying to eavesdrop on the conversation. "What do you want here?" he asked as she approached. "Do you want to study the wedding couple?"

"Even if I wanted to study," Rukhame replied, "is that a crime? But why are you peeking through the keyhole? Perhaps you're the one trying to learn something!"

"You little hussy!" shouted Gasan, only half in anger because the crowd was so entertained by her answer. "What have I done to you? Why are you so set against me?"

"May I never do to someone else what you're doing now! Don't you know that allowing something to be done to someone is worse than doing it yourself?" asked Rukhame as she turned and left the house.

Gasan rolled his eyes and went over to the table and sat down beside Meyshe Shneyur who was sitting like the perfect son-in-law writing out the bride's part of the engagement contract. Golde's nephew, Aron Yude, was writing the contract for the groom. Aron Yude was twenty-one years old and facing military service. He knew that if this match were successful and God helped him become an in-law to the head of the community council, his future prospects would certainly improve.

Roza and the groom sat like two silent statues. Roza was not talking because her heart had died, and there was nothing left to say. If she were in her right mind, she would tell him she was not ready to marry and explain in a very friendly way that she was not her usual self today. But now with her mind no longer functioning, she could not speak. Her situation was like being thrown into a pit where lions are kept. As the wild-eyed young lions looked on in wonder at her lovely appearance, the older lions prepared to tear her apart without mercy.

The groom had no idea of how to begin a conversation. Although his married friends had tried to help him, all the prepared words had vanished from his mind, and he was left with nothing to say. When Roza saw Rukhame return to the garden, she awakened a little, excused herself, and started for the door. "Wait, what's the hurry?" asked the groom.

Roza regarded him. Who was this person speaking to her?

"Tell me, how will you write to me?" asked the groom. "You could write your letters in German, but I'm more fluent in French. So it's better if you write to me in French. And you must write to Father in Russian. He knows Russian very well. But you should write to my mother in Yiddish. I can't think about Yiddish!"

"I don't know any French," replied Roza. Again, she tried to go out, but he stopped her and asked, "What's your name?"

"My name? Why do you ask?"

"Why do I ask? How will I write to you? I'm Faybesh, but in Russian, they call me Seriozsha."

Roza tried to leave without answering, but the groom blocked the door. "Wait," he said abruptly. "You're a woman. My teacher told me, better to follow after a lion than a woman," and Faybesh quickly slipped out the door.

Roza wanted to cry, but could not. Soon the mother-in-law came in and started kissing her. She told Roza to come and listen as the contract was read, then she took her by the hand and led her into the other room.

During the reading, the mother-in-law scolded Yude the *shammes* for bringing in a clay pot to break at the end of the ceremony. Gasan agreed and added, "The father of the bride, thank God, can certainly afford to break a porcelain service on such an occasion. He didn't make a match with just anybody! Yude, go into the kitchen and take whatever you see."

Yude went into the kitchen and grabbed a dozen porcelain plates before the maid ran him off with an iron stove poker. He returned just in time to hear the final words of the contract and began throwing the plates on the floor. The broken utensils resounded like rifle fire, and Roza suddenly remembered where she had seen this scene before. My nightmare has become a reality, she told herself as her face turned white as snow.

Hearing the noise, Rukhame rushed into the house and tried to push her way through the crowd that surrounded her sister. One of the groom's in-laws, the busybody Sterne Gute, was standing in front of Roza, relating her lineage. More than once she mentioned her relative, Yosef.

"It's official! Meant to be!" exclaimed Sterne Gute. "Roza, I never believed you were Yosef's intended bride. Everyone knows

God sits on high and makes matches below. *Nu*, Roza, what does Yosef write to you?"

When Rukhame heard Sterne Gute's question, she thought her sister would faint. But Roza's heart was frozen, and she remained indifferent to everything going on around her. "Come, Roza, Mama is calling for you," Rukhame said, and she gently led her sister from the room.

As Tevele and Gasan's sons-in-law served themselves drink after drink, the crowd began to sing. But in Golde's room, anyone arriving with a heart of stone would have left with it melted like soft wax. Roza was on her knees with her head on her mother's lap. She sobbed, and her heart screamed, Yosef, Yosef, what have you done to us?

Rukhame could not watch any longer and left the room. When she saw the drunken crowd celebrating the engagement, she thought, Oh, Yosef! You once told me there are people in the world like the ancient tribes in America who eat the flesh and drink the blood of their victims. I didn't believe you then, but now I understand what you meant. Here is a gathering of fine Jews, everyone a saint. They recite the blessings, then drink the blood and eat the flesh of my innocent sister. How can You watch this, God, and be silent?

By dawn, the guests were gone. As they staggered home, they all agreed it had been a long time since they had enjoyed such an engagement party.

Part Four

OUT OF JAIL

Long and difficult days stretched out as Yosef spent his time in jail. He became almost used to his bitter circumstances, yet in the damp darkness and lonely solitude, he never forgot his Roza. How could I ever forget you? he asked himself. How could I forget my dear love as long as my brain is still alive and my blood pulses through my veins? Oh, Roza! Neither the walls of this cruel fortress nor the terrible darkness that rules my life will ever remove your sweet face from my memory. I see you before me with your lovely smile and bright glances, and you alone are my light in this dark pit. If not for your sweet voice that still rings in my ears, I would be lying in the Petersburg cemetery free from the sounds of the chains and groans coming from the prisoners in the other cells. Without the single hope of seeing you again, and knowing you're as true to me as I am to you, I could never have survived this torment. You must believe that all the crimes against me were invented. I had no dealings with counterfeit money.

Yosef told these words and many others to the investigator who pursued every possibility of bringing light to the truth. On the same day that Yosef was first brought before the investigator, the police also detained the doorman from Reb Itsik's office and sealed all his possessions. Upon examination, it appeared that Yosef's suspicions were correct. Several of Yosef's letters to Roza and Roza's letters to him were uncovered, and when translated into Russian, provided enough evidence to prove that Yosef had innocently fallen into a trap.

Reb Itsik also returned from Leipzig where he had spent several months trying to complete a complex business transaction. Unable to intercede on Yosef's behalf while out of the country, Reb Itsik was now doing everything possible to free him. He spared no expense or trouble but could not get in to see the prisoner.

The prosecutor who read Yosef's letters was sympathetic and worked hard to determine the truth. He even put Yosef in a room where his voice could be heard by a certified Yiddish-speaking recorder who wrote down everything he said. But this still did not provide enough evidence to free him, and the process dragged on for months.

Finally, God took pity, and the thug who had switched Yosef's coat landed in jail. During the investigation, they confiscated his things and found Yosef's coat with his two letters still in the breast pocket. This was presented to the prosecutor who compared it with Yosef's original statement. Seeing the similarities, he decided to show Yosef the two coats—the one with the letters and the one with the counterfeit money. Yosef immediately recognized his coat and added that the sleeves had the same lining as the frock coat that was hanging in his office.

Without delay, the police brought in the frock coat, and it proved Yosef was correct. But since the thug refused to confess, the prosecutor had no choice but to keep Yosef in jail while the investigation continued.

Early one morning, Yosef heard the rattle of keys. His cell door opened, and he was told to come out. Five soldiers followed behind him as he made his way through the darkened corridor. Having been prevented from walking for nearly a year, he was weak, and his jail clothes restricted his movements. As he stumbled along like a small child, he endured the frequent jabs of the soldiers' rifles urging him forward. They took him to a room in the new jail where the doorman from Reb Itsik's office was sitting. He, too, was wearing a jail uniform.

"Khaym!" Yosef shouted. "What have you done to me? You're an old man already and will answer to God for this. Look at me. Look at my eyes and face. Am I the same Yosef who was so good to you? Khaym, where's your heart? Have pity on a young couple; have pity on my poor parents. Don't murder me! You, of all people, knew how precious Roza was to me, yet you kept her letters from me. Remember, Khaym, God gave you a soul, and you'll have to stand before Him. I swear my innocent blood will not be stilled even if they put me back in that dark hole for the rest of my life!"

Khaym took Yosef's hand and said, "Don't cry for me, dear Yosef, and don't beg me. I asked for you to be brought here so I could confess my sins to your face. I've spent fifty-eight years living as a thief and murderer, and now I'm ready to face the gallows. My only wish is to see you freed. Our plan was to drown you if the trick with the counterfeit money didn't work. But every night since I've been in jail, I've seen you in my dreams. Sometimes you're weeping; sometimes you're dead. And every morning I wake up sick. Now I admit everything. I beg you to forgive me. I've committed a terrible sin against you. Please ask God to forgive me after I'm dead."

"I forgive you from the bottom of my heart," replied Yosef. "And if you wholeheartedly turn back to Him, He'll forgive you, too!"

The guards suddenly came to attention as the court prosecutor entered the room. Khaym confessed that he was one of a group of thugs led by Leyb Sorkin and that he had worked as an office doorman to throw off suspicion. The prosecutor took Yosef by the arm and told him he would be taken back to his cell until the evidence could be presented in court. Yosef thanked him and was led away by one of the guards.

The next morning, Yosef was handed a certificate that allowed him to live in Petersburg until he could receive papers from home. Following a brief meeting with the prosecutor, who promised to send him all the confiscated letters and a copy of his entire investigation, Yosef was permitted to step out into the street without a guard.

Giddy with happiness, he immediately took a cab to Reb Itsik's office. Thank you, God, for your loving kindness, Yosef thought. You have shown me Your love, and I am free again. Is there anyone in the world who appreciates the word "free" as much as I do? While I spent a whole year in jail, these streets were filled with the noise and bustle of a thousand people. Yet in my dark little cell, the whole world was dead. I feared my life was like a breath on a mirror that disappears without leaving a trace and that when I died, not even a shadow would remain. But as long as one lives, there is still hope of freedom. Oh, how I want to live. I want to live for my Roza!

When the cab stopped, Yosef entered the office with great joy, but the bookkeeper did not recognize him. "What do you want?" he asked sternly.

"I want you, Shapiro!" said Yosef, barely able to hold back his tears. "I want you and the owner, Reb Itsik."

"Who are you?" the bookkeeper inquired as he studied Yosef's ragged appearance.

Hearing his name, Reb Itsik came to the door. "What's going on out here?" he asked.

"God in heaven!" cried Yosef. "Have I changed so much that even you, Reb Itsik, can't recognize me anymore? Oh, Reb Itsik, I'm your Yosef!"

"Yosef, dear Yosef!" shouted Reb Itsik as Yosef collapsed in his arms.

When Yosef awoke, he was lying beneath many blankets in a large bed. Reb Itsik sat beside him with a worried look on his face. "How are you, dear boy?" he asked when he saw that Yosef had opened his eyes.

"Reb Itsik, is it really you?" replied Yosef, barely able to speak.

"You don't recognize me, Yosef? What's wrong? Should I send for a doctor?"

"No, no, dear Reb Itsik. I recognize you. I just can't believe you're here with me. You can't guess how many times I've fainted and fallen on the cold brick floor where I laid for hours not knowing whether I was alive or dead. When I awoke, I would burst into tears as I looked around my dark cell where no ray of light and no spark of hope could penetrate. Now I have fainted in your arms, dear friend, and awakened in your bed with you beside me. The bars are gone! Please, help me to the window. I want to breathe in the fresh air. I'm free, Reb Itsik! Today I want to run through the streets of Petersburg. God, how good is Your freedom!"

Reb Itsik let Yosef talk and cry. He knew that if he stifled what was in his heart, it could harm him more than his agitated ramblings. When Yosef finally quieted down, Reb Itsik said, "So now, my son, you must get better. God Himself pulled you out of the pit, my child. Not I or any other person could help you. God saw your innocence and loneliness and took pity on you. He alone revealed your truth and set you free. I pray that God will not take His hand away from you, Yosef, and will guide you to goodness and joy for your whole life."

"What you say is like oil on my wounds, Reb Itsik. While I was in jail, I tried to find someone from my studies who suffered for nothing. When I recalled Yosef's story in the Torah, I compared myself to him. He was once loved by people just as I was. He was the boss' favorite, and although he was innocent, he was thrown into a pit and left to die. The only difference I could see was that Yosef consoled himself by thinking he had sinned by speaking ill of his brothers and that God was punishing him for it. But I asked myself, 'What sin have I committed? Who have I wronged? Who have I slandered?' No one! I was only imprisoned for my love of Roza. Tell me, what is sinful in that? Didn't God create the world with love? God is not guilty, but why did He make snakes and people who can poison our lives?"

"That's how our little world is made," said Reb Itsik with a sigh. "People are not angels. You can't know who is guilty or innocent. The Law was not given for evil. Thank God for sending you a good judge and honest people who discovered the truth. You suffered for your true heart, dear Yosef, and I cry for your suffering. Thank God, I can now cry with joy for your freedom. Now you must forget, dear Yosef. Forget everything, and be happy. Be a *mentsh* and don't seek revenge."

"Dear Reb Itsik, you ask me to forget while my wounds are still open. How happy I would be if I believed everything bad was over, but I have a terrible feeling that my enemy is not finished with his evil plan. God knows what is happening in Mohilev. What have you heard? What do you know about Roza?"

"Yosef, I don't blame you for being agitated. A year in prison can make a person fear the future. I'm sorry I don't know anything about Roza. I've been in Leipzig the whole winter. I could not get away, and my people here did everything they could for you on my behalf. I've only received one letter from Fridman, and he asked me to do whatever I could for you. The other letters were kept here in the office for me. That's why I was silent. Your good friend, Shapiro the bookkeeper, decided not to forward the letters to me. One of my beloved grandchildren died, and I was going through a very bitter time. Yosef, when the time is right, I'll explain everything to you. In the meantime, as far as I know, Roza is well. I can show you letters from your parents, and Shapiro has a letter from Roza that he took from the doorman."

Yosef read his parents' letters which helped him understand what Reb Itsik had tried to do for him. "How can I ever thank you?" he cried as he kissed Reb Itsik's hand. "I didn't know there was so much goodness in the world!"

"Yosef, if you want to thank me," said Reb Itsik, "ask God to let me see you happy. Come now, you must be hungry. Let's get something to eat. I'm hungry myself."

"I don't want to eat," replied Yosef. "My heart is too full. Right now it might be better to see a doctor. The cold and damp have eaten me alive, and I have a pain in my chest. God knows what I've brought here from that cursed place."

"Don't worry," Reb Itsik said, "and don't be discouraged. I'll send for a doctor, and with God's help, your health will return."

"Yes, I believe I'll get back my health," Yosef answered with a sigh, "but how will I ever get back the lost year of love with my Roza? My imprisonment has made me sick; I can pardon them for that. But if they've taken away my Roza, I will never forgive them!"

"Don't worry, Yosef, your Roza is as true to you as ever. And don't pain yourself about the year that was lost. Just thank God that you've survived. The murderers who did this to you didn't just want to rob you of one year. They wanted to take your whole life. That dark Moor is an assassin; he wants to bathe in your blood. When I think that you must spend your whole life with him, my heart weeps for you. When I recall how God created that lovely Roza among all those hurtful thorns, I tremble for her; and I tremble for you, too, dear child. I'm not capable of driving that snake out of your garden, but if I could make you happy in any other way, I would lay down my life to do it. Your suffering has only drawn you closer to my heart, and until you are well, I will not allow you to return to Mohilev to confront your enemy. God knows what else he has in store for you. You are in danger and must protect yourself."

As Reb Itsik spoke, he began to bang his fist on the table. "Turn him over to me, and I'll show him what it means for blood to flow! How does that poisonous snake get away with it? He bites and runs, and no one can catch him."

"Don't worry, dear friend, he's not so bad. I'll go to him and tell him I forgive him and that I'll forget everything he's done. I'll promise to leave him alone and not disturb a hair on his head. All I want is to take my Roza and be happy with her wherever God leads us. What can he do to me? No, Reb Itsik, no person can be that evil!"

Yosef said this with conviction because his own pure heart could not admit that many people become enemies for their own petty interests. Once they begin their persecution, they do not relent, even after they have won, but continue to pursue their prey until devoured. Yosef did not accept this view and hoped he could convert his enemy's hatred into friendship, or at least turn an angry wolf into a quiet lamb. He refused to acknowledge that a snake dies with the poison still in him, and a wolf remains a wild animal until its final day. If Yosef had thought it through, perhaps he would have realized that the ambitious Meyshe Shneyur cared less for money than he did for honor, and having Yosef as his brother-in-law would jeopardize his standing in the family and the community.

The Dark One's anger towards Roza also meant he would stop at nothing to make her life miserable. Love made Yosef blind, and his joy at being released made him forget that a year had passed and a great deal of water had flowed under the bridge. He did not stop to consider what the waters may have carried away with them.

Reb Itsik's servant came in with food and was sent to bring the doctor. Yosef began to eat but tears clogged his throat, and he could not swallow.

"You're crying again, Yosef?" asked Reb Itsik.

"This piece of bread reminds me of my troubles in jail, but now I'm shedding tears of joy. I just took a bite and did not search it before chewing. More than once I broke a tooth on a bit of stone that had been baked into the bread. How can I ever explain all the things I suffered?"

"But you cry so easily now," said Reb Itsik. "It's like you've become a child again. Enough already. Tears are a shame for a reasonable man."

"I've said that to myself a hundred times," admitted Yosef. "I know life's troubles should make us stronger. But now I wonder if my troubles and broken heart have weakened me. Whether or not my heart is broken, I know it has been badly wounded. They say tears are the blood of the heart. Maybe that's why I can't stop crying, Reb Itsik. But someday I hope to become a *mentsh* again."

"And you will, Yosef," said Reb Itsik. "I know your heart is full and you haven't had anyone to talk with for a very long time. But eat now; your food is getting cold."

As they finished their breakfast, the doctor arrived and told Yosef he needed to get plenty of fresh air. He suggested he go for a long walk and do something amusing. He also recommended that when he was feeling stronger, he should leave Petersburg to avoid the damaging air.

A flash of hope passed through Yosef. Perhaps he would see Roza very soon.

Two

FROM PETERSBURG

Yosef remained in Reb Itsik's house for the entire first day following his release from jail. On the second day, he was provided with new clothes, and soon after breakfast, Reb Itsik took him for a walk in the neighborhood to show Yosef how pleasurable life could be and how important it is to go on living after a catastrophe. That evening, Reb Itsik's friends called, and each one expressed his joy over Yosef's release. Many brought gifts, but the best gift of all came from Reb Itsik's bookkeeper, who brought a packet of Roza's letters that had been stolen by the doorman.

Yosef read the letters tearfully. Oh, God, he thought, how much you've suffered, too, dear Roza. But it's over now. The darkness is past, and I must fly to you. I know your heart has stayed true to me, and I'll go without waiting for an answer.

Reb Itsik tried to dissuade Yosef from taking such a long journey before his strength had returned, but it was of no use. The moment *Shabbes* ended, a cab arrived at the door. Reb Itsik accompanied Yosef to the train station and tried to convince him to stay a little longer.

"Please obey me, Yosef," Reb Itsik pleaded. "Don't go yet. Wait until I can come with you. It'll only be a month or so, and then we can travel together. Or I can go ahead of you, see what the situation is like, and offer you some advice. Please Yosef, I beg you to reconsider."

They heard the first call from the platform as the cab arrived at the station. Yosef sat with Reb Itsik until he could endure it no longer. "I've got to go, Reb Itzik. Thank you for everything, but I can't turn back now!"

"Then go in good health, my son," said Reb Itsik, "but write and tell me everything that happens to you. Be a *mentsh*, Yosef; be strong. You must strengthen yourself to stay a *mentsh* no matter what happens. May God protect you, and may things turn out as you hope. Just keep in mind that the world is not coming to an end. You're only nineteen years old and can still have many good things in your life. Guard your health because you're precious to many people. I don't have to emphasize that I've always treated you with loving kindness, but now I'm afraid for you and must give you a warning: Protect yourself! Don't be ungrateful and don't forget me. In the worst case, call on me in a letter, and I'll do whatever I can for you."

"How could I ever forget you, Reb Itsik? Be well, and be certain that your words will never be erased from my memory."

Reb Itsik bought a ticket and handed it to Yosef. He then pressed him to his heart and kissed him. Yosef did the same in return. As the train began to move out of the station, Yosef waved and called out, "Be well."

Reb Itsik shouted, "Travel in good health, dear boy. I'll see you in good health!"

Before Yosef could answer, Reb Itsik was out of sight.

THREE

A GOOD SIGN: A WEDDING IN TOWN

Yosef's impatience was so great, he barely survived the three-day journey. Only rereading Roza's letters shortened the long hours. Finally, the awaited moment arrived, and on Tuesday at six in the evening, Yosef saw the church spires of Mohilev rising up in the distance. He was now traveling in a wagon, and his heart pounded with anticipation. It was good that the road was all downhill and the horses running unimpeded. As the wagon passed through the city gate, the driver shouted, "There's a wedding in town. Can you hear the musicians? That's a good sign!"

"God grant what you say is true!" said Yosef. Suddenly realizing his unannounced arrival might startle Roza, he got out of the wagon and asked the driver to follow along quietly as he looked for someone to deliver a letter to her.

"Reb Osher," Yosef called out to a passing Jew who was leading a cow tethered to a rope. The Jew stopped and looked at him for a long time. "Is that you, Yosef? How are you, dear boy?" the old man asked.

"Tell me, dear friend," replied Yosef, "what's happening in the Fridman household?"

"The Fridmans? They're all well, thank God. Those who were rich are still rich, and those who were paupers are still paupers. I was a poor teacher, and I'm still a poor teacher. The world goes on, and I haven't seen any miracles lately. But to your question, 'What's going on at the Fridman's today?' Roza is getting married!"

"God in heaven!" shouted Yosef, and grabbed Reb Osher by the arm. "You've made a mistake. It can't be true."

Reb Osher the teacher, a very honest Jew, had only told Yosef what he had heard in the city. Realizing the news was like a bullet to Yosef's heart, he quickly replied with an embarrassed smile, "I must be mistaken. There's a wedding in town today, but it must be with one of the other families."

"Reb Osher, will you go and tell the Fridmans I've returned?" asked Yosef.

Reb Osher could see the wild look in Yosef's eyes. "Follow me," he said. "Drive to my house, Yosef, and we'll take you in as a guest. Then we can figure out what to do."

"Thank you, Reb Osher," said Yosef.

All at once, a crowd of men and women came pouring out of the study house. From a distance, it looked like a merry gathering of Jews coming from a wedding. As Yosef studied the scene, he suddenly shouted, "I see my Roza!" and threw himself against Reb Osher.

As passersby ran to see the bride and hear the famous musicians, Reb Osher held on to Yosef with both arms. Although no tears appeared in Yosef's eyes, the old teacher knew his heart was weeping.

As the bride was led down the street, she fainted at every fifth step, and people said the fast must have weakened her. As they passed, no one noticed the poor teacher holding up Yosef who had also fainted. Which of the two, wondered Reb Osher, was more miserable?

The wagon driver took Yosef to Reb Osher's house. There he sat, his heart like a stone, listening quietly to the old Jew who had always been so kind to him. Reb Osher told him of the talk he had heard in the city about Yosef's imprisonment and the rumors that Roza was not in her right mind. How similar, thought the good teacher, was Yosef's experiences to those of Job and Kohelet. In Job, God punished an innocent man; in Kohelet, the one who sang the Song of Songs with so much love and joy was turned into a beggar and treated like a transgressor in his own land where no one recognized him.

That night, just like Kohelet who could only pass by his lovely palaces and gardens but was forbidden to go in, Reb Osher took Yosef to all the places he had loved so much. More than once they passed by Fridman's windows and Yosef heard the music, saw the dancing, and saw his beloved Roza for whom he had suffered and shed so many tears. He saw her in a beautiful white dress, but her face was covered with a veil. He thought if he could only get a look at Roza's groom, he could determine with one glance whether she would be happy or not. But he never saw him.

Yosef could have stood there all night, and at first, Reb Osher did not have the heart to pull him away. But when he saw the anguish in Yosef's eyes and how deathly pale he had become, the poor teacher dragged him home.

"God, why am I still alive?" Yosef sobbed. "Why can't I die?"

From inside the house, people heard the voice, but no one came out to see where it was coming from. It is always easier to look into a lighted house than to look out at a darkened street. Thus, poor people are quicker to look into the fine, lighted homes of the rich than the rich are to look into the shabby dark residences of the poor. So Yosef saw all the happy wedding guests, but no one in the house noticed his dark, sad face.

"My heart," Yosef said quietly as the teacher led him home by the arm. Then he cried out, "God! You watched and let me suffer! All those dancing, happy faces; faces I once loved and who once loved me. Roza certainly loved me, but now she's married to another. She's no longer mine, and still I live. All that talk we hear and believe is false! How many times did I say that I would die without her, and here I am still alive and still in pain!"

Reb Osher brought Yosef back to his little house. A small candle flickered on the table. The teacher's wife and children were already asleep, and Reb Osher invited Yosef to lie down on a blanket near the stove. But Yosef said he could not sleep and had to write. Reb Osher, afraid that Yosef might take his own life, gathered up the knives and tools he used for making smoking pipes after his students went home from *cheder*. Then he sat down on a chair and drifted off to sleep.

Yosef wrote until daylight. The candle went out, and the pale light of dawn entered through the shutters. Exhausted from not sleeping for three nights, Yosef finally fell asleep over his papers.

When he awoke, Yosef found Reb Osher reciting the Psalms in a sad, heartfelt trope. Feeling each word tearing at his wounded heart, Yosef wept and continued writing his letter. When his eyes had no more tears left, he ended the letter and gave it to Reb Osher to give to Shimen.

Reb Osher did as Yosef requested, but Shimen was so distracted by the wedding activities, he accepted the letter without opening it. He put the letter into his coat pocket and completely forgot about it. When the teacher came back after morning prayers in the study house, he found Yosef lying ill with a terrible fever.

Four

RUKHAME

No one at Fridman's house knew that Yosef had returned to Mohilev. Reb Osher had heard that Fridman and his family were still very angry at Yosef, and seeing how miserable Yosef was, he realized it would be of no use to move him back to the place where he would be confronted by his lost love at every turn. When Yosef asked him not to tell anyone, the good teacher assured him he would not.

Yosef lay in bed at Reb Osher's for a whole week. He gave up on life and waited for death. His pain at knowing that no one in Fridman's house would recognize him was worse than death. Yet Yosef did not die. A person lives one's life unwillingly and dies unwillingly. One's will cannot bring about death any more than it can bring about life.

Why not? Yosef asked himself. I've known some goodness in this life, and I haven't been a fool. I've loved my Roza and was prepared to die for her. But now she's gone. So why do I keep on living? What is left for me to hope for? I've lived enough! Then Yosef stood up and walked out of the house.

It was *Shabbes* evening. On the street, a light rain fell, and a cold wind blew. Reb Osher had gone to the study house to say the evening prayers, and his wife was rocking their youngest child. Yosef stood in the courtyard for a long time thinking about what he should do. Should he go to the river and throw himself in? Or should he wait? Wait for what? Now that Roza was married, everything was lost.

I'll end it tonight! he told himself. Tomorrow I'll be free from these wounds that torture me. But first I want to see Roza one more time and remind her that there was a Yosef in this world who loved her, and whom she loved, and who suffered torments in jail for her. A man who loved her with all his heart and whom she's now forgotten.

But as Yosef stood at the door of the Fridman house that once opened happily to him, he was afraid to go in. Golde, who had called for the doctor to come see Roza, was sitting by the window. Hearing a cab pass by and footsteps near the entryway, she ran to meet him. Opening the door, she found Yosef standing before her.

"Mother!" cried Yosef.

Golde shuddered. "Yosef, is that you? What evil spirit has brought you here?"

"Mother!" answered Yosef, and took her hand to kiss it, but Golde angrily pulled her hand away.

"Listen, Yosef," she cried, "if you have even one spark of conscience left in your heart you'll go away and not say another word to me. You're sinful! After all the trouble you've caused, what do you want from me? My health? My life? Get out of here, you heretic. I don't want to know you anymore!"

"Mother, tell me, how have I sinned against you?"

"You're a wicked heretic, Yosef. You've lost God. Go away. Don't talk to me anymore!"

"Please hear me out, dear Mother. You loved me once. Let me explain, and you'll see I'm completely innocent. Even God receives the sinner. Let me say a few words to Roza. That's all I want. I won't ask you for anything more."

"May God pay you the way you've paid us for our hospitality and loyalty! Don't you dare enter this door. I don't ever want to see you again. You're a spiteful heretic, riding in a cab on *Shabbes* to boast that now you can do whatever you want. Get out! You have no merit to speak one word to Roza. Get out, you Satan!"

"I only want to say that I forgive her. I forgive her everything. What have they invented about me here to make you treat me this way? How could Roza so completely forget me?"

Golde slammed the door and locked it from the inside. Yosef stood like a statue. When he finally pulled himself away, he headed to the river.

As he walked along the riverbank, he cried out, "Oh, God, what has become of me? How have I ended up like this? All my hopes have been turned into wretchedness. Waiting until tomorrow will only bring new wounds. God, you know I can't bear this anymore. Tonight I'll write my final words to Roza, and then end my life forever."

Yosef returned to Reb Osher's house and recited the evening prayers with a feeling that only God could understand. Then he sat down to write.

Miserable Roza!

Who is more miserable, the reader or the writer? Only you will know. Right now I think there is no one more miserable than I. Roza, before my death, I wanted to experience the taste of revenge for the very first time. So I went to your house to tell you that you had sinned before God by not keeping your vow to me. I blamed you for my suffering and early death, but now it has become clear you are not guilty and that I must confess to you. Forgive me, dear Roza, for sinning against your faithfulness because of my own pain and suffering. But know that throughout this whole ordeal, I have been pure and innocent.

I forgive your mother for her reception; she is not to blame. I see now the hands that planted counterfeit money on me in Petersburg and threw me into a dark hole for a year, also ruined my name here in Mohilev. Meyshe Shneyur and his people are skillful at destruction and can be proud of their workmanship. Tell your mother that I did not ride in a cab on *Shabbes*. What she said had nothing to do with me.

Roza, if you want to do something for me, please write to my parents and tell them my troubles have led to my death. I am sorry for the pain I have caused them.

Rukhame said she would protect you from your brother-in-law Meyshe Shneyur. Her heart, I hope, is still loyal to me, and her unhappiness calls up the last few tears I have remaining inside. My letters, which will be sent to you by the police, will show my innocence. But I cannot wait any longer because I have nothing left to wait for. I lost everything when I lost you.

I send greetings to your father, Shimen, and the dear, good Rukhame. I send greetings to everyone. I want to be in good standing since after my death I will be unable to make things right.

I say after my death because, by the time you read this letter, I will be lying in the ground. It will no longer matter whether people believe I was innocent or not. I have lain sick these past two weeks at Reb Osher the teacher's house after arriving from Petersburg just in time to witness your wedding. I had flown to you on the wings of hope, but then I became ill. I wrote to Shimen, but he did not answer. The whole world seems to hate me now.

Be well, my dear Roza. I request that my things be left with Reb Osher, my best and last remaining friend. I would like to write more—it is so hard to part with my pen—but there is no more to say. Be well, Roza. I write to you now for the last time.

Your innocent Yosef

Yosef felt exhausted when he finished the letter, but was determined to put it in Roza's hands himself. Hoping to see her on the street, he headed to Fridman's house and trembled as he waited by the door. When it finally opened, Rukhame came out. He called to her without using her name, and she replied, "What do you want?"

Yosef came to her and said, "Dear child, here is a letter from a close friend. Please give it to your sister Roza. She will know who wrote it. Be well, dear child!"

Rukhame heard the bitter emotion in the man's voice. Although she did not recognize him, the voice sounded familiar. "Who are you?" she asked, and tried to look into his face, but Yosef did not answer and quickly walked away. Rukhame started to go after him, but when she saw him heading towards the city bridge, she went back inside. Opening the letter, Rukhame was surprised to find Yosef's handwriting and immediately ran out to find him.

As Yosef arrived at the bridge, his leap into the river was delayed by the lamplighter who was slowly moving from side to side doing his job. A group of young people merrily strolled by, then a whole convoy of wagons took another half hour to cross.

"Even death begrudges me!" he cried out angrily as he walked down to the riverbank. "Why should death be such a sin? Why should someone be tormented forever? They say a living person always has hope, but what hope is left for me? Will I ever forget Roza? Will my suffering ever end? God, how can I go on living?"

As he gazed into the rushing water, Rukhame raced towards the bridge. Out of breath and with her heart pounding with fear, she imagined a crowd of people pulling Yosef's drowned body from the river. At the bridge, she heard his voice, and running to the water's edge, she threw herself on him.

"Who are you?" exclaimed Yosef. "Where did you come from?" He tried to pull the woman's arms from around his neck but realized she had fainted. Lifting up her pale face into the lamplight, he gasped, "Rukhame!"

Carrying her onto the bridge, Yosef tried to revive her, but her lovely face did not move. Her eyes were half-closed and sightless. Yosef kissed her, and his hot tears fell on her face. He looked around for help, but the bridge was empty.

Several minutes passed, and Rukhame began to stir. She opened her eyes and found Yosef holding her in his arms. "Yosef, don't die," she cried.

"Be quiet, dear child. Calm yourself."

"Yosef, I read your letter. Don't die, dear Yosef. You haven't lost all hope yet. I know about your misery, but Roza is not to blame. Believe me, she never sinned against you. She wept and mourned so much for you, but it didn't help. Yosef, are you still a Jew?"

"What kind of question is that, Rukhame?"

"Poor Yosef," Rukhame answered with a wail. "You didn't write that letter about being baptized?"

"Baptized? What are you talking about?"

"I told them the letter was a fake, but no one believed me. Everyone said it was your handwriting. Oh, that letter made Roza so miserable. That's when she stopped crying, but I knew her heart still wept for you. She was sold, Yosef! Put into the hands of a coarse and ignorant fool who doesn't have the sense to know who she is. Yosef, she has chains around her neck. She's as unhappy as you are."

"Rukhame, who did this?"

"Meyshe Shneyur, the thief! Why doesn't God punish him?"

"It was Meyshe Shneyur who took all my letters and had me thrown into a dark, damp hole for a whole year. He made up the whole story that I had converted and taken your father's money. But worst of all, he sold my Roza! Don't you see, Rukhame, I have no hope left and can't live with this grief any longer. Don't try to stop me. I want to die."

"Oh, Yosef, please, don't do it! If you die, I will die too. Look at me, Yosef. You still have a heart that lives for you, that is full of love for you even in this terrible moment. Yosef, I love you! Don't make me suffer like Roza. If you jump off the bridge, I will follow you into the water!"

"No, Rukhame! Your life is not over yet. It'll take you years of living and suffering to come to the place where I am now. Don't ask me to live when there's nothing left to live for."

"Yosef, don't speak of death when I've just begun to live in the world. Once I loved you like a brother. Now, Yosef, I love you. Do you hear me, I love you!"

"Rukhame, what are you saying?"

"Yosef, never doubt that God opened my heart to you. I'll do everything I can to make you happy. Stop thinking about death. I know you love me, Yosef, and don't want me in an early grave. I love you, Yosef, and will make you happy again!"

"Dear Rukhame," cried Yosef, "what can possibly come of this? Has Meyshe Shneyur changed his ways? As soon as he knows I'm here, he'll try to kill me. Why would you lead me down that same thorn-filled path again? Yes, Rukhame, I love you, but I still have the strength to separate myself from you. Dear God, haven't You put me through enough troubles already?"

"Remember your parents, Yosef. What joy have you given them from your life? My parents will soon know of your innocence and will also weep and mourn for you. No, I won't let you do it! You have no right to spoil things for everyone. I will not live without you; and without me, Roza will be seven times more miserable than she is now. You must live for her sake. You can still be a good friend to her even if she can't be your wife anymore. And let me remain alive for her, so she knows there's still a heart in the world that feels her suffering!"

"Oh, dear Rukhame, I never would've expected such words from you. When I left, you were still a child. Now, I see how you've changed."

"They say, 'Trouble makes one wise,' " answered Rukhame. "Yosef, I've taken your troubles to heart, and Roza's miseries have taught me to love you. I'll tell you the truth: your kiss when we were saying goodbye gave me a feeling I'd never known before. I tried to hide it, not wanting to understand what that feeling really meant. The moment you took your lips away from mine I began to miss you, Yosef. I'll confess: I was jealous of my sister, but I did everything possible for her and you. I defended you and insisted the letter was a fake, but no one believed me. When Roza became depressed, I tried to cheer her by talking about you, but this only made her more upset so I stopped. Then they arranged her marriage. You can't blame Father, Yosef. No one heard from you for months, and there was a rumor you'd been baptized. Mother forbade us from mentioning your name, but I know she never forgot you and often cried alone in her room. I didn't think Roza would survive her wedding day. She fainted several times, but no one said a word. When the wedding was over the cruel beast was done with her. Now she has no one in the world to heal her heart."

Rukhame looked into Yosef's eyes and saw the tears streaming down his face. "Yosef, if you throw yourself into the river, you'll not only kill yourself, you'll kill both of us. I won't leave you, even if you don't think I'm worthy of your love. Swear to me that you'll stay alive, dear Yosef. If you can't, I'll understand. Just know I'll only live as long as you live. If you kill yourself, I'll do the same. But I must tell you: I want to live!"

"Beloved Rukhame! What can I say? You're worthy, and I have nothing to offer but the burden of a great sacrifice. I still face grave troubles and will suffer torments every time I think of Roza. I gave her my whole life and can't take that back. If what you say is true and my friendship can be a consolation to her, perhaps then I can also be yours."

"Just don't kill yourself," Rukhame pleaded.

"For me to live, Rukhame, you must agree to let me part from you. I don't want you to suffer, and I don't want to suffer either, but it turns out I'm a good student and want to learn a profession. Reb Itsik has promised to support me, but it could take five or six years. If you can agree to wait that long, dear Rukhame, I will pledge my love to you. If not, you must leave me."

"Dear Yosef, do whatever you think is best. Do what's right for you. But promise me you will not die."

"I promise," replied Yosef. "I swear to you."

"I believe you," Rukhame said. "No one in the world believes you as much as I do. Will you write to me?"

"No. It will be easier if no one knows. Your brother-in-law must not know; it'll be better for both of us. Don't tell anyone, Rukhame. I'll go away, and in your house they'll mourn or curse my name. When the time is right, and I'm in a position to do so, I'll come for you and never leave you again. Go home and be at peace. You have a lot to take in, but I know with your good sense you'll carry it off. You'll have to wait five or six years for my return. Not receiving a letter will be the sign I'm still alive. The first thing I'll do when I arrive at my destination is order that you be informed in the case of my death. You can be certain that no one else in the world will take my heart—you have given me back my life. If it weren't for you, dear Rukhame, I'd be dead and floating in the river. And because Roza is your sister, I hope that someday I can be of help to her as well. Please go home now, Rukhame. God Himself is our witness. Rest assured that I will return to Reb Osher's house, and early in the morning, I'll leave on my journey without saying a word about what has taken place between us."

Yosef walked Rukhame to her door and said goodbye. He then went to Reb Osher's house, put his things together, and before the break of day was already far from the city.

FIVE

GOLDE'S LAST KINDNESS TO YOSEF

The news that Yosef had been in Mohilev spread quickly and eventually reached Roza's ears. When Fridman received a message demanding that Roza be brought to the police station, Golde would not permit her daughter to go alone and accompanied her. The police chief read to them the history of Yosef's past year, then handed over all his confiscated letters, including the last two written to his mother and Roza. Golde was stunned. Roza fainted.

When they returned home, they did not say a word to anyone. Roza read Yosef's letters, and by morning the doctor was called who prescribed several bottles of medicine. Roza's heart weakened. She was unable to leave the house until the end of summer. Although her husband loved her, he was an unsophisticated boy who did not understand or appreciate her. She rarely talked with him, and only hoped to die soon so she could end the torture of old memories.

In the city, people talked. They said that Yosef had jumped off the bridge and drowned himself. When Roza overheard this, she began walking along the riverbank hoping to find his body. More than once she thought of drowning herself, too, but now that she was pregnant, the thought of robbing someone else of life kept her from killing herself. She knew her husband's groom support from her father was coming to an end, and with no head for business, he had few prospects for making a living. So what? she asked herself. Having a husband who makes millions won't help me now that I'm dead. I died a long time ago, and am just a restless spirit awaiting her arrival in the Next World. Tell me, God, when will it end? The torments of hell can't be any worse!

And so our miserable Roza spent her time weeping for Yosef. Her love for him lived on inside her, and she never suspected he was still alive.

Golde did not fare much better. She was plagued by the thought that Yosef had drowned himself because of her. If I hadn't treated him so harshly, her heart told her, he might not have done it. It's worse for me than for Yosef's parents. They've only lost one child, but I've lost two and must watch my Roza die over and over again.

One afternoon, while Golde was emptying Shimen's pockets before *Shabbes*, she found Yosef's letter in his coat. She recognized the handwriting and called her son to read it:

Beloved brother, dear Shimen!

A year is not such a long time. However, if one breaks that year down into seconds, and if each second brings a new trouble or plague, then a year's time is an eternity.

Shimen, I was only in prison for one year, but for three months before that, I did not get a single letter from Roza. I tried to figure out what was going on between us, and the minutes passed like bitter years.

While sitting alone in my room, I cried quietly as I wrote to Roza until dawn. God, where did all those letters go? Your brother-in-law, my unjust enemy, did all this to me and more. He had counterfeit money planted on me, and for this, I spent a full year suffering in a hole as dark as Egypt. But even there I did not forget my love for Roza. With every bite of prison bread, with every rising up and lying down, I remembered Roza. This gave me strength and I refused to die. I hoped and waited for the truth to shine down into my dark pit.

When I remembered Roza's goodness and loyalty, the wet walls, filthy floor, and wails of prisoners did not seem so terrible. I sent my warm wishes with every little bird that flew by the bars of my window. With every prayer I recited in that awful place, my heart called out for Roza.

And so I began to look back to see how I had fallen into this pit and realized it had all come from Meyshe Shneyur's hands. Now that I was out of the way, he could do whatever he wanted to Roza. Then, dear Shimen, I would get wild with rage and throw myself against the cell door to break it down. I would pull at my hair and rip at my face in frustration. Yet I never felt any pain because the wound in my heart was so much worse.

Reb Itsik did not want me to travel here alone, but I had to come. The hours on the train and the wagon seemed endless. I barely survived long enough to see the city gate when the driver said there was a wedding in town. I heard the musicians playing, and if someone had told me it was Roza being taken to the wedding canopy, I would have come running to prevent it. I would have died before I saw her sold to another man! But I did not know what was happening. When I learned it was Roza's wedding, I lost all my senses and stood dazed as Roza was led away by a crowd of Jews. Every note the musicians played was like a dull knife being thrust into my heart. While my heart was still alive, all I wanted was to talk with Roza one last time and then die in peace.

All this, dear Shimen, happened in just one year! I lived out my whole life in it, lost all my happiness in it, and was robbed of all hope. That is how I lost my heart.

Shimen, my candle is going out. It has melted down to a tiny blue flame that rises up and sinks back down like someone drowning. The little flame flickers as if looking for help, but there is no help to be found. I cannot watch it anymore. I have to put out the light and make an end to it!

My soul is like that little flame. With one leap off the bridge, I can extinguish my soul in the river. With one leap I can end all my troubles. Why, I ask, should I wait until death has the mercy to free me? Why should I keep suffering in this world?

So it will be. I will drown myself, and when they find me, they will cover me with a sack. The good and pious Jews will say, "He killed himself; you must bury him outside the cemetery wall!" Jews with a modern education will say, "What a fool! He had nothing better to do than drown himself?" But my heart knows that none of these people understand my wounds. They do not know that day and night I have drowned in my own tears. If they felt the pain themselves—and I do not wish it upon them—they would do the same because there is no other way to end the heartache.

It is too bad that no one will know the truth about me. I will go down with a stone around my neck so no one finds me. My truth will remain forever at the bottom of the river. Of course, God knows my truth, but He is often silent. This is my truth, Shimen: I am innocent. I did not break my vow to Roza.

Shimen, my heart is deeply wounded. Tell me, can I still turn to you now that Roza is no longer mine? Will you help me, dear brother, now that I have forfeited all my happiness and I must lose my life as well?

I must talk to Roza. I must talk to your dear mother. I do not want to die with such bitter feelings between us. I want to remember their last words during my final seconds of life.

I cannot write anymore. I will not read this over or correct any errors. A sick person is forgiven a mistake, and I am very sick and not far from death. Come to me, dear Shimen. I just want to prove that I am still faithful to you and your family. Perhaps this is the last time I will write. And you are the one to whom I write my last letter. Please come see me.

Requested by your Yosef

After lighting the *Shabbes* candles, Golde wept like a mother mourning the death of her only son. Devoured by guilt, she told herself, The dear child had only wanted to cry his heart out to me, and I pushed him away with both hands. I poured salt on his wounds and drowned him with a heavy, bitter heart! God will punish me for this.

At dinner, she could not eat, and when she laid down to sleep, she had a terrible dream. She was standing outside, and the streets were dark. She was alone, and in the distance, she saw a lonely ghost appear. It was Yosef, and as he approached, he called out, "Mother! Do you believe me now? I did not convert. I did not ride to your house on *Shabbes*. I have drowned and will get no comfort for killing myself. One is not even allowed a *Kaddish!* If you want to do me a kindness and redeem yourself from sin, hire someone to say *Kaddish* for me." Suddenly, a terrible storm swept in, and Yosef's ghost was carried away in a whirlwind. Golde screamed until Rukhame rushed in to awaken her.

The next morning, Golde sent for Shmayahu the Talmudist and told him to study a chapter of Mishnah and say the *Kaddish*. When he asked for the name of the deceased, she let slip the name "Yosef," and, unable to stop herself, revealed the secret of her dream. Shmayahu was an upright Jew who admired Yosef for his ability to explain difficult commentaries which Shmayahu's Chassidic head found hard to comprehend. An honest Jew without pretensions, he found Golde's request a suitable reason for being obligated to say *Kaddish* and decided on his own to observe several fast days to speed Yosef's passage through hell.

There was no discussion about money. For one thing, it was *Shabbes;* secondly, how could he accept money for reciting *Kaddish* for someone he considered—as he put it—one of his teachers. Golde, however, hated asking anyone to do anything for free, so when *Shabbes* was over, she sent Shmayahu's wife a generous contribution. Shmayahu, of course, never knew anything about it. He never asked his wife where she got the money to buy a loaf of bread because he was certain that Elijah the Prophet, with whom he walked every night in his dreams, would never abandon him and always provide abundance in the pot.

Six

ALMOST TOO LATE ALREADY

From that *Shabbes* on, Golde was different. She often fasted and recited additional Psalms after reading the Psalm of the day which she never missed. She assisted poor widows and frequently went to the cemetery. She visited those who were ill and consoled unfortunate parents who had lost a child. She helped anyone in need whenever she could.

On the day before Yosef's *yortsayt*—as Golde had calculated it in her mind—the community busybody, Sterne Gute, stopped by for a visit. "Golde," she said, "have you heard who's dying?"

"Who?" asked Golde as a dark cloud passed over her face.

"Don't be frightened," chuckled Sterne Gute. "It's no great loss for the community."

"Who, Sterne Gute?" Golde asked impatiently.

"Grune, Sorele's mother," the busybody replied. "Leyb Sorkin's mother-in-law, the worst mother in the world!"

"Feh, indeed!" said Golde. "What is your connection to her?"

"I was visiting the sick; I heard she was on her deathbed. *Oy,* what kind of children did she raise? The rule is: if you're good and pious, your children will be good and pious, too.

"May I say something about your children, Golde? How could they not be pious with a mother as pious as you? Of course, I never much cared for that teacher you brought in, even if he was a relative of mine. And certainly not after he got himself baptized, may the demons take him! But at least God sent Roza her intended one. So what if he's not so smart? Does everybody have to be a King Solomon? What good was all of Yosef's learning when he just used the Talmud for deceit? Better that God took him out of the world and out of your life, may he rot in hell!"

"I have no more time to chat," Golde said after listening to Sterne Gute's poisonous tirade. "I've got guests coming and must see that the house is in order. But tell me, is Sorele's mother dying?"

"All I know is that I went by Grune's place before *Shabbes,* and while I was there, she asked me to bring you to her. She said she had something to tell you. Honestly, for someone like that, it's better to give a lecture on ethics than listening to a confession."

"Have you seen her since *Shabbes?*" Golde asked.

"Don't worry; she's still alive," answered Sterne Gute. "Someone like that doesn't just die in an instant like Moses our Teacher. They have to suffer until the Angel of Death finally steps in. Sorele's mother asked me to send you after *Shabbes,* but I'm afraid it went in one ear and out the other. Thank God I remembered! Now you can go see her for yourself. When it comes to death, it often comes without an announcement."

Barely waiting for Sterne Gute to finish, Golde threw on her coat and went to visit the dying woman. When she arrived, the house was empty. Neighbors said Sorele and her husband were at the fair in Makaria. Others said Leyb had been caught by the police and Sorele was trying to get him released from jail. When Golde went into Grune's room, she found a small boy who called out, "Grandma, Golde Fridman is here."

"Golde, may you be well," said Grune in a weak and trembling voice. "I sent for you several times last year, but no one obeyed me. Now that I'm hanging by a thread, you are my last bit of consolation."

"Hush, Grune, don't strain yourself. I'll listen to whatever you have to say," said Golde as she took the old woman's hand.

"I have no time to spare," answered Grune. "Thank God you're here, and I can talk to you. Oh, Golde, I have been plagued with such terrible children, may God protect you from such sorrow in life. I speak of this now with my last breath to tell you that I have a terrible daughter and son-in-law and that your son-in-law is no better!"

Golde sighed heavily as the old woman rested for a moment.

"Don't hold it against me," Grune went on. "I don't mean to speak evil gossip right before my death, but you know me, and know that God has punished me with terrible children. I was going to remain silent, but since it concerns the happiness of your daughter, I must tell you everything. A year ago during Shavuos, your Meyshe Shneyur came here to see my son-in-law. I've known Meyshe Shneyur since he was a boy. Only sons are never quite right in the head. He came with Tevele and Gasan's son-in-law, and they played cards and talked about all kinds of obscene things on that holy night. Then they talked about someone named Yosef who they wanted to keep from marrying your Roza. Your Meyshe Shneyur didn't want him because he wanted Roza to take some fool for a husband. Everyone gave him advice on how to start a rumor about Yosef not being so trustworthy and about making fake letters. Your son-in-law didn't like any of it until Leyb told him that they could kill him and 'the rooster would never crow.' Which means no one would ever know about it. Golde, you would be heartsick if you heard what was said here, and the evil expressions Meyshe Shneyur used. He even wished for you the same end as mine! I tell you, Golde, get rid of him. He's a scoundrel!

"Just tell me, dear Golde, has your Roza married Yosef or someone else? Or has Yosef, God forbid, met with a terrible end? I wanted to tell you a year ago, but God is my witness, they wouldn't let me. The next morning my son-in-law tried to give me poison because he realized I had overheard everything. And if I didn't take it, my daughter and son-in-law said they were going to throw me out on the street or beat me until I was speechless. Since then no one has been allowed to see me. I asked the boy to go for you, but he's afraid of Leyb and refused. Now tell me, how is Yosef?"

"May he intercede for us in heaven," answered Golde with a wail.

"*Oy*, there's nothing left to live for," cried Grune as she fell back on the pillow with her eyes closed. She lay there for several minutes, then opened her eyes and looked at Golde. Slowly, she closed her eyes for the last time.

No one in the world cried as many tears for that lonely old woman as our deeply grieved Golde. She remained for the ritual washing, dressed the body in burial clothes, walked behind the casket, and smoothed the earth over her resting place. And when everyone else had left the cemetery, Golde went back to the new grave and moistened the fresh mound with her tears. With deep sighs, she poured out her heavy heart to God begging Him to have pity on Yosef's drowned soul.

The city talked about this at length, although it was not unusual to see Golde at funerals anymore. But seeing her weeping and mourning over a person of such bad reputation made people wonder. For Sterne Gute, trying to find the reason gave her something to talk about for many months.

Golde's blood boiled every time she saw her dark son-in-law. What can I do? she asked herself. I'm like a sick person who sees his hand start to rot but prefers to let his whole body die before cutting it off. It's too late. There's no one to help, and no hope left. He's already destroyed Yosef, buried Roza, and pushed Shimen aside. God only knows what will happen to Rukhame.

SEVEN

A DOCTOR IN THE HOUSE

Days and rivers never stand still. Even while people sleep, rivers follow their own course flowing farther and farther on. Even during the winter months, when covered with thick ice, the waters below move on. People may drive across the solid ice, build on it, even hold markets on it, but the activity underneath never stops. Is it not unlike the difference between our human deeds and the deeds of the Almighty. Everything a person does has its particular time and place. A clock may stop for a day or even a year, but the year speeds by while the clock stands still. God sets His clock once, and everything goes forward without stopping, continuing on its course for as long as He wills it. Even when we forget about time, it runs on. Even when heavy ice presses on our hearts, and we think the whole world has stopped living, time goes on until we awake, and are stunned by what has flown by without our even noticing.

Time went by at its own speed for Roza. She lived a life almost devoid of feeling, so it did not matter whether the day was bright or cloudy, because time simply ticked away. But the same time passed very slowly for Rukhame who tried to satisfy herself with the knowledge that each passing day was adding to the five or six years Yosef required for his education. As the remaining time decreased, the final day came closer and more clearly into view. At first, she counted the days, then weeks, months, and years.

When the sixth year arrived, and Yosef had not returned, Rukhame became sad and restless. Summer went by, then winter, then Passover came and went, and she began counting single days again.

In the meantime, marriage proposals were being offered for her. Rukhame listened calmly and never opposed her parents. She dressed up for the prospective in-laws, went strolling with the prospective grooms, and was not uneasy because she knew she would not be forced to marry without her consent. When she told her mother, "I don't like this one" or "I don't want that one," Golde never said a word. She just told the matchmaker to stop the negotiations.

The Dark One did what he could to persuade Golde, but soon realized she was doing exactly the opposite of everything he advised. So he stopped interfering but secretly laid out a path for Rukhame to get a husband like Roza's so he would remain the inheritor of the business. Shimen had already married in another city and was engaged in a completely different work, so Meyshe Shneyur no longer feared him. But Rukhame, he knew, would not be so easy to get rid of, and he began to plot his trickery.

If we got Roza to put on the veil for such a fool when she was so in love with Yosef, he thought, this should be easy. I just need to torture my father-in-law a little by telling him people in town are starting to talk about his situation. "Rukhame is nearly twenty-one and still unmarried. Maybe it's a sign that Fridman's not so rich after all." He'll hate hearing that and will be forced to find her a match.

And so the day came when Rukhame's father spoke very sternly to her about getting married. She listened without saying a word.

She knew what she hoped for and wanted, and was determined to wait. When her mother begged her tearfully to explain why she would not accept any of the grooms who had been offered to her, Rukhame replied, "I have decided not to marry until I am twenty-one." Whether Golde believed this or not, she decided not to argue. Rukhame had always been her happiest child, but she had become increasingly sad lately. Fearing she was falling into a depression, Golde remained silent.

During this time, Rukhame did not mention Yosef once, but Roza spoke of him often and always mournfully. One fine morning during the first bright and joyful days of spring, Roza and Rukhame went out for a walk as the doctor had instructed. The whole city was still asleep, and all the shutters were closed. Far off in the distance by the woods, they saw a mail coach approaching the city. The coach stopped at the top of the hill, and a passenger climbed out. Pensively the man walked around studying everything. Stopping at a young tree, he said to himself, This is what time does: transforms all things. I still remember the first time I came here. It was winter, and everything was dead. There were no green leaves, and no happy little birds to accompany me with their sweet songs. How sad I was back then and how much happier I am now!

The passenger climbed back into the coach and requested the driver go slowly down the hill. Spring has arrived, he told himself. It was winter then; winter for the world, but inside my heart it was spring. Now it's just the opposite: gay, warm, and light, but inside I feel the darkness of winter. Oh, dear God, what storms I've sustained in my life! What terrible blizzards have blown over me, and the ice that surrounds my heart has not been broken by a single happy sunbeam. Yet, in spite of all the old pains, new feelings seem to be tugging at my heart.

As these thoughts drifted through his mind, the passenger saw two women walking towards him. Not wanting to be recognized by anyone, he turned away, and the women walked by without noticing who was in the coach. How often do people pass by their own happiness by turning away and not noticing?

"Do you hear that?" the passenger asked the driver as they headed through the city gate.

"Hear what?" answered the driver.

"Is it music? Is there a wedding in town?" asked the passenger in alarm.

"A wedding?" replied the driver. "It's too early in the morning."

"I'm not crazy, I hear music playing!" said the passenger.

"Yes, yes," said the driver. "I hear it now, too."

"Drive faster!" shouted the passenger.

The driver cracked his whip, and they soon saw where the music was coming from. A company of soldiers was marching into the city with their band. The passenger relaxed and breathed more easily.

When the coach arrived at Fridman's house, the passenger told the driver to go in and ask if he could stay there. The doorman came out and carried the passenger's things into a lovely, well-appointed room. The guest rewarded the driver handsomely and entered the house.

The doorman asked the driver, "Who is he?"

"A German doctor," said the driver.

"How do you know?"

"While we were at the post office, I saw him write a prescription for a sick child."

Half an hour later as family members entered for breakfast, they asked the doorman who had arrived. He said a doctor. "It's always a good sign when there's a doctor in the house," replied Golde with a smile. "You know what they say, 'If there's bread in the house, no one will go hungry; and if there's a doctor in the house, everyone will be healthy.' Nevertheless, I'm going to ask him about Roza's condition."

"I'll tell you the truth," replied Fridman, "I don't consider doctors worth a pinch of snuff. Most of them are charlatans. God is the real doctor, and that's all there is to it."

The doctor stayed in his room the entire day, but by evening the baby was crying so pitifully that Golde insisted Roza take the child to see him. Roza sent the doorman to inquire if the doctor would see them, and he came back with the answer, "Come in a few minutes."

Roza spent the time waiting outside the door to the doctor's room and was surprised when a scene came to her mind: the time she waited to see Yosef on the morning after they declared their love to one another. How different that morning had been, and she wondered where the memory had come from.

She remembered Yosef once telling her, "A person's heart is like a telegraph. It sends messages in advance of something good or bad, but we rarely understand the secret language. How often do we think about a forgotten friend and, just a few minutes later, find that very person standing in front of us?"

Roza began to think deeply about what had become of her, and what had become of Yosef. I'm still alive in any case, she told herself, but God knows if there's even a memory left of him in the world. Roza became so absorbed in her thoughts, she did not see the door open in front of her. A handsome young man in European dress stood before her in the doorway.

When the doctor saw her with the child in her arms, he could barely control himself. He stepped back into the room and sat down on the sofa, weak and exhausted. Roza stood at the door hardly noticing. Realizing he was in no condition to help, the doctor gathered his strength, and said in a shaking voice, "My good woman, I beg your pardon. I fear I'm not yet ready to see patients."

Roza immediately snapped out of her reverie and recognized his voice. She heard within it the old, sweet music she listened to with such love. She lifted her beautiful dark eyes and screamed, "Yosef, my Yosef!"

Roza grabbed the door frame to keep from fainting. Seeing that the baby was in danger of falling, Yosef stood up and took the child from her. He then took Roza by the arm and led her to the sofa. She stared at him in disbelief.

"Roza, calm yourself. I'm still the same old Yosef—'your Yosef.'"

"But I'm no longer 'your' Roza!" she replied tearfully. Seeing her baby in Yosef's arms, she said in a bitter voice, "Yosef, I can't be your Roza anymore!"

Tears welled up in Yosef's eyes. "Yes, Roza, that's how it is now. They separated us, but our hearts are just as pure and true as they ever were. Our enemy put me in jail and sold you to a stranger. He tore us apart and nearly killed me. Yet he never touched our faithful devotion. Roza, I'm the same now as I was back then, and if you're happy with your husband, I'm happy too."

"Happy? Yes, Yosef, I'll be happy from this day onward because you're still alive! I still have a person in the world who knows me and is true to me. That's enough for now, Yosef. God did not permit the happiness I desired, but He's not to blame. We can't put all human blame on God. Meyshe Shneyur is the tyrant. As God lives, I will not be silent!"

"Roza, introduce me to your husband. Tell him I'll be the best brother in the world to him. Where is he?"

"My husband? Ask Meyshe Shneyur. That Moor has done everything in his power to ruin my life! I didn't know my husband for two years. Now that I've come to know him, I see how completely unfortunate I am. Yosef, I can't explain it to you now, but soon I'll tell you everything. But please, tell me what happened to you? Why did people say you drowned yourself? Did you write that in a letter?"

"If I'm alive today, Roza, and if I have anything to hope for in the future, it's because of our Rukhame. She practically pulled me from the river."

Yosef told her everything, and Roza listened intently.

"You deserve her, dear Yosef," Roza said solemnly, "and you'll probably be happier with her than me. She's more educated than I am, and she's been reading and studying this whole time. I can see that you've changed, too, Yosef, while I've become a simple housewife."

"Roza, remember when I told you that anyone who strives to learn can become an educated person? I know you, Roza, and can never forget your heart and feelings. Be certain that I'm the same as I was. Should we tell your parents?"

Roza left her child in Yosef's arms and ran to bring Golde and Fridman. "Yosef is alive, alive!" she shouted in a voice that rang through the house the way Serach the daughter of Asher announced that Yakov's son Yosef was still alive.

A great commotion broke out in the house! Rukhame came running in and wrapped her arms around Yosef's neck. Golde kissed him and cried out, "I can't believe my eyes! Oh, children, tell me this is not a dream."

"Be sure, dear Mother, you see me with your own eyes," said Yosef. "You're not dreaming, I promise you. To the world, I'm a doctor now, but to you, I will always be your Yosef who loves and respects you as a mother!"

The joy in the house was unrestrained. Even Fridman greeted Yosef with fatherly kisses. Yosef told his story, and when he was through, Golde put her arms around Rukhame and Yosef. She kissed them and exclaimed, "What a God we have!"

Only Roza stood at a distance playing the role of a caring sister. But as she looked on, her wounded heart wept.

EIGHT

WHO ARE THE MODERN DEMONS?

If there is a person in the world whose happiness can make her forget the great suffering she has endured, it is the lover who has been assured by her beloved that he will never leave her again. So it was with our happy Rukhame, who had borne so much for her love.

Rukhame had loved Yosef when he was in the arms of her sister and she had no hope of having him. She had loved him when the rumors spread about his baptism, and when she read the letters Meyshe Shneyur had forged. Although she had not believed the lies, each word pierced her heart. She had loved Yosef when he returned and was still in love with her sister, yet she vowed to sacrifice her own life to keep him alive. Finally, after that terrible dark night when her soul sensed a spark of hope that one day he might be hers, she suffered through six more years of waiting. In that time, she grew from fifteen to twenty-one and would accept no other love and no other passion in her life.

At last the happy day arrived, and her love for Yosef was revealed. Her mother was comforted by it, and her father, seeing everything clearly, offered no resistance. He did not want to lose

Yosef again and gave Rukhame to him with great pleasure. He would have preferred things to be like before, and wondered, now that Yosef was a doctor and spoke German, if he was still a good Jew. Would he keep Rukhame from wearing a wig and force her to go around with her own hair like all the other doctors' wives? That one thought gave him no peace. He also feared Yosef might take his daughter away to another city where he could earn thousands of rubles a year. Yet he saw that Rukhame could not live without Yosef, so he thought it better to remain quiet and let Golde manage the arrangements.

On her side, Golde was delighted with Yosef's new occupation. She could never forget how she wept and wailed as a young bride when they cut off her long beautiful hair and clapped a wig on her head. She felt sick every time she looked at her bare forehead in the mirror. She could never understand why an unmarried girl was allowed to show her natural hair but a married woman was not. She had even asked knowledgeable people if there really was a prohibition against showing your own hair. Some said it was written in the Talmud that a married woman should not show her hair even within the walls of her own home, and God would bless such a woman with good children. Yet some of the most modest women she knew had terrible children. She had also seen many wealthy women in the city who no longer wore wigs, so why should one of her children do any less? If one of her daughters wanted to wear her own hair, Golde decided, it was no great crime, and no child would die from it.

Golde's only concern was if Yosef would keep a kosher kitchen. But since he was not the type to do anything that would make others suffer, she was optimistic. Rukhame, unaware of all the foolishness, happily spent her time with Yosef, showing him all she had learned and how much she had changed over the past six years.

But just as some bad must always mix with the good, and every sunny view must have a few shadows, so it was with Rukhame's happiness. The pain came from Roza's husband who had lost all his money through Meyshe Shneyur's deceptions. It was not enough for the Dark One to deepen Roza's misery by selling her to a person who did not understand her, he went to great lengths to destroy her husband's happiness too. Eventually, Faybesh had no choice but to flee to Petersburg where his debtors had handed his promissory notes over to the court. One fine morning, several police officials came to Roza's home to appraise her property. Roza steeled herself and gave away her jewelry, clothes, and wedding gifts, even though she had not seen one groschen of the ill-gotten money enjoyed by her husband, the father of her beloved children.

Yosef marveled at her strength as she turned everything over without complaint. After the police had left, she pulled her children close and said, "Oh, my bright little stars, now you are as alone and poor as your unfortunate mother. Now we have nothing."

When Yosef overhead this, he hurried to Roza, took her hand, and said, "Dear Roza, have you forgotten I'm still alive? Why do you say you're alone? Can't I be a father to your children? Or at least a teacher? I swear to you that nothing kept me from drowning myself more than Rukhame's telling me how unhappy you were, and the thought that I could be of comfort to you if I lived. All I wish, Roza, is to make you happy. You would give me the greatest joy by not keeping me at a distance. Involve me; I will never require any accounting from you. And I hope that Rukhame will be happy with this, too."

"Thank you, Yosef," Roza answered with tears in her eyes.

When Rukhame came in and found them crying, Yosef told her what had happened and what he had proposed to Roza. The good Rukhame was pleased with the arrangement, but she worried about Yosef's health and his determination to get Roza's husband back on his feet. Rukhame was not, heaven forbid, jealous, but she was concerned that Yosef would never be completely happy until Roza was happy, and she knew that would never be, especially now that her sister had lost everything.

Two weeks passed, and the family began to plan the engagement. The Dark One, who had been in Warsaw and unaware of the recent events in Mohilev, returned in the middle of the night without anyone hearing him come in. In the morning, he learned that Yosef had come back as a doctor and was now living in the Fridman house. Alarmed by the news, Meyshe Shneyur dressed quickly, got control of himself, and went to see Yosef.

When Meyshe Shneyur entered the room, Yosef almost did not recognize him. The limp little Chassid now looked like a big African trader, as black as ink, with a closely cropped beard. He had replaced his long frock coat with a short jacket and was wearing glasses. Only his crooked nose remained the same. Coming in, he saw Yosef sitting in a chair reading a book. He went to him with his arms spread wide, fell on him, and kissed him. Yosef could hardly tear himself away.

"You haven't washed your hands," Yosef said, "and it's dangerous to kiss someone before you've rinsed away the demons."

"Who believes in such nonsense anymore?" asked Meyshe Shneyur. "There are no demons in the world."

"I used to say the same thing," said Yosef, "but I don't deny it anymore. I've seen enough devils at work in my own life to rival any described in our most frightening folk legends."

"But I stand by the Talmud," answered Meyshe Shneyur, pretending not to understand Yosef's meaning. "The Talmud says that all the demons were driven into the wilderness, and here in the city we have no need to fear them."

"Yes, back then they played a trick on those demons. But the modern ones make the city into a wilderness. Don't you know that if a bride is injured at the wedding canopy, they pull her away from the groom and sell her as a demon? The groom is also spirited away to who knows where. Don't you believe in such things?"

"I say, toss the demons aside, who needs them? Let them all go to hell!"

"Hell is where they come from," said Yosef. "You talk about tossing them aside? Tell me, how do you get rid of them? At one time people said the night prayers helped, but today only God Himself knows what to do. I hope someday He'll release me from their grip."

"Enough already, Yosef," said Meyshe Shneyur. "Come now, tell me, how are you doing? You appear to be a great success. I take pleasure in knowing that."

Yosef turned away, no longer interested in talking to his enemy.

"Look, Yosef," said the Dark One in a conciliatory tone, "I know at one time you thought I disliked you because I didn't allow your engagement to Roza. Believe me, I didn't disapprove of you. I was really doing you a favor. I saw that you could grow into a great person and I couldn't allow you to fall into ruin. I knew that Roza had flaws and that she was crazy, and that Rukhame would be the kind of wife you needed. I couldn't allow myself to stand at a distance. Remember, you were still an idler in the study house. Who was the first person to welcome you into this house? Who made a good name for you? Who, in the end, saved you from a life of troubles? However bad it's been for you, remind yourself that you could now have three children and a plague of a wife, and be as bitterly poor as Roza and her husband."

Enraged, Yosef replied, "Oh, I know what you've done for me, Meyshe Shneyur! I know and will never forget! I can pardon you for everything but making Roza unhappy. For that, I will never forgive you. You're an assassin, Meyshe Shneyur! I know you, and everything you've done, and I now have it in my power to make you miserable. Only our father-in-law's good name and mother-in-law's health prevent me from destroying you. But one day, God will provide your reward! How true the saying: a wolf can change his coat but not his nature. You're the same deceiver as you were before in a different guise. You may trim your beard, but you haven't changed your heart. I will never be your friend, now or ever. Get out of my room; I can't stand the sight of you anymore! Go seek people of your own kind. I will do you no harm, Meyshe Shneyur. I will simply forget you!"

Yosef opened the door, but Meyshe Shneyur did not move. He glared at Yosef, but before he could say another word, he saw his mother-in-law coming down the hall and decided to leave before she could see him in such a humiliating situation.

"Get out of here, you snake," said Golde when she saw him. "Do you think things will remain as they were? Just wait, justice will be done!"

Meyshe Shneyur pretended not to hear, but his dark heart seethed with rage, and he swore he would soon take his revenge.

NINE

THE ENGAGEMENT EVENING

Several days later, the Fridman house was full of joy and merriment. The engagement contract between Yosef and Rukhame had been written as is done among Jews. There were many invited guests and family members, but one in-law was missing. Meyshe Shneyur's dark heart would not permit him to look upon the joy of his father-in-law's child for whom he had sought only misery. People who knew him well understood his absence. Those who did not, accepted his excuse of a headache. And, indeed, at that very moment, he was suffering from the painful thoughts that raged through his head. He lay in bed with the blanket drawn over him, knowing that he would soon see Yosef and Rukhame standing under the wedding canopy. There he would be called up to give a blessing, and Yosef would become his brother-in-law.

No, it will never be! he told himself as he got up and left the house. In an overheated state with his fists clenched, he walked down the street and shouted in a wild voice, "It's my life or his!"

What a fool I've been! he scolded himself. Why didn't I take his head off when I had the chance? Now it's time to finish this business once and for all. Leyb Sorkin's in jail, but there is still Tevele and Zoyrek Kopel Karinov. I'm ready to pay them whatever it takes to get the job done!"

Heading to Karinov's house, he found the thief's mother painting a white chicken she had stolen from a neighbor's henhouse. "What do you want?" she asked him.

"I want my advisor Zoyrek Kopele," said Meyshe Shneyur.

"He's in jail."

"I just saw him today."

"They give him credit for everything," she said, bursting into tears. "Someone set a shed on fire, and they took my baby boy to jail. Why do you want him?" she asked, wiping her eyes.

"He's been very helpful to me in the past," said Meyshe Shneyur. "I want to discuss an issue with him. He could earn a little cash—or maybe a lot."

At first, Karinov's mother wondered, Is this a trap? Then she thought, Maybe the Dark One really needs my son's help. She knew who he was, and although she was afraid of him, she saw that he needed her more than she needed him. And why pass up the chance of making a little income? So she instructed Meyshe Shneyur to go into the city to visit Libe Reytse. She gave him a password to get in and promised to send her son as soon as he got home.

Meyshe Shneyur headed to Libe Reytse's. As he passed by his father-in-law's house, he heard shouting and fighting but refrained from going inside. "Bang your head against the wall!" he cursed as he continued on his way.

The fight at Fridman's was the result of Meyshe Shneyur leaving the door open when he departed the house. While everyone else was enjoying themselves at the engagement party, Zoyrek Kopel Karinov was pulling off a robbery. For some time, the thief had designs on the house, in part because he was angry at Fridman for catching one of his sister's trying to steal a *mezuzah* while visiting the house for charity. In seeking revenge, Karinov wanted to break into the house and "impoverish them a little," as Dvorah Basye the tavern keeper liked to say. He had been waiting for a night when everyone was in the main part of the house so he could empty the other rooms, and he got his chance when Meyshe Shneyur left the door open.

In a matter of minutes, Karinov went into a chest, grabbed a little box he assumed had money in it and took Meyshe Shneyur's good fur coat. He then went out the window and over the fence. But before he could get away, Kuzmo the butler caught him and shouted for help. Karinov tossed the box aside and threw the fur coat over Kuzmo's head. By the time people came running out of the house, they found Karinov punching the butler. The half-tipsy guests gave Karinov a good thrashing while he screamed, "Let me go!" They dragged him inside to see who he was; and when they pulled off his black mask, they were shocked to discover it was the well-known criminal, Zoyrek Kopel Karinov. Everyone knew that Karinov was capable of anything: setting fires, murdering people, and viciously taking revenge on anyone who crossed him.

Fridman was the most rattled of all. Knowing it was not always possible to get insurance for his business, he was anxious to mollify the thief to prevent any repercussions. He gave Zoyrek Kopel a big glass of whiskey and stuffed his pockets with treats. Then he pulled out his wallet, shoved a pile of money into his hands, and sent the criminal home.

Later that night, when Meyshe Shneyur learned what had happened, a plan began to form in his mind. Good, he thought, this is what I've been waiting for. Now, no one will suspect me.

Just before sunrise, while everyone was sound asleep from wine and weariness, the butler began banging on Fridman's shutters. "Fire! Fire!" he shouted.

The quarters where Roza and Rukhame were sleeping were engulfed in flames. Barrels of fuel oil in a nearby storeroom had caught fire and spread to the house. Half-awake people scrambled out of windows and doors. People were panicking as the heat and thick black smoke from the burning oil prevented anyone from getting close enough to extinguish the blaze. Suddenly screams were heard from one of the rooms: "Save us! Save us!"

Yosef came running out and ignoring the smoke and flames, climbed through the bedroom window. He grabbed Roza and her children and brought them out. Handing the children to Golde, he headed back for Rukhame. Finding her lifeless body, he lifted her up in his arms and carried her out. With their clothes on fire, he ran to the gate where people poured buckets of water on them.

Yosef coughed up blood and collapsed. Rukhame revived but struggled to breathe. She had escaped the flames but was now drowning in water.

TEN

GOD DESIRES A SACRIFICE

The fire left Yosef gravely ill. From the cold water that had been poured over his weakened body, he contracted consumption. Half-crippled and barely able to get out of bed, he felt himself sinking with each passing day. As a doctor himself, he doubted he would survive the summer.

The doctors said his broken health could only be healed with great effort, and they suggested he go to Italy to recuperate. But Yosef was certain he would die on the way and preferred to be buried in the Mohilev cemetery where his friends and loved ones could follow his casket and visit his grave. So he remained in the Fridman house and waited for death to arrive rather than travel to meet it.

Rukhame was also ill but could still get around. Golde wept and mourned. Roza forgot her life and focused on Yosef who had become her only consolation. Now, as he lay dying, all the sorrows and troubles of the past were lost in the pain of the present moment. Day and night she remained by his side, trying to make him happy. But she could not lift his spirits. Yosef knew he was leaving Roza, and lamented his poor, lonely parents. By now they should have had some satisfaction from all their efforts and tears, but he had only caused them worry and grief. Most of all, he wanted to live for Rukhame.

He wept bitterly with each passing day as he looked at his unfinished papers and work. His heart had been full of high ideals, and his head had developed many ways to heal his ailing people. Now his valuable ideas were destined to die with him.

Leaving an unfinished work in the world is worse than leaving an ungrown child, he told himself. A child will grow on its own, but my work, my first-born ideas, will be buried with me and no echo of them will remain in the world. Grant me, God, just one more year of life and I will devote it to my people. I will not take any benefit of Your world other than to set my ideas free.

Rukhame suffered silently. She knew that if Yosef died, she would die too, but was determined to stay alive until he was gone. She could not bear to cause him any more pain.

Golde tried to comfort her. "With God's help," she insisted, "you will both be healthy again." But as hard as Rukhame tried to act reassured, her half-dead heart reminded her at every step that her life hung by a thread. She felt her strength waning as her agony grew, and she completely lost her appetite.

Rukhame and Yosef were often seen talking together. They encouraged each other and refused to reveal how desperate they felt. Although he was a doctor, Yosef did not perceive Rukhame's true condition. The lovely colors on her beautiful face still glowed as before, and her speech was just as lively and playful. But when Yosef held her hand, he noticed her pulse racing. When he questioned her about it, Rukhame always replied that she could not be at ease when she saw him in such distress.

One day, as they sat looking into each other's eyes, their hearts weeping silently at the thought of leaving this world to lie in a cold, narrow grave, Yosef said with a bitter sigh, "Dear Rukhame, I want to make a request of you."

"Ask anything, dear Yosef," answered Rukhame, giving him a warm kiss.

"But I must tell you first that I'm not asking for a small thing. This will be very hard for you. But I still want it," Yosef said as he began to cry."

"Dear Yosef," Rukhame said as she caressed his cheek. "I swear to you that nothing in the world is too hard for me if it makes peace for you. Not even death."

"But life, Rukhame?" he asked, squeezing her hand.

"What do you mean, Yosef?"

"I mean that you must live even if I die."

"God in heaven!" Rukhame gasped, and tears poured from her eyes.

Yosef did not try to comfort her, and they cried together. Rukhame held his hand and would not let go.

"Oh," said Yosef bitterly, "what a miserable person I am! Once my heart was so distressed when I saw the funeral of a lonely old man who had no one to shed a tear for him. I was so afraid of such a death. Today, dear Rukhame, I'm envious of that person who died so peacefully. Oh, how painful it is to know that my death is the reason for your early aging and that I'm the cloud over such a lovely, precious rose."

"Yosef, you must live," Rukhame said. "It cannot be otherwise. God can't be so terrible. Why would He punish me, a pure and innocent person? Hasn't He punished you enough? Haven't you suffered enough for both of us?"

Rukhame's words stirred angry feelings in Yosef. He thought of cruel taskmasters who ordered their slaves to do things without revealing their purpose, and parents who punished their children without explaining their reasons. He had always hated teachers who taught him things with a wink and a nod and then left him to guess at the answers on his own. Or those who punished a child unmercifully for not grasping some Talmudic teaching that was beyond his understanding. How could he compare the Creator of the Universe with such people? As these ideas mixed in his head, tears fell from his eyes.

"Yosef, put your sad thoughts aside," pleaded Rukhame. "This must not take up your last shred of health. Is there a person in the world who hasn't asked these questions of God? I remember hearing the words of a wise friend of my father's who said, 'God punishes the ones He loves.' That is, He doesn't tell us in advance what good will come from the difficulties we're facing. We must trust that what comes will be better at the end. God wants to surprise people with the goodness that awaits them in the World to Come. Yes, Yosef, I admit that at the time I laughed out loud at such a thought. Today that laughter comes with great pain. When I was first learning mathematics, it didn't grieve me if I couldn't complete a lesson. What bothered me most was not yet having the knowledge to accomplish the task. What bothers me now is not knowing what our lesson is or how to resolve it. But enough! I beg you, Yosef, don't give yourself over to such dark thoughts. Better health will improve your spirits. Life is calling you back!"

"Rukhame, you know we have no say over our thoughts. How fine my few remaining minutes would be if I could forget everything. But all the days of my life and all my troubles are passing before my eyes. How I spoke with Roza for the first time, and how happy I was with her. How my enemies almost killed me in a dark prison. And how I stood ready to jump off a bridge until you, my dear Rukhame, yanked me back to life. Oh, God, why didn't you make that the full measure of my troubles? Why did you let me live only to stab me in the heart with fresh wounds? For what purpose? The dark grave?"

When Golde entered the room, she found Yosef and Rukhame holding each other tightly. Both were sobbing. "My dear, good children," she said, swallowing back her own tears. "I see you're getting better. God is our doctor. I'm praying to God for you, and everyone who knows you is praying to the Holy One for your precious lives."

"Yes, dear Mother, pray to God," said Yosef as he kissed Golde's hands. "No one but God can help me now."

"No one but God," agreed Golde. "The One who gave us life."

"Yes," said Rukhame, "He gave us life and has the right to take it. And we are forbidden to ask Him why He gave us life, or why He takes it away once it has become so precious to us."

"If only I could stop reminding myself that tomorrow or the next day will be my last," Yosef said. "Death is staring me in the face. This is the curse God put on people after Adam ate from the Tree of Knowledge. But Adam never ate from the Tree of Life, so we will never know the answers to life's riddles: What is our purpose here? What do we bring with our existence? What do we leave when we're gone? These are the questions that torment our souls. All we know for certain is how it ends."

The sad little group talked until late in the afternoon. As Golde pulled Rukhame away, Yosef asked weakly, "Dear Mother, would you please spend the night in my room?"

That night, Yosef's sleep was feverish and restless. Golde could hardly wait until morning before sending for Shmayahu the Talmudist to gather a *minyan* of Jews to recite Psalms for Yosef. She told him to change the patient's name so the Angel of Death would not know who they were praying for.

Six years earlier, Golde had asked Shmayahu to recite a year of *Kaddish* for Yosef. During that time, he had also fasted and studied

Talmud to help Yosef's soul transmigrate. Every night he dreamt of Yosef's lifeless drowned body, and when he learned that Yosef was alive, he was certain that his Psalms had helped him transmigrate into a doctor.

When Shmayahu saw Yosef for the first time after his return, he looked under his clothes expecting to find him dressed in a burial shroud like other transmigrated souls. He hoped to show that a miracle had occurred and this was the body of the drowned Yosef. Of course, he found no proof. Underneath Yosef's clothes were only a fine pair of socks. But Shmayahu was undeterred. Finding nice socks instead of a shroud was not a hard problem to solve. He knew why the shroud was missing: Yosef had drowned himself and had not been given a proper Jewish burial.

Shmayahu was eager to help when Golde told him that Yosef was deathly ill and needed him to recite Psalms. He went straight to the ritual bath, performed ninety-five immersions, then went home and picked up his singed book of magic which he had thrown into the Fridman's house to help extinguish the fire. Thankfully, one of the firemen thought to rescue the book by hosing it down with water in order to earn a drink of whiskey from Shmayahu as a reward. Due to that fireman's merit, the book of magic was saved, and as Shmayahu began digging through it, under the heading "Transmigrations" in a section called "The Tree of Life," he found everything he needed to cobble together the best remedy for Yosef's recovery.

ELEVEN

THE REAL VALUE

Rukhame wiped away her tears and prayed, prayed without words, for words could not express her feelings. She prayed with her whole heart and entire mind so that her prayers echoed in the *Ayn Sof,* the Divine Infinite Nothingness. Praying made her feel lighter.

Roza prayed more fervently than anyone else. By dawn, she was already standing at Yosef's door. When he awakened, he called to her and asked her to open the window. The fresh air was invigorating, and Roza smiled lovingly as she said, "Look what I have found under the house, Yosef," and held up a small wooden box. "I didn't want to open it without you. Whatever it is, I want you to have it. Or we can give it to the poor to help you get well."

When they opened the box, instead of money, they found their letters, the ones that Meyshe Shneyur had stolen from them. This was the box that Karinov had tossed away when Kuzmo the butler had caught him. They began reading their letters, and the whole strange story became clear to them. When Roza came to her last letter, she read it aloud to Yosef.

Yosef, beloved Yosef!

You alone can answer me—why is my wellspring of tears exhausted? I have always been lucky that I could cry. My tears always calmed me and softened any hard feelings. Now I am alone, a person of stone with a living heart. I hear and feel, see and suffer, but cannot talk or cry.

I am no longer your Roza, Yosef. You would not recognize me and would tremble if you saw me. Crazy as it may seem, I still feel I will see you again someday. I will not believe the words of your enemies who say you were only an imposter. I will not believe your letters which I read with my own eyes. I will not believe the whole world if it speaks against you.

Yosef, my heart is still yours, and always will be. My heart screams for you, but you do not hear or feel my pain. Still, I know you are innocent! Why do you not answer my letters?

It was not for nothing that your words, "We must part," tore at my heart before you left. If I had only known what was going to befall us, I would have never let you go. I would have held on to you for as long as I lived. Then, after my death, you could have gone to Petersburg and forgotten your Roza. I would have been happy then. But now I live and cannot die!

I am so lonely, Yosef. Every night I am terrified by awful dreams. I hardly sleep, and my head is affected. I hear people talking to me but do not understand them; I look at things but do not see them. Yosef, my mind is too weak to bear all this! I am losing my strength, and my senses are shaky and uncertain. I have stopped believing in myself, and make up tests to see if I am still in my right mind. I am sinking, Yosef, and God only knows how much longer I will be able to write to you.

Day and night, the house is full of matchmakers and prospective in-laws. I try but have no words to use against my father. He has letters which he believes are from you. Mother is ill, and I have no one to pour out my heart to.

Yosef, please come home. Come, rescue me! I fear I am losing my mind and will be sold off, unknowingly and unwillingly. If that happens, Yosef, you will be guilty! But how can you be guilty of anything?

I beg you, come quickly before it's too late. Come, Yosef, while I still have sense enough to keep the wolves at bay. Yosef, do not forget me while I am still yours. While I can still sign,

Your Roza

Roza could not stop herself. She read the letter through to the very end. Her heart melted, and she fell on Yosef's chest. "Oh, my worst fear arrived in all its dark colors!" she sobbed. "Yosef, let me cry on you; no one knows my torment. God, why have You begrudged me my only wish?"

"That savage, Meyshe Shneyur, achieved everything he wanted," Yosef said. "He stole you from me and left me alive to see it. At least God allowed me to hear your letter. My whole heart pours itself out in my tears. Pull back the curtains, dear Roza, and let me see this lovely world for the last time."

"Yosef, don't talk of death. You will get well. You must get well! Look, look at the world and see how everything wants to live. Listen to the birds, how cheerfully they sing. Come to the window, dear Yosef, and see the beautiful new day. And listen, there's good news from your parents. They intend to come visit. They will set out after

Shabbes, and when they arrive, we'll all go out to the country. We've rented a summer house where you'll get your strength back. We can act like children again, running and jumping without worrying about whether it's appropriate or not. Give me your hand, Yosef. Live, and I will live, too!"

"Roza, please, let's not fool ourselves. What must come will come. I know I won't see another tomorrow. Why do you still try to comfort me? I can tell my blood is cooling and my feet are already cold. I know that death is not far off. Be calm, and I'll be calm, too. I beg you to write to my parents and tell them not to come. What's the point of causing them more pain? Their anguish will only seem worse in a strange place. They don't know you yet, they don't know Rukhame, and they don't know the real reason for my death. Why should I make new wounds for them? I beg you, dear Roza, ask them for a pardon right after my death, but don't invite them here now. Leave them to cry their bitter hearts out in their own home. Write and tell them it's my last request. Give me a pen, and I will write a few words, then you can finish the letter."

"Yosef, dear one, how can I listen to such talk from you? Better to live and get well."

"Roza, do you think that if I let you convince me that I will live that Death won't do his job? No, it's better to express my feelings now than die with them locked in my heart. I tell you, frankly, that it grieves me to leave this world—to leave all this joy and love, to leave you and your children so alone, and to leave my Rukhame so devastated.

"Oh, Roza, look at how the sun plays with me through the window. Why does Nature tease me with her love when I can no longer enjoy it? Why isn't today dark and cloudy? Oh, God, is this what I have earned for myself?"

Roza wept, and Yosef held her hand to his heart. "I wish you could stop the clock, Roza. If only for one very long day so I could finish just one of my manuscripts. I give them all to you, dear Roza. It will comfort me to have you read them. I know your good heart will feel what I wanted to say. Now, I must write to my parents."

Roza gave Yosef a pen, and he wrote in a trembling hand:

Beloved Father and dearest Mother!

First, settle yourselves, and then read this letter. I want to tell you myself that I have died. Oh, God, that is such a terrible word! But it is so. I am writing this with my own hand and will leave it for someone to send to you when I have taken my last breath. My last thoughts are of you, dear parents; my last wish is to comfort you. Although I cannot live any longer, I am not dying alone, thank God. I am under the care of precious hands and accompanied to the grave by a river of tears. I know this is God's will.

Father, I remain your virtuous child. If it brings you any comfort, I die an observant Jew, and that is how I will come to God. Do not cry too much for me for I am satisfied. Father, bless me after my death, so God will hear your voice and comfort my dear ones here who mourn for me.

Be well, my parents! I send greetings to everyone. Please assure them that they are not forgotten. I would like to say more, but the time is short, and it is difficult to write. I wish you peace and happiness, your dying son,

Yosef

When Yosef finished the letter, he glanced at the clock. It was twelve-thirty. He threw himself back on the pillows and handed the pen to Roza. "Here, Roza, you may add whatever you like. Please call in your children. Let me say goodbye to them."

Roza went out and hurriedly returned with her three children and Golde. Yosef kissed each child, then asked for his white silk scarf, the one Roza had given him before his trip to Petersburg. Putting it around the oldest boy's neck, he said, "Rivetchke, once I wanted to be buried with this scarf around my neck but among us Jews that would be disturbing. The community would put the question to the rabbi, and that would cause a lot of discussion. So let it be. Rivetchke, please remember that once there was a man named Yosef who wanted to take care of you and your mother. He lived and gave this to you before he died."

"Enough, dear Yosef," Golde pleaded. "Children, leave him now so he can calm down."

Everyone went out, each to cry in his own corner. As Yosef fell asleep, Golde saw the cold sweat on his forehead and knew the end was near.

As the sun paused at the edge of the sky, Yosef awoke and looked around in confusion. Seeing Golde sitting beside him, he said, "Good Mother, I want to see Rukhame. Please, indulge me this one last request."

Golde went out and was so distraught she could barely make her way through the house. When she finally found Rukhame, she brought her to Yosef's room, then went for Roza.

"My dear Yosef," cried Rukhame, "you're still alive!"

Yosef opened his eyes and whispered, "Rukhame, come closer."

Rukhame gave him her trembling hand, and said, "Yosef, I gave you six years of pain and suffering. You're supposed to be free now."

"Rukhame," Yosef answered, "don't speak about the past. I will soon be leaving you forever, and I need you to tell me you won't ruin your health over me. Tell me you'll get well and be happy for your future husband. Promise me, Rukhame, if you can. But I won't bind you with a vow. Be free. Know this is my last wish."

Rukhame answered through her tears, "I promise, Yosef. I promise anything you ask!"

Yosef laid his head back down on the pillow, and a dark, sad stillness filled the room. Rukhame leaned forward to kiss him, but his lips were cold as death itself.

Yosef opened his eyes and glanced lovingly at the three women who gathered around him. "Be well and happy," he whispered, then closed his eyes for the last time.

All hearts wept, and tears flowed silently as Yosef's life went out like the final flicker of a candle. At the edge of the sky the last rays of the sun disappeared, and in the house, the last spark of a precious life was extinguished.

"He's gone," Golde said quietly.

Outside the window, a gust of wind gave a mournful howl and inside a wailing lament began. Family members came and took the women away. Roza tore out her hair and screamed; Rukhame and Golde wept quietly.

People from the community came, lifted Yosef up and dressed him in his eternal clothes. Sterne Gute was among the women, and while she sewed the burial shroud, she kept singing Yosef's praises: what a saint he had been, what a fine child, and she shed a few tears as well.

Rukhame watched as they carried Yosef out and tore up the engagement contract over the casket. No longer able to control herself, she ran into the street and began screaming like a wild woman, "Yosef, my Yosef, you won't have to wait long! I will be coming to you soon!"

* * * * *

Two weeks passed, and before the deep wounds could heal, a new woe appeared in the Fridman house. At the dawn of another beautiful day, Rukhame put on the dress she had worn when Yosef had first returned from Petersburg. When asked why, she replied, "I will see Yosef soon." Although some people wondered if she planned to take her own life, her calm voice and sweet demeanor seemed to alleviate such fears. Her words made Golde uneasy, but Rukhame refused to say anything more.

Gradually, Golde saw the color leaving Rukhame's face. When she threw herself into bed still wearing the dress, Golde hid her tears and did not reprimand her. Then Rukhame read Golde the letter Yosef had written to Roza on the day he intended to drown himself in the river. It was the letter he had handed to her on the night she rescued him.

"Look, Mother," Rukhame said, "Yosef writes and tells me to beware of Meyshe Shneyur, so he won't do to my beloved what he did to him. Oh, God, why did You set that snake on us? It's so true what Yosef said that we can still see the story of the Garden of Eden in our own lives today. We were driven out of the Garden of Eden because of that evil snake. Mother, do you remember how we once lived in a Paradise? Do you remember how joyful our life was and how happy we were? How your motherly love used to accompany Roza and me wherever we went? Remember what people said about me, Mama? That I was born to laugh. There was so much joy and pleasure in our house until that snake, Meyshe Shneyur, arrived and brought us tears and pain. Dear Yosef, what you said is true. I see you now in the real Garden of Eden, and you see how wounded I am here. Give me your hand, Yosef, and take me to you."

"Rukhame," Golde cried, "you're my last consolation in life. Please don't give me any more pain. Oh, God, why am I such an unfortunate mother? How have I earned this?"

"Oh, Mama," replied Rukhame, "I've asked God the same question a hundred times. I've sent Him a whole list of questions. My Yosef is happy now. He knows everything and is at peace. Soon

I will be at peace too. Then Mama, the first thing I'll do is plead with God to comfort you."

"My precious child," cried Golde in despair. "Better that God takes me instead of my precious jewel!"

"No, Mama," said Rukhame tearfully, "You must stay alive. You have children and grandchildren who depend on you. God has given you a higher task, and you must help Him build His world. You're like a tree in the forest with a much greater lifetime than mine. I'm just a flower that bloomed for someone else. Now, like a flower that can only live for one summer, I must wither away."

"Oh, my dear child, my bright little life," said Golde, clasping Rukhame to her heart. "You can't wither away. Your summer is just beginning!"

"Mama, perhaps it's better to say I'm a flower broken off before its prime. As a child, I was so mean. I used to pull young flowers out of the ground. I watched them wither in my hands. I put them in a vase with fresh water, but it didn't help because I had torn them out by the roots. Mama, what good is the best medicine if one's heart has been torn out by the roots? I must be with Yosef, Mama. Please forgive me, but I must go now. See how cold my hands are already?"

Golde grabbed Rukhame's hands and began to kiss them. She held them to her heart to warm them, and in her pain cried out, "God, help us!"

"I beg you, Mama, be comforted by the fact that God only created me for a short time; a blossom in the world that bloomed but did not thrive here."

Golde could not talk. She held her daughter and poured out her tears. Finally, Rukhame said, "Mama, please call Father."

When Fridman came in, Rukhame saw the tears in his eyes and began to cry, too. "Father, dear Father," she said reaching for his hand. "Forgive me! I have given you so much suffering in your life."

"No, my child, you have only sweetened my years," said Fridman. "My life will be poisoned if you leave me!"

"Father, this is God's will. He took my Yosef first, exactly two weeks ago, and now He's calling me. Oh, pray for us, Father. God sees the tears of an old man."

"My daughter!" cried Fridman. "Would you like to recite the confession? Say it after me; I'll lead you in it."

Rukhame was silent. She raised her lovely blue eyes to heaven and said, "God, You alone know my rights and wrongs. You can lead me in my confession. Father, I have not sinned against Him or anyone else. I've never done harm to any person. I pray for everyone's pardon."

Roza entered and saw her parents at Rukhame's bedside. "What's wrong?" she asked.

"Roza," said Rukhame. "What greeting will you send to Yosef?"

"Oh, dear sister," cried Roza, "may God put an end to my life, too!"

"I will tell him," said Rukhame, "then Yosef and I will go to God and plead for you. Bring everyone in; I don't have much time left."

As people entered the room, Rukhame kissed each one, and tears flowed. She laid her head back on the pillow, and said, "Be well, everyone." Then added, "Yosef, you'd better come to meet me!"

Rukhame closed her eyes and became very still. Her breathing became difficult, and after a few minutes, her pained expression changed to one of quiet contentment as the light of that precious life went out. They washed her pure body and pulled on the sad white burial clothes, and everyone wept. More weeping followed on the day they laid that sweet blossom with the lovely eyes and smiling lips down into the grave and covered her tender body with cold, dry earth.

As Golde left the cemetery, she cried, "Oh, my children. How will I ever bear my life with such pearls in the ground?"

*   *   *   *   *

Those who come to visit the Mohilev Jewish cemetery may not notice the two graves that lay a little to the side of the other graves. They certainly would not expect to find such saintly souls buried there. But those who knew the dear young lovers, never leave without sighing deeply or shedding bitter tears.

The only happy person to visit the graves was Shmayahu the Talmudist, who hoped to bring the dead ones into Paradise with his *Kaddish*. Shmayahu hoped that Yosef would appreciate his efforts and intercede on his behalf in the World to Come.

Even happier than Shmayahu was the man who proudly strode through the streets of Mohilev with his beard shaved and dressed in a short coat with a pair of glasses over his foxy eyes. Now that his advice was sought from far and wide, this Dark Young Man gloated in his victory. He strolled with a walking stick in his hand and trod heavily as though the earth danced with joy knowing that such an important man was stepping on it. And, indeed, he could be happy. When he went home, there were no thorns to contend with; everything was under his control. He had become a fine person and a trustee at the study house. People referred to him as "Reb Meyshe Shneyur" and granted him the best honors and fattest rewards. He was also a politician, philosopher, astronomer, doctor, and advisor, and it never occurred to anyone that his dark heart was a thousand times darker for the pains he had taken to dig those two graves in the Mohilev cemetery. His only wish was to send his father-in-law's other children into the Next World as soon as possible.

No one gave a second thought to Karinov the thief as he was led to the executioner's scaffold. Although he protested that he was not guilty of this crime, he was still hanged as the Dark Young Man looked on from the crowd, smiling at the knowledge that he had fooled the world.

The solitary Roza was the one who mourned Yosef's death most deeply. She felt the spider on her neck but had to keep quiet. The Dark One tortured her with a dull knife without killing her, and she had to bow down to him because he now controlled the Fridman business. Her husband earned no money, and when her dear children begged for food, she had no choice but to seek help from Meyshe Shneyur.

Golde saw everything. Her heart ached, but she could not turn a cold shoulder to her daughter Leyke's husband, the father of her grandchildren. Even Fridman had to bite his tongue now that Meyshe Shneyur had taken over the business. But he no longer silenced Golde when she cried, "That evil snake has driven all the joy out of our household. He's laid our blossoming children into an early grave and made our Roza penniless and miserable. Only God knows what he has in store for us!" Fridman knew she was right, but what could he do? How could he turn to public funds in his old age?

The Dark One had brought himself so far. Once a poor only son, he committed so many wrongs, yet the land still tolerated him, and Mohilev society did not spit him out.

Reb Itsik, who had Meyshe Shneyur in his grasp and would have paid all he was worth to take him down, knew he could do nothing without hurting the people he loved. So he remained silent and followed the request in Yosef's will that was found among his papers asking him not to fight with Meyshe Shneyur. Although Reb Itsik suspected the will was another forgery by Yosef's adversary, he could not prove it. Only God could reveal the truth.

The same guest who had given that once happy child the name Rukhame now made a gravestone on which he chiseled this sad lament:

Ha-ne'ehavim veha-ne'imim b'chayeihem uv'motam lo nifradu.

Those who are beloved and pleasing in life will never be separated by death.

ACKNOWLEDGMENTS

Many people must be thanked for their help in preparing this book for publication. Tina Lunson for her English translation of Jacob Dinezon's original Yiddish novel. Arthur Clark for his thorough reading of several drafts, his invaluable editing advice, and his friendship. Maxine Carr, Michael Bassman, Linda Fineman, Josette Chmiel, Eileen Fetters, Kathleen Southern, Wende Essrow, and Nan Watkins for their proofreading assistance and manuscript suggestions.

Special thanks to Robin and Jim Evans and Carolyn Toben for their ongoing love, encouragement, and support over the many years we have worked to bring an English version of Jacob Dinezon's *The Dark Young Man* to twenty-first-century readers.

GLOSSARY

akh. An interjection like "ah" or "oh."

Av. A month in the Hebrew calendar that falls between July and August in the Gregorian calendar.

Ayn Sof. Without end. In Kabbalah, the Infinite Nothingness or Infinite Divine.

bashert. Predestined; also, a person's predestined marriage companion.

basherter. A man predestined to be a person's marriage companion.

basherts. Heavenly-decreed marriage companions.

bimah. The raised platform in the synagogue or prayer house on which the Torah scroll is placed for public reading and where the service leader often stands.

bobke. A sweet yeast cake.

bris. The ceremony of circumcision performed on a Jewish boy when he is eight days old.

Chassid. A follower of the Chassidic movement.

Chassidim. The followers of Chassidism, a mystical Jewish religious movement founded in the eighteenth century in Eastern Europe.

cheder. Traditional religious elementary school for boys.

Cheshvan. A month in the Hebrew calendar that falls between October and November in the Gregorian calendar.

cholent. A traditional stew started before the beginning of Sabbath that is served as a hot meal on the following day after services.

Der shvartser yungermantshik. The dark young man.

Eighteen Benedictions. The eighteen blessings that are recited during the weekday prayers.

Elul. The month in the Hebrew calendar that coincides with August and September in the Gregorian calendar.

fräulein. German word for "Miss" or an unmarried woman.

groschen. An Austrian coin; one-hundredth part of a shilling.

Ha-ne'ehavim veha-ne'imim. The beloved and pleasing.

Haskalah. The Jewish Enlightenment movement.

Havdalah. The ceremony that concludes the Sabbath and holidays.

Kaddish. An Aramaic prayer of praise to God; a version is recited by mourners in public services after the death of a close relative.

Kedushah. A prayer recited during the third part of the Eighteen Benedictions.

Kohelet. Ecclesiastes; a chapter in the Hebrew Bible attributed to King Solomon. Sometimes translated as "Teacher" or "Preacher."

kosher. Food prepared according to Jewish law. Also, genuine and legitimate.

l'chaim. A toast meaning "to life!"

mazel tov. Good luck; congratulations.

mentsh. A moral person of dignity and worth.

mezuzah. A box or case that contains a small parchment scroll with two blessings from the Torah. The *mezuzah* is fastened to the doorpost of a house or building.

minyan. Ten men needed to hold a public Jewish prayer service.

Mishnah. The portion of the Talmud that contains the original version of the rabbinic oral laws.

mitzvah. A commandment or good deed.

nu. An interjection similar to the words "so?" "so what?" or "well."

oy. Similar to the expressions "Oh my!" or "Oh dear!"

rabbi. A Jewish scholar, teacher, or religious leader.

Shabbes. The Sabbath.

shammes. Caretaker of a synagogue.

Shavuos. A major Jewish festival held in the spring that celebrates the day God presented the Torah to the Jewish people at Mount Sinai.

shtetl. A small Jewish town or village in Eastern Europe.

Shtrafnoi. A popular novella by the Jewish-Russian writer, Osip Rabinovich (1817–1869), about the forced recruitment of Jewish soldiers into Tsar Nicholas I's army.

shvartser. Black or dark.

Sukkos. An eight-day holiday that celebrates the fall festival and commemorates the escape from Egypt and the forty years spent dwelling in the desert. During Sukkos, meals are eaten in a temporary outdoor structure called a *sukkah.*

Talmud. The collection of Jewish law and tradition consisting of the Mishnah and the Gemara.

Talmudist. A person who studies the Talmud.

Talmud-Torah. The traditional, tuition-free elementary school maintained by the community for the poorest boys.

Tishah b'Av. A fast day on the ninth day of Av to commemorate the destruction of the first and second Temples in Jerusalem.

Torah. The holy scroll on which is written the five books of Moses.

vey iz mir. Similar to the expression, "Woe is me."

yeshiva. Jewish institute of higher education and Talmudic learning.

yortsayt. The anniversary of a death.

Yosefke. Affectionate name for Yosef.

THE DARK YOUNG MAN
By Jacob Dinezon

A Reader's Guide

ABOUT JACOB DINEZON

JACOB DINEZON was born in New Zagare, Lithuania in the early 1850s. His father died while he was a young teenager and he was sent to live with an uncle in the Russian town of Mohilev.

An excellent student, Dinezon was hired by a wealthy family to tutor their young daughter. While living in their household, he became a trusted member of the family and was soon promoted to bookkeeper and manager of the family business. Through this family, Dinezon was introduced to the owner of a famous Jewish publishing company in Vilna called The Widow and Brothers Romm, which published his first novel, *The Dark Young Man,* in 1877. The book became a runaway bestseller.

Moving to Warsaw in the 1890s, Dinezon quickly became a prominent figure in the city's Jewish literary circle. He befriended almost every major Jewish writer of his day, including Sholem Abramovitsh (Mendele Mocher Sforim; 1835–1917), Sholem Aleichem (1859–1916), and I. L. Peretz (1852–1915). These writers are the classic writers of modern Yiddish literature, and Peretz became Dinezon's closest friend and confidant.

Over the next twenty years, Dinezon published several works of fiction, including *A Stumbling Block in the Road, Hershele: A Jewish Love Story, Yosele: A Story from Jewish Life,* and *The Crisis: A Story of the Lives of Merchants.* He wrote sentimental novels about urban life in the Russian Empire and focused on the emotional conflicts affecting young people as modern ideas challenged the traditional religious practices of their parents. As in *The Dark Young Man,* the plight of his characters often brought tears to the eyes of his devoted readers, and remained in their memories long after they finished his stories.

During the First World War, Jacob Dinezon helped found an orphanage and schools to care for Jewish children made homeless by the fighting between Russia and Germany. He died in 1919 and is buried in Warsaw's Jewish cemetery beside I. L. Peretz.

LEARN MORE ABOUT JACOB DINEZON'S

LIFE AND CAREER AT

www.jacobdinezon.com

QUESTIONS AND TOPICS
FOR DISCUSSION

1. At the very beginning of *The Dark Young Man,* Jacob Dinezon provides an almost cinematic view of the streets in the Jewish section of Mohilev, the dire life of the underpaid watchmen, and the contrasting conditions between rich and poor. How does this establish the novel's mood and tone?

2. When we first meet Yosef, he is living the life of a poor yeshiva student—an "idler"—in the Mohilev study house. How does Yosef's poverty and social status affect his prospects as a potential bridegroom?

3. Dinezon tells us that people always called Meyshe Shneyur by his two names. Dinezon goes on to say, "His countenance, dark as a Moor, made an impression on people when they first met him. This impression was so strong, they immediately forgot his two names, and referred to him instead as 'the Dark One' or 'the Dark Young Man.'" What cultural associations and stereotypes are associated with these terms? How does Dinezon's description of Meyshe Shneyur influence our understanding of his character?

4. Yosef's father wants his son to become a Talmud scholar and rabbi, but once Yosef moves into the Fridman household, he begins to have second thoughts. On page 73, Yosef admits to himself, "I am bound by love to my parents and their wishes." Why do you think he is so concerned about his parents' feelings regarding his decision to end his religious studies?

5. Why do you think Yosef ultimately leaves the study of Talmud and the possibility of becoming a rabbi to enter a trade or profession? In the end, do you think he made a wise choice?

6. On page 41, Dinezon writes, "In these times when the slave trader is almost unheard of anymore in Europe, and when we are horrified to hear how they conducted their business in Africa, we seem not to notice that family slave traders are still at work in our Jewish communities." How did you react when you read Dinezon's comparison of arranged marriages to slavery and matchmakers to slave traders? How did you feel about the process of matchmaking as it is depicted in the novel?

7. What was your reaction to Golde's memory of falling in love with her cousin, Leybl, and how devastated she was when he married another woman?

8. Dinezon introduces us to several mothers throughout the novel, including his own mother, Golde Fridman, Sterne Gute, Dvorah Bayse, and Sorele Sorkin's mother Grune. How does Dinezon contrast "good" and "bad" mothers?

9. In your opinion, why did Dinezon spend so much time describing "the enviers" Sterne Gute the busybody and Dvorah

Basye the tavern keeper? What role did their characters play in the unfolding of the story?

10. How did you feel when Meyshe Shneyur spent Shavuos eve drinking whiskey and playing cards with Leyb Sorkin the criminal, his wife Sorele, Gason's son-in-law, and Tevele the Ale Man? What was your reaction to their discussion of the "Laws and Customs of the Son-in-law"?

11. On page 196, Dinezon writes about truth: "Although it may be wrapped up in the most abominable lies and treachery, truth is like the sun shining in the sky. A lie is no more than a cloud that hides the light for awhile, but the truth will always break through the darkest clouds that cover it. The problem is that we do not always see the sun through the darkness, and often the sky must clear completely before the sun reveals itself again. The truth is like that, too. It is never lost, but may not reveal itself at the right time." Why didn't Dinezon reveal the truth of Meyshe Shneyur's crimes in the novel? Why didn't he punish the Dark One for his evil deeds?

12. On page 198, Fridman discusses the differences between Jews and Christians: "What girl doesn't like a boy, and what boy doesn't like a girl? But Jews can't have anything to do with falling in love. This is just another way for young Jews to follow lockstep after the Christians. Once Gentile ladies started strolling about with parasols, Jewish women wanted to do it, too. . . . Soon they'll want to allow men and women to dance together at weddings the way Christians do." Do Christian customs influence Jewish life today? If so, in what ways?

13. Letter writing—both real and forged—plays an important role in the novel. Yosef and Roza use letters to reveal their deepest

feelings for each other. Did you ever write long letters to a loved one or family member that revealed your deepest thoughts? How has our modern technology changed the way we correspond with people today?

14. At Roza's engagement party, Gason says, "I've always said your Roza belongs to the old order, but your Rukhame belongs to the new." What were the major differences between the two sisters and how were they exhibited in the novel?

15. On page 253 in the chapter, "A Doctor In the House," Yosef tells Roza how Rukhame rescued him and that he is now going to marry her. Roza replies, "You deserve her, dear Yosef," and goes on to say, "You'll probably be happier with her than me. She's more educated than I am, and she's been reading and studying this whole time. I can see that you've changed, too, Yosef, while I've become a simple housewife." Why do you think Roza said this? How did Roza's words affect you?

16. How did you react to what happened to Rukhame at the end of the novel? Did you expect it? How was it foreshadowed by her words to Yosef on the bridge?

17. What was your reaction to Jacob Dinezon's portrayal of Meyshe Shneyur at the end of *The Dark Young Man?* Why do you think the author chose to end the novel in this way?

18. What do you think happens to the remaining family members once Meyshe Shneyur has complete control over them?

19. Dinezon describes the lives of wives, mothers, daughters, and sisters in nineteenth century Jewish families, and depicts the constraints placed on them by the Jewish traditions and ex-

pectations of that time. How have women's lives changed since Dinezon wrote his novel? Are there still limitations and restrictions based on gender in Jewish communities?

20. *The Dark Young Man* is set in the Russian Empire in the 1840s. What lessons does it offer to us today about how to live a modern life while still holding on to our Jewish identity and values?

ALSO AVAILABLE FROM

JEWISH STORYTELLER PRESS

MEMORIES AND SCENES
SHTETL, CHILDHOOD, WRITERS

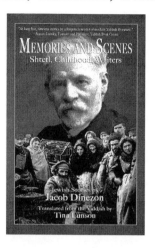

"Jacob Dinezon's newly translated masterpiece belongs next to Sholem Aleichem's works."
—*Jewish Daily Forward*

"With Dinezon's *Memories and Scenes,* we happily encounter a master writer who deserves to be ranked with Sholom Aleichem and I. L. Peretz."
—*Hadassah Magazine*

"Highly recommended."
—*Association of Jewish Libraries Reviews*

In August of 2014, the English-speaking world received access to a short-story collection by the once-beloved author Jacob Dinezon, a central figure in the development of Yiddish as a literary language in the second half of the nineteenth century.

Amid poverty and strict adherence to Jewish law and customs, Jacob Dinezon's characters struggle to reconcile their heartfelt impulses with age-old religious teachings as modern ideas encroach on traditional Jewish life.

This profound and delightful collection, translated from the Yiddish by Tina Lunson, paints a vivid portrait of late nineteenth century Eastern European *shtetl* life and provides readers with a treasure trove of Jewish history, culture, and values.

HERSHELE
A JEWISH LOVE STORY

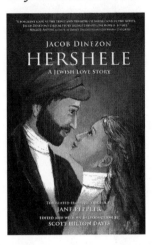

"A gripping tale with a realistic adolescent love story,
a complicated plot, and an unexpected ending."
—*Association of Jewish Libraries Reviews*

"A sweet, ageless romance that has stood the test of time."
—*Foreword Reviews*

In 1891, the Yiddish writer Jacob Dinezon crafted a tender love story exploring the budding romance between two young people separated by class and tradition. This compelling fable, created with equal measures of hope and despair, charmed his many readers, but until recently has remained inaccessible to modern audiences.

Hershele is the bittersweet love story of Hershele and Mirele—he a penniless yeshiva student with no family, she the lovely daughter of a widow who provides a weekly charity meal to poor students.

Their unlikely meeting generates a strong attraction that gradually overcomes the powerful obstacles of social norms and class status. But determined forces are arrayed against them, and their first tentative steps towards modernity are challenged at every turn.

Hershele, translated from the Yiddish by Jane Peppler, is at once a fascinating glimpse into the daily life of Eastern European Jews in the late nineteenth century, and the extremely personal and poignant story of two young lovers trapped in the clash between existing traditions and social change. It is simultaneously a historical novel and a timeless tale of romance. In its own way, *Hershele* is the Romeo and Juliet story of the *shtetl.*

YOSELE
A STORY FROM JEWISH LIFE

"A must-read in this area."
—*Donald J. Weinshank*

In 1899, Jacob Dinezon's short novel, *Yosele,* exposed in vivid detail the outmoded and cruel teaching methods prevalent in the traditional *cheders* (Jewish elementary schools) of the late 1800s. The novel was so powerful and persuasive, it transformed the Jewish educational system of Eastern Europe.

Writing in Yiddish to reach the broadest Jewish audience, Dinezon described the sad, poverty-stricken, and violent life of a bright and gentle schoolboy whose treatment at the hands of his teacher, parents, and rich society is shocking and painful. The pathos and outrage resulting from the story's initial publication produced an urgent call for reform and set the stage for the establishment of a secular school movement that transformed Jewish elementary education in the early 1900s.

Translated into English for the first time by Jane Peppler, Jacob Dinezon's *Yosele* presents a rarely seen sociological and cultural picture of Eastern European Jewish life at the end of the nineteenth century.

JACOB DINEZON
THE MOTHER AMONG OUR CLASSIC YIDDISH WRITERS

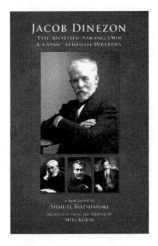

"A literary biography with summary, gentle analysis, and evaluation of Dinezon's works."
—*Jewish Standard*

Was there a fourth classic Yiddish writer? This is what the renowned literary historian Shmuel Rozshanski asserts in this insightful and well-documented biography about the beloved and successful nineteenth century Yiddish author, Jacob Dinezon

(1851?-1919), called by the *Jewish Daily Forward*, "The Greatest Yiddish Writer You Never Heard Of."

Credited with writing the first "Jewish Realistic Romance" and the first bestselling Yiddish novel, Dinezon was closely associated with the leading Jewish writers of his day, including Sholem Abramovitsh (Mendele Mocher Sforim), Sholem Aleichem, and I. L. Peretz—dubbed the "Classic Writers of Modern Yiddish Literature."

Dinezon's poignant stories about Eastern European *shtetl* and urban life, focused on the emotional conflicts affecting young people as modern ideas challenged traditional religious practices and social norms. He was also a staunch advocate of Yiddish as a literary language, and a highly respected community activist.

In this extensively researched Yiddish biography written in 1956 and translated into English by Miri Koral, Shmuel Rozshanski makes the case for including Jacob Dinezon in the "family" of classic Yiddish writers. If, as scholars suggest, Sholem Abramovitsh is the grandfather, I. L. Peretz the father, and Sholem Aleichem the grandson of modern Yiddish literature, then Jacob Dinezon, Rozshanski insists, should be considered the "mother" for his gentle, kindhearted, and emotional approach to storytelling and his readers.

An important new research book for scholars of Jewish literature, history, and culture.

Made in the USA
Middletown, DE
09 April 2019